THE ARMY OF NAQUIOR
Book 4

THE NIVIAN KING SERIES BOOKS

The Nivian King: Book 1
The Ice Scabbard: Book 2
The Arvinstrum: Book 3
The Army of Naquior: Book 4

SELECT NONFICTION

Persons Artificial
The Earth-Colonizing Handbook of Generation Stelan
God is DNA
The Science of Reality
Grand Robot
World War C

THE ARMY OF NAQUIOR
Book 4

PARIS TOSEN

Tosen Books

The Army of Naquior: Book 4 is a work of fiction.

ISBN: 978-1-926949-23-9

www.tosen.ca

Book design and cover by Paris Tosen

THE ARMY OF NAQUIOR

Life is an exponential mountain of results. —
Nahkli-li-Zorath

Chapter 1

THERE WAS a cryogenic luminosity about the head office of Technomicon, the worldwide technological leader of consumer gadgetry in the Vale of Arvicity north of the urba Batall.

Technomicon was founded as a small operation 92 tios ago by Director Jicama, an entan without a history or family, when a series of new technological wonders were made profitable in the rapidly developing markets at a time when denizens were being converted into consumers. The company first made flamma burners for home cooking and extended their product line into slow burning ovens. It was the first company to prove that mass marketing using a suitable level of technology designed for the average Seronian could sustain a viable market. They succeeded in tapping the residential consumer who preferred to eat at their unamid. Flamma technology has evolved since then and the company sold its cooking products division as new technological products came about.

Twenty tios ago, shortly after the death of Jicama, Technomicon became a holding company with three strategic corporate entities covering; communications, mediamenta, consumer arvonics and military. Expansion financing came from a suspicious and unidentifiable source that provided all the necessary zorn required to launch a massive business operation. Each entity was enabled with their own mission and fed sufficient resources to keep them operating profitably including the ownership of subsidiary companies like Narcophalin (actually a new acquisition), an export trading arm, but the connections were so distant that they were invisible to the numularian eye.

The murderous acquisition of the palpazine Querist was never proven and did nothing to mark the company. When Technomicon's subsidiary, Malkar, stole plans and six new prototypes ready for production from another organization, the 30 denizens who were angered by such action were all found dead in their residences the next morning. No further complaints came, and from that point on, the company has prospered by introducing arvonic gadgets and devices on a regular basis.

Today, Technomicon produces 90% of all consumer arvonics; virtually all mediamenta, content and entertainment used in consumer persuasion and distraction; and 70% of the communication tards, a figure which has been on the decline over the last three tios from competitive activity.

The newly-constructed head office towered over the previous building. Five main buildings were joined together to one central tower that rose up from the ground into a sharp pyramid, a polyhedron joined at the top by one vertex. The headquarters was centered in the Vale of

Arvicity with a number of smaller corporate enterprises not connected by business or partnership. In all there were fifteen companies and were growing by one every week.

Unlike the traditions of the past that made buildings artistic and comfortable, Technomicon was an aberration that defied Seronian beliefs and may have worked as its promotional keel as the ocean of consumers deepened.

Under late Director Jicama, Technomicon took advantage of the planetary changes and created a new kind of tard based on a numerical encryption system for communications while maintaining the use of arvic weight (AW) for identification.

The first series of tards, used extensively by all, were encrypted by entan scent, a singular, non-duplicable identification system personalized by every individual entan and impossible to break. Arvic and elemental shifts from within the planet had changed entans' scent and; therefore, made tards largely useless. This was perfectly timed with a newly modified tard based on mathematical formulas. The incorporation of AW had been consistent throughout the development of technology since it was unique to all beings and did not change as it was based on the birth code. AW was the amount of arvicity that was conducted and its passing frequency through a body. Lower frequencies suggested a closer tie to the first generation of beings on Seranor. But the birth code, referred to as AW in common, was fixed as the time the seedling was separated from its mother.

In total, there were 98 entans on Seranor in the beginning, 49 of which were lutos and 49 lutas. Stories had circulated among urbas that some of the original beings, born 13,000 tios ago, were still alive. Bodies of the first generation were a hollow white, bone smooth, the purest conductors of arvicity and had abilities not found today. It was said that all beings had a natural regenerative ability, as Seranor herself once had, before being enslaved and that they could adjust their translucence.

The latest tard was white-faced on one side and black-faced on the other with a clear crystal slotted in the center. The white side was used for communications. The black for identification and zorn-based transactions.

Weight had been a problem for tards from the very beginning. All technological devices were powered by ganium chargers that accepted, stored and discharged arvicity from the planet into the device and back again. Ganium was a heavy ceramic compound and using it in smaller devices such as the hand-held tard made it bulky to carry around. Even the original zorn card used ganium. Chargers generated a lot of heat if used for too long and this hampered communication.

The new dual-purpose tards used kium as both a cooling agent and a transactions medium. Kium was a permanently cold ice that was cool to the touch but was effective in drawing away heat from objects, including bodies, if contact was made. It was also almost indestructible by normal means. Technomicon developed a technique with which to manufacture kium to be used in a whole host of devices. This enabled the tards to work for near indefinite periods of time without heat and with a reduced weight. The limited tard name was replaced with TARC to complement the new transaction-communication card. Normal tarcs were still limited to urba-based communications. Some were seen carrying around special versions, smaller in size, made by House Levin.

Technology proliferated in all places and manners. Kitchens for cooking became smaller and a simple ceramic plate only thirty centimeters in diameter could cook any range of clay food in a fraction of the time conventional devices needed, using a patented flamma bubble. And the clay tasted better.

The Photonic Translator (PT), a 30 cm long cylindrical receiver and emitter of photon-based information that projected a sharp visual image on a screen made entirely of photon-level flamma, became a popular device and was originally launched to supplement the palpazine giving a stronger visual performance to news and information. Those who owned a PT watched them religiously and had all of the latest information of what was going on.

Technological devices had their uses and were accepted by most in Casus, as well as other urbas. Politics, the official body of order, was not so easily digested by the locals. Orders and rules were put to things in daily life and it was like binding an entan's feet and telling them to run as fast as they could. Ceramin were tripping left and right. Many didn't like the changes to their freedom. All of sudden their lives had become restricted as if they were still seeds and this was told to them by a select group of leaders who weren't fully elected, rather were placed in position by those of greater wealth and influence suggesting that this meant they knew better for the average entan. As if they really knew better.

Politics infested everyone's life, demarcated it, captured it; and once Seronians began to accept that their choices were removed, they too began to incorporate politics into their lives. Began to accept its rules. The voices of the strong rang out only for a short while, at which point it was discovered that there was a relationship between a strong voice and a quick death. Voices began to diminish. Assassins, even the amateurish, looked for work as demand took off.

Politics needed a weapon in order for it to strike its enemies. The Seronian Guard grew in number to support them as it did in brutality. The connection between them and leaders were like brother and sister.

Seronians, instead of pushing for death, turned their attention to technology and demanded more enicoys, tech-toys, to simplify their unhappy lives. Technomicon was happy to oblige and rake in the financial reward for their audacity.

Clearer lines began to be made between the variations in society from entan to ventan, luto to luta, foreigner to resident. These greater strained the receding relationship in society and sent Seronians on a path of independence. It was a time of technology that had begun. Technology and arvicity.

Devices grew in use and stories of arvic battles became the popular thing to talk about. Many entans took to studying how to manipulate arvicity, schools with the strangest names opened across urbas. In Casus, the two largest schools, Pellanomica and Tyz-arc, took in students by the hundreds.

Chapter 2

NAQUI ZOLDIERS frequently entered Casus led by a Sint crusader on business for the self-elected, planetary King. Zorath had restrained his overt actions across all borders and was directing his energy elsewhere as his synthetic troops marched in his absence. The local leaders did not try to stop the Sints or zoldiers; instead, talked about finding ways to cooperate.

Ira took advantage of the situation and studied their military methods and their arvic traits. Ira had accumulated an exorbitant amount of data and went through an exhaustive analysis in pain-staking effort to find a weakness in Zorath's forces. When he had narrowed down the variables and identified their greatest fighting weaknesses he prepared the land's most famous Kozotian fighter in attacks that would counter those of the Sint.

When the fighter, Teramon, a plate-armored warrior wielding a wide bladed black batier and a thick shield on his left arm, was ready, a strategy was implemented to test Zorath's right hand. An attack was staged on Avar-Sint, a greedy Sint who took much more in lives and wealth than he deserved and had incensed the kind of kozotians who had the power to make big decisions.

Teramon challenged Avar-Sint to a battle of arms. The two of them met on a low hill just outside a patch of cora trees not far from Zahara on the southern most tip of Seranor. Many came to watch but none interfered in what transpired.

Weapons of the two heavily armored giants clashed. Arvic rader against arvic batier sung their song and rang out their pains in a wide radius. Teramon was trained by the best and was the military leader of the Terium of Seranor, now famous as the renegade society where politics were looked upon as a plague.

Teramon started strong and fast using the techniques taught to him by Ira himself, and as they started Teramon did seem to have an upper hand until something unexpected happened. The Sint changed its fighting pattern to effectively defend against Teramon's attacks while maintaining a strong range of attacks. Avar-Sint and Teramon fought for more than an hour, twenty minutes more than the maximum that the Kozotian had been trained to do.

By the sixty-eighth minute Teramon was losing his strength and the Sint had already pierced his armor twice to Teramon's single blow. Milk poured out profusely without a chance to fully heal. Another two strikes and he would die for certain. The third came as his shield was ripped into two and an arvic rader gouged into his left pallette. He dropped to one knee, nearly finished. From his behind a cloaked figure flashed in, parried the killing blow with a translucent weapon, and, touching Teramon, flashed the both of them to safety.

Avar-Sint turned his head from left to right, sensing for any other danger then walked away slowly to his original destination inside the urba. Utter fear followed the victor after he had beaten the best fighter on Seranor. The battle would be told a thousand times and each time the story was relayed the entire ceramination would clutch their lives closer and donate risks to the foolhardy.

THERE ARE those who believe that learning is made through close observation and study, as well as analysis. Then there are those who would take a minute of experience over an hour of study because they would swear that the benefits of experience far outweigh any derived from close observation. Ira Levin was a believer of the latter and a user of the former. He was not disturbed by the event with Avar-Sint, and had guaranteed Teramon that although he may become injured, he would not die, and it was why Ira himself had pulled him to safety.

His experiment, while casting terror in others, gave him the confidence he needed to beat the synthetic oratic creations of Zorath who was weakening Seranor, and would eventually pluck all of life away. More study was needed. The recent battle had given him valuable data that he began to ream through. Unfortunately, he was limited by his own genius intelligence. "Cerbi," he had always said, "are the limited creations of all natural beings." He required additional cerbi if he was going to beat the Ice King, and when he had discovered that a new technology was being developed by his competitor it brightened his eyes and fired him up once again.

The Levin wanted to study Technomicon's latest intelligence prototype, called RATIO, to learn its capacity.

Fed by well-informed servants, Ira became intrigued by a
device that offered synthetic intelligence. He wanted the
Ratio.

Ratio was a 5 cm thick and 20 cm long cylindrical
intelligence device that combined the storage properties of
ganium, flamma, and newly developed arvic intelligence.
Nietsn Dl, a half-entan, genius-level mathematician,
developed a complex mathematical formula that
harnessed the hidden intelligence contained in arvicity.
The Ratio's arvic intelligence had limited artificial
managerial abilities and House Levin wanted to know
what they were.

Khan, Boon, Griz and Alexan were Ira's first pick to
obtain the device, but Khan declined in order to give the
members of his party a rest and the freedom to indulge
their own ideas and implement their own plans. Ira had
found others to do the job for him. A second group, this
time made up of three mercenaries, was hired including
Mosp, a renowned thief. Mosp was a ventan who had re-
learned the ability to camouflage his skin against any
color surface and to emit no presence. It gave him
ultimate stealth as a thief.

The party of three was discovered, charmed by Napia-
Sint, and obliterated at the Lorrat Inn. She cast several
incendiary balls of fissile gamma energy upon the
unsuspecting party. Three large holes were seen the next
morning at the Lorrat and it became a place where
seedlings went to play after it closed down.

Gamma energy was the second most powerful flammic
energy known only to the highest level arvicians and
ancient devices lost to the land. Zamma energy was the
purest and the most deadly. Zamma spells, if they could
be cast without killing the spellcaster, would cause
damage not only to the target but also to those around the
target from a decaying sickness that would infect all of

those in a sufficient radius. At present, there was no cure or protection from zamma. The Sints were not capable of such power. Zorath's ability to manipulate arvicity would have surely reached the level of zamma without endangering himself.

Ever since the battle with Teramon, the Sints had increased the levels of their power. They had turned up the heat of the fire and the mortality rate went up as they did. Ira guessed that Zorath had been experimenting with Seranor up until now and it also seemed that his power was multiplying giving rise to his previous claim that Zorath was absorbing the cosmic energy of Seranor. It was inconceivable for any one or a range of devices to be capable of such a feat, but Zorath must have found a way to absorb large amounts of arvicity. As he grew in power so too did his closest minions.

Nietsn, a day later, was marked for assassination after a seminar demonstrating the power of the Ratio device and letting slip his next great work, an upgraded model that nearly simulates real intelligence, as well as combines communication abilities.

Sarcophagi, the master assassin hired to kill Nietsn, was left for dead hours before his attempt, an attempt that would most certainly have killed the mathematician.

The Khan party considered themselves lucky of the Nietsn affair except for Griz who wanted the chance to face a Sint again, this time on fairer grounds. With his anger unsatisfied, he hacked a fat morb into three pieces in a senseless argument at the Ice Scabbard.

It was not known who had marked Sarcophagi for assassination. What was well known in the circle of those who knew was one basic idea – there were only two other assassins capable of killing him. One of those was Zorn. The other was a female assassin who used the name AAA (pronounced 'Triple A').

Zorn was ruled out as a potential killer because Zorn was Sarcophagi's student and the unwritten rule was to never kill your teacher. Zorn was blamed for another assassination having this time to do with the corporate leader of Narcophalin, Borius. He had taken over from Director Jicama and had done a very impressive job up until his untimely death. Technomicon could not retaliate directly because it was not supposed to have any official business links with Narcophalin. Indirect methods suited the underground society and sellers had a new contract to sell.

Chapter 3

ZORATH'S EXPRESSION on the wide PT screen held
Denar'ka's attention captive. Shell as black as the
darkest night, hairless, parts muttering unintelligible
sounds as he moved his limbs to accent his gestures, eyes
of translucent orange, the only physical memory of who he
once was. Thickly muscled arms ended in three fingered
hands with four knuckles each. His glimmering golden
tongue, long as his hand from wrist to fingertip, slid out
between the time he raised his voice. A dull-tipped horn,
turned downward, extended itself from the top and back
of his head just to the level of his eyes.

Zorath was calm and focused as always as he made his
demands to Denar'ka on the PT. Denar'ka listened more
than he spoke as his cerbi worked on solutions for his
king. Denar'ka had just finished explaining the current

production situation at Vatu to Zorath who was not satisfied with deadlines not being met under any reason.

"THE S4S, DENAR'KA, ARE *STILL* NOT COMPLETE." Every word spoken slowly with a resounding echo ever so faintly as if he were talking from an icy underground cave. "I EXPECTED BETTER RESULTS FROM A NIVATON. YOUR ACTIONS DISAPPOINT," said Zorath.

"King Zorath, I will have results for you soon. Our time is devoted to it as to all tasks under the Ice Timor," said Denar'ka. A splinter of apprehension in his voice.

"CONTINUE TO DISAPPOINT AND YOU WILL NOT ONLY DISAPPOINT ME BUT NIVA AS WELL. COUNT YOUR DAYS CLEARLY."

"I understand."

Plans fitted into structure like mouths to aqua. The plan had been set, not served. Nivian cerbinds could not comprehend the unfulfilled nor the unstructured. Zorath, because of his long stay on Seranor, understood better than others but rarely accepted such behavior unless for special reasons unannounced. His weakness, if such words could be used when describing a god in progress, was to things devoted to ice. Nivatons were the worshippers of Niva, the ice spirit, and were the closest representation of what he once was – a Nivian. Not what he had become – a kium black monster.

"AND MY S3 ZOLDIERS?"

"The next batch of 20,000 S3 zoldiers are being prepared. I estimate ten more weeks of naqui gestation and they will be ready but we will need more crystalloids from Narcophalin. You will be pleased with the enhancements."

"NARCOPHALIN. AN IMPORTANT MATTER. THE FALSE TRADING ARM THAT SUPPLIED ALL OF THE CRYSTALLOIDS HAS BEEN SMASHED."

"I know."

"BORIUS IS MURDERED BY ZORN. IS THIS TRUE?"

"No. It was not Zorn. We still do not have that information."

"FIND OUT WHO HAS HALTED THE TRANSFER OF OUR MATERIALS AND SUBSTRACT THEM. I DON'T WANT ANY MORE DELAYS, DENAR'KA."

"When will I have my chance to kill Khan?"

"SOON ENOUGH."

"He must die from the ice. From my ice hand, my king." Denar'ka had made known that he wanted to kill Khan to revenge what Nao did to him and, more importantly, to earn Zorath's respect. Zorath had said at the beginning that Khan would not be so easily killed. Denar'ka did not agree and was eager to prove it.

"NO. I WANT KHAN ALIVE FOR A SHORT WHILE LONGER. YOU WILL HAVE YOUR CHANCE TO TASTE HIS MILK IN DUE TIME."

"He walks on cracked ice yet the ice remains."

"HIS IS MY PATH. MANAGE VATU AND HE WILL COME TO YOU.

"What if he chooses not to come?"

"THEN YOU WILL ENSURE IT, DENAR'KA!"

"I understand."

"A SHIPPING TRACK NOW LEADS TO VATU. YOU MUST PUSH THE PRODUCTION AHEAD TWO WEEKS. DISREGARD THE PAIN."

"It will require more crystalloid shards."

"MORE THAN ENOUGH WILL ARRIVE ON THE MORNING OF THE SECOND WEEK. TELL KOZO OF ANY OTHER NEEDS."

"A list will be arranged. How else can I serve you, master?"

"A RICH VENTAN, WEREWUL, NOT UNDER THE ICE TIMOR, HAS HIRED A MAKESHIFT PARTY OF THREE MERCENARIES TO RETRIEVE THE SMALL WHITE BOX. TO THINK THAT THEY HAVE A CHANCE TO GET THE ITEM IS AN ENIGMA. SO FAR,

THE DULL-WITTED VENTAN KNOWS THIS TO BE A FACTORY AND NOTHING MORE. BUT YOU WILL SHOW THEM DIFFERENT."

"They will not pass the gates alive—"

"THEY WILL PASS — ALIVE AND CAPTURED. YOU WILL FIND OUT WHAT OTHER KNOWLEDGE THEY HAVE. TORTURE THEM IF YOU DESIRE BUT THEY MUST REMAIN ALIVE."

"As you wish. Superiority in structure."

"BE WELL PREPARED, DENAR'KA. OUR PLAY IS IN ACTION. SOON MY ARMY OF NAQUIOR WILL STRIKE AT THE CORIUS OF THE TERIUM AND THE HOUSES, AND SECURE THE EXECUTION OF OUR PRIMARY STRATEGY. ALL ELSE IS ARRANGED BUT THE ARMY OF 20,000 MUST BE READY AND PLACED IN POSITION. YOU HAVE A FURTHER THREE WEEKS TO COMPLETE AND EQUIP THE ZOLDIERS. THAT IS 11 WEEKS FOR WHAT I REQUIRE. THIS DUTY I LEAVE IN YOUR HAND. FAIL ME AND VATU WILL BE YOUR GRAVE."

"It will be done," Denar'ka said, confident of his ability. "Is her fate sealed?"

"SHE SPEAKS SOFTLY IN HER DYING MOMENTS."

"Then it is true that she will soon die."

"I HAVE SEEN TO IT."

"Arvicity will be on your horn, King Zorath."

"THESE ARE STERILE DAYS."

"But—"

"AS LONG AS SHE LIVES, CHANGE IS POSSIBLE. STAY WELL PREPARED AND TREAT NOTHING AS I·N·S·I·G·N·I·F·I·C·A·N·T. NOTHING. WHEN SERANOR CASTS HER INFLUENCE, HER MOVES WILL BE SUBTLE AND INCONSPICOUS. ARTFUL AND INVISIBLE. THEY HAVE ALWAYS BEEN HER METHODS."

"I will alert the staff."

"DO NOT WASTE TIME. FOCUS ONLY ON THE TASKS I HAVE TOLD YOU."

"Yes, my King."

"I WILL ARRIVE AT VATU TO SETTLE OTHER SENSITIVE MATTERS WHEN THE TIME COMES. BEFORE THEN YOU WILL GO TO TECHNOMICON AND TAKE AN OBJECT THAT MUST BE CARRIED BACK TO VATU. IT IS FRAGILE AND WILL BE USED FOR THE S4S."

"Yes, my king. I shall arrive in two days to retrieve it."

"I ALSO WANT YOU TO MEET THE NEW DIRECTOR OF NARCOPHALIN. HIS NAME IS OMNITACUS." Even from the PT, Zorath read Denar'ka's facial expressions, unachievable by any other looking at the deformity. "I CAN SEE IT IN YOUR FACE DENAR'KA. SOMETHING RATTLES IN YOUR CERBIND."

"Yes. It is the Terium, my king. They are developing an underground rebel force and it is hampering our actions with the zoldiers. I have sent V-Non to proliferate the IceFist in the main urbas but the Terium still strikes each time harder than before under the command of the Houses of the North."

"DO NOT CONCERN YOURSELF WITH THE TERIUM. THEY ARE MY DECISION."

"I understand." The connection closed down.

TIME TO the Kozotal was immortal when on their home planet. But outside, the physical laws changed and reduced their mortality evaporating their atomic bindings. Still they did not care about age even on Seranor where their life spans normalized and they assumed the mortality rate of about three entans combined if they remained for a long time. Kozo was one such Kozotalian. He arrived here by indirect decision and became the last of the flamma beings to exist on Seranor. He had been imprisoned for his betrayal 1,100 tios ago. In his view, this still left him with approximately another 1,000 tios of

life. There was no need to be concerned and more than
enough time to do what he wanted.

Many Kozotalians had visited Aquanomicus in its early
formation. All had returned to Mettadi-di Flamma except
for two; Escarotian, the one who stole Orbis Inigra, and
his wife. Lamatia. Kozo was sent back to the planet when
it was found that he had assisted in the thieving of the
Orbis, and it was also known that he had secretly mated
with Lamatia. Orbis Inigra was the majestic storage
device shaped into a ball and capable of holding
immeasurable levels of arvicity.

Escarotian became fired with a misguided and angered
emotion, and locked Kozo in the air's temporal lobe in an
inconspicuous spot inside of the Halinari Woods to forever
live his limited hours in view of the outside world, but
without being able to interact with it ever again.

It was this reason that Zorath had found him inside of
the Halinari Woods between Gaze and Zahara. There had
been no formal record of Kozo's imprisonment. Lamatia
was killed by her husband who then himself disappeared
in the southern region.

The Seranivas had assisted Zorath in his quest for
historical information. He was not aware of the details of
this planet. It had never been necessary until after his
accidental arrival. Until after he transformed into who he
had become. A new identity. And it was important in his
strategic plan to strike back at his Nivian brother for the
betrayal, for the vengeance and for the love he had lost.
The Seranivas, bribed by his lustful power and charmed
by Zorath's empty promises, divulged all that he needed to
know and had given him a lead on the local competition.

On Seranor, Nivians were demi-gods by nature. That
wasn't enough for Zorath. He wanted to become a
supreme being: A god (granted omniscient dominion). He
wanted to play the strings of the Versos with his fingers.

He always achieved what he wanted on Nivata. Seranor had shown him that there were actions that were not predictable, and could alter the efficiencies of his executions. Actions that could affect his control. It improved Zorath's tactics.

Kozo appeared in Zorath's chambers. Something urgent.

"Zorath, there has been a new development." Kozo knew to continue. "An artus lock has been opened and it was not by our command."

"WHAT?"

"One of the lower points was released. It is a miracle of miracles. There is no knowledge of the artus points on Seranor. I am certain of that. All of those who knew have died. And my brothers have been gone for a millennium."

"MAYBE NOT ALL OF THEM HAVE DIED."

"It was Shev'la Khan and his three friends."

"IMPOSSIBLE! YOU YOURSELF ARE NOT AWARE OF THEIR LOCATIONS."

"It was them. The wanderer does wander to places none should know. And in his wandering his seeds do sow."

"KHAN CONTINUES. IT IS AS THE SERANIVAS HAVE SAID."

"Yes. One of her disguises."

"IF HE IS CAPABLE OF SUCH A MIRACLE THEN HE MUST BE KILLED SOONER RATHER THAN LATER."

"It is impossible to predict his next actions, Zorath. He rides a twisted, venomous wind."

"HE IS ONLY NEEDED FOR ONE MORE THING. HE IS THE ONLY ONE WHO HAS OPENED THE WHITE BOX. AND MUST FINISH HIS WORK."

"None other will ever be able to open the box."

"IT IS WHY I HAVE NOT MARKED HIS DEATH YET."

"But now…"

"HE WILL WORK HIS MIRACLES FOR US. THE ARTUS POINT IS IN OUR FAVOR, KOZO. DO NOT CONCERN YOURSELF TOO MUCH. HE HAS DONE US A FAVOR."

"The elements favor him, Zorath. They lead him and his crew. The Kozotalians created the seragons to do such wonderful things and when they became the elements I even thought that their fate had been sealed. Now the elements have spoken and they go against our plans."

"SERANOR HAS ONLY ROUSED THEM. SHE WILL DIE SOON ENOUGH AND THE ICE TIMOR SHALL HAVE HER POWER. I SHALL HAVE IT!"

"And of Khan?" Kozo started. "He is dangerous as long as he lives. He is a wind follower and none could ever control the wind. It is the spirit of this planet that cannot be controlled. Cannot be moved against its will. He must be killed before his own ability is awakened. Before he becomes the wind," Kozo said with a rising intensity.

"KHAN IS WEAK OF CORIUS. HE FAILS AT FOLLOW THROUGH AND WITHOUT IT, MY WORRISOME KOZOTAL, HE CANNOT SUCCEED. THAT WAS THE PROBLEM WITH HIS FATHER AND BROTHER."

"But he is different. He is not entan..."

"INFERIOR TO ANY ONE ZOLDIER! INFERIOR TO THE ICE!" Zorath roared. He walked up to Kozo, black face and all. Kozo quickly bowed his head down slightly and took a step back.

"I am only informing my king and nothing more," said Kozo, head still bowed. "It is information that is relevant to our future plans. The ceramination can be controlled. You have proven that. Seranor and Seragorn will die. That is certainty. But Khan is an aberration. There is cosmic force in unpredictability."

The Nivian belief in structure and control could not fathom unpredictability. Entans in general did not possess such skills. Only Nata. The rebellious spirit who could not be killed. Considering the magnitude of Khan's unpredictable behavior and actions, Zorath needed to be concerned. If the windy wanderer could unlock a lost artus point without planning, then his actions had to be reduced. The only way to do that would be to remove him and his dangerous luck from the equation. Zorath did not think of him as a major threat and he was intrigued that Kozo did. But Kozo was a poor example of what divinity should be. He failed to pass for anything but an information gatherer and compiler devoid of independent ideas. What was his opinion worth?

"Kozo, continue our plans for Seranor and her seed. Khan will die at Vatu. He begins to bore me. To think that he discovered me. Make sure that Denar'ka keeps his goal to kill him once he has done what I want. I shall overlook it myself."

"Will he come so eagerly to his death?"

"Khan does not see death."

"He will suspect that he is endangered."

"Sometimes I think that your existence on this planet has made you like them," said Zorath. He lectured on. "Khan's optimism corrupts him. His persistence occupies him entirely. There is turbulent madness in him and it grows. He will come and not see death. He will only believe in obligation: To his family, to Seranor and, maybe, against me." Zorath smiled. "Foolish Khan."

"Then unpredictability will soon be sowed and only predictability will remain."

"What is more foolish than a dedicated fool?"

Two large hands clasped one another, smacking each other gently. Kozo had already left Zorath alone; his orange eyes gazing at a distant place inside of the only organic part that remained: His cerbus. There was a time, even for him, that he played the fool and in the end

lost his wife and his previous kingdom. Passion was his
folly. There was an inverse relationship to the absence of
passion and the presence of foolishness. He had abolished
this passion. Destroyed it when he destroyed his former
body. But the kium that housed his kol could not
experience passion. Could not caress it as he once did.
This inability comforted him in his moment of
recollection. For who could have estimated the effects of a
Nivian female gone against him. Who could know the
depth of deviant beauty? A fool no longer. Zorath was
now the fool maker.

Chapter 4

EXACTLY TWO days later Denar'ka arrived in Batall with a small armament of zoldier troops. There was displeasure on his already unpleasant face. He hated to interrupt his arkti training. He was working on the next level in arkti state, his own form, it required intense concentration for a period of not less than seven days and had to break it when Zorath called him for that important discussion. Zorath did not often contact him, and so, when he did there was no way to prevent the intercourse.

Denar'ka promised himself to settle matters quickly and then return to Vatu to solidify his arkti state. Soon, he predicted, he would achieve the highest ice form ever attained by an entan and one that could not be copied by any other. If he could achieve it, the form would squeeze the naqui from his body into the vessels which circulated his milk and would permanently, as a Nivian, have naqui for his milk. This would give him unlimited fighting and

even arvic abilities, diluted but similar to those of a
Nivian. It was Zorath who had led him this far and it was
up to him to finish the last stages. He had discussed it
with V-Non because he wanted his best Nivaton to
develop his skill to such a point, but V-Non was not ready.
It would still require many tios of practice to reach the
point where the Nivaton could try without obliterating his
body into a pool of naqui.

Batall was a pristine urba with a growing port that
connected Maffin and Zahara together in a triangular
shipping route. A further trip to Ravada could cover 70%
of the planet and many importers and exporters set up
operations here to facilitate low cost shipping. Casus was
another major port but it was far more dangerous than
Batall.

Travel across land was made by a combination of
flashing and talins. Industrial flashport devices, limited
in production and use, were commonly used at Ice Timor,
and Denar'ka had flashed him and four cohorts to a flash
depot inside the Omon Woods. From there they took to
talins along with a score of zoldiers and rode into Batall.

Denar'ka detested business negotiations and
relationships. He was a fighter, a physical warrior and
not suited for politics or position much unlike Zorath who
probably trusted him for those very reasons. It made him
loyal to his words. Politicians were useful but their very
nature was to politic, and without the intellect of a
Nivian, the domestic politicians were not the most reliable
unless their greed was constantly satisfied. It was what
led Denar'ka to create and insert a number of synthetic
politicians in the urbas. They were the dedicated.
Loyalty was the driving force behind the Ice Timor. The
Ice Timor was largely *Vian*, of synthetic ice beings.

Denar'ka was not surprised then to find that
Omnitacus was an artificial creation. He could tell by the

markings on the skin and confirmed it when he shook hands, despite the requisite gloves they wore. He was surprised to find that it did not originate from Vatu which, until then, had been the primary source of synthetic beings. Was there another production site? How many Vians were on the planet? thought the Nivaton.

Standard greetings were made and the two of them talked about the current operations at Narcophalin. Omnitacus had a new strategy for the company that Denar'ka welcomed since it eased off of his demands at Vatu and would allow him to focus on manufacturing the Army of Naquior. He could not help to wonder, in his conversation, of where his future lay at the Ice Timor. Once the S4s were completed there would be nothing to do. And the time for completion was drawing very near.

"I think that you will agree, Denar'ka. Once we can control the entire processing of crystalloids here and then load them in refrigerated special containers that I have shown you then you will only have to use the *crystine* pods, which contain pure arvic energy suitable to our production machinery," said Omnitacus.

"Am I to believe that you can deliver all the energy that I require when I require it," said Denar'ka, not willing to so easily go along with the plan that may phase him out.

"No." Pause. "Before you require it."

"What do you mean?"

"Because of the structure of the crystine pods they are compatible with the current flashport technology. This was not possible before but we have extended the code and now can take advantage of a new distribution model."

"You are asking me to reengineer our whole production process."

"Yes. Our king has advised you, I am sure."

"Yes."

"Then it is no problem."

"I will arrange it. But I want to test this system before I come to rely on it so easily. Any further delays in the production will cost me my head and if you are responsible maybe even your head, Omnitacus."

"Will two weeks be sufficient to win your approval?"

Denar'ka's tard lit up. A masked informant was on the other side. His image did not project upwards and Omnitacus could not see who it was. "Yes?" said the Nivaton.

"I have information," said the masked voice.

"Speak," said Denar'ka.

"An old enemy of yours has been resurrected."

"Who is it? One of Ira's?"

"No. Much further than that."

"I am too busy to play. Tell me."

"Nao."

"Nao Li-Grum?"

"Yes."

"Where?"

"In Casus. But he is sick."

"What do mean, sick?"

"He is weak and has forgotten his skills. He roams the streets not knowing what is what. As I have said, he is sick."

A sick Nao was of no use to Denar'ka. He must wait. "Monitor him but do not interfere. He still owes me."

"I will contact you." The connection was cut.

Omnitacus had not waited idly. He had given instructions to several of his employees during the time that Denar'ka was using the tard.

"Is it two weeks then?" asked Omnitacus, referring to his last question and eager to go about his business.

"Two weeks are sufficient only if Narcophalin can convince me that it is as or more secure than the current model, and that your crystine pods can do what they say they can. It is in your hands."

"Very well, Denar'ka. I will have the first shipment sent in 60 hours. A follow up shipment will arrive every 96 hours according to your current and future use of crystalloid energy. These schedules will be adjusted according to your needs."

"Day day, Omnitacus," said Denar'ka coldly and left.

TECHNOMICON HAD been under heavy security lately. This happened at about the time of Nietsn's death. Technology had turned into a game of possession and the more one possessed the more potential power they had in the market. Technological innovations were rapidly evolving and Nietsn's new artificial cerbus that was to be incorporated into the Ratio device was reengineered into a spin-off technology suitable to operations of zoldiers that would enable a zoldier to have independent thoughts rather than networked thoughts as they were now.

The head of innovation at Technomicon was a ventan named, Per Pix. He was able, by thought alone, to evolve ideas exponentially into plausible alternatives. It was his original idea that triggered the development of the Zoldier Manufacturing Mechanism (ZMM). He had also influenced every other idea to come from Technomicon. His latest work was the unfolding of Nietsn's mathematical processor and reworking it to fit the head of a zoldier.

Director Rajahira, who replaced Jicama, spent most of her time outside trying to sell the concepts into the cerbinds of the mass consumers while her employees did all of the real work at the company.

Denar'ka was welcomed by Per and taken on an exclusive tour of his latest project. Per had been able to take embedded lutium concepts from the Ratio and spliced them together with shattered crystals. The resulting material was a rounded, sponge-like white matter that sparkled from the crystal specks inside.

Per did a masterful job at covering the technology. He said: "It is the first step into the next and final step of life." Per did not strike Denar'ka as a ventan capable of such creation. He was an oddity and it was no accident that this artificial cerbus was created.

"What makes this one different than the others in use?" asked Denar'ka.

"Well...ah...well...many components are different. It's all about the function. I—I mean, we, have been able to make a shift from one deep-seated concept into another. The beauty of the Ratio was that it did not require a source from which to 'think'. Our S3s need the photon network. This network feeds back to the base which feeds once again to the zoldiers. Networks are finished once this new technology gets..."

"Slow yourself, Per. What do you mean that the network is finished?"

"Nivaton Denar'ka, allow me to ask you one question?'

He nodded in agreement.

"What makes the current beings – choose entan or morb, any really – what makes these beings, living entities, special?"

"You tell me."

"Okay. What makes us and others special is our ability to create. There are two aspects: creating something from pre-existence and creating things to destroy existence. We are beings of creation. We create then destroy then create once more. Some entans call this cycle evolution. I like to call it a waste of time." He laughed but Denar'ka did not find it as funny as he. "Anyway, evolution has been thought to propel life forward. Creativity is the driver."

"Where are you going with this, Per? I'm reaching boredom."

"I almost there."

"Quickly, will you."

"Yes, yes. We create—"

"I understood that..."

"This new discovery, a technology far ahead of its time, is capable of using information on a continual basis with no need for a network or a high amount of memory. This cerbus, molecule to molecule, is not as powerful as yours."

"Then why do you say it is better if it is not really better?"

"It is better. It is far better than we ever imagined."

"How is this?"

"Many believe that in order to be smarter one needs higher intelligence. As if they were comparing it to physical things, like mountains. A mountain is bigger than a hill therefore it is greater than a hill. But when we are discussing the ability of a thinking device such as a cerbus this theory does not hold true.

"A cerbus, in fact, is made powerful as a temporary storage device. Like ganium. You see, ganium stores arvicity then releases it then discharges it once more."

"But intelligence is not arvicity."

"But it is."

"What?"

"Beyond us, I mean outside of our physical shell is an ocean of intelligence. It is the roadway on which arvicity flows. We have not seen it before because we have been so mesmerized by arvicity and its power that we have blinded ourselves to the obvious.

"After finding this ocean of intelligence, I have created a device that is capable to access its natural intelligence reservoirs."

"Cannot others do the same?"

"They do not have our technology. This new 'brain' can download what it needs from the reservoir, use it and then recharge itself. Each time it does so it 'learns' something, a skill perhaps or an idea. Skills, once learned, are kept until no longer needed: new skills replace old skills at some point. So there is no reason to hold information indefinitely. This is where we have failed before. We have been trying to create a brain that has a massive amount of storage capacity and processing power when all we needed was a brain that could access, utilize and learn from the intelligence reservoir." He took a breath. "That is where we are now. This brain can do such things."

"This soft piece of matter can do what you have said?"

"It is soft because so that it can be permeated by this intelligence reservoir which, by the way, is flamma based and another reason why we did not see it."

"Enough already, Per. Tell me one last thing."

"Yes, Nivaton Denar'ka?"

"Is it finished? Is it perfect?"

"Nearly. These prototypes are ready for testing." Per Pix smiled and mystery filled the air around him as he prepared the cerbi for travel.

The Nivaton studied one of them closely. What he saw was the end of the future. The place for entan and Kozoty, cerbor and morb was diminishing. The borders of life were being crossed and he knew then that achieving a goal in life was the pity of natural beings. It was their delusion. And, by thinking that, he clutched his goals more closely than ever before. It was all that he had and despite its insignificance in the natural order of things he had yet to accomplish all that he wanted. He could not prevent Nao's image from forming his head. It forced him to drop a few degrees in temperature.

Three synthetic cerbi were put into small protective cases and given to Denar'ka who then gave them to his guards just before they exited Technomicon. Razafon, a potent arvicerer, was sent with them to shield their priceless packages.

Denar'ka started to care less for technology and thought more of his enemy. It was the last of his pain. He would focus harder on his training and arrange to meet this Nao, but Zorath would certainly not approve, so he would wait and prepare until all vertices met as they should.

THE SPEED that information began traveling was becoming dangerous. Communications would soon be the future battlegrounds. Melee could, in theory, disappear within one or two generations at the current rate of technological development. Actions were being taken via communications, enemies were beings weakened, strategies planned, data taken and physical responses initiated.

The tard connection that Denar'ka had accepted was a decoy. The *ta* ("call") was made by Jasoko, an informant for the Ice Timor. But Jasoko had two jobs and only one of them was for the ice king; the other was for a distant branch of the Terium. The ta confirmed Denar'ka's presence at Technomicon, knowledge of the presence of an artificial cerbus had already been acquired.

A team of eight, seven heavily armed and one lightly, was sent in to obtain the object. Razafon detected them early on and had alerted Denar'ka.

The ambush took place not far from the head office of Technomicon with the tall pyramidal peak in the background. The Terium team sent in were well prepared and countered several of Razafon's spells to flash away with the items in tow by casting a spell in the shape of a giant hemisphere around them that prevented flashing out or into the area. Any others would have to approach them by foot and that would still leave them enough time to finish their task.

Razafon abandoned the idea of dispelling the shield above them all and decided to focus on the other spellcaster who challenged him. Razafon was not the most powerful arvicerer but he was skilled in the art of arvicity. The Terium arvician, a rogue spellcaster named Caladartian, threw up a yellow disk-like device into the air and when it landed the ground opened and five large yellow snakes, more than 5 meters each in length, ripped out of the earth and onto the ready zoldiers. Raders and scales met in a gore of red milk and naqui.

Denar'ka engaged three of his enemies as the others took to his personal guards. The Nivaton became naqui and froze the first opponent into a block of ice before he shattered it with a fist. The other two jumped in wearing special shields that were heated and protected them, at least temporarily, from the liquid beast.

Caladartian faced his challenger and spells erupted from their hands as arvicity was shaped into the destroyer of entans. The ground shook as elemental noxy fires burned the landscape and left the blackened markings for others to remember. Razafon would have quelled his foe by liquefying Caladartian's entire skeletal structure if not for black spike that raced through the air and into his rear shoulder blade that knocked his concentration allowing Caladartian to recover. A shadow moved on one of the opposite buildings and a searing hot noxy ball flew onto the rooftop to explode in a wide radius, but the assassin was long gone.

The snakes, now dwindled down to three, had massacred and squashed eighteen of the twenty zoldiers who had turned to aqua and made the ground slippery. They now approached Denar'ka who still fended against the shielded warriors. The box containing the cerbi had fallen to the ground when guard and enemy died together. Razafon cast a spell at Caladartian that stunned the arvician and bought him enough time to grab the box, and get close to Denar'ka. He handed the Nivaton the cerbi.

Once ready, Razafon raised his hands in an arc high above his head. Arvic energy flowed around his palms and started to collect and increase in density. The fields moved violently and as his hands clasped each other in front of his chest, all arvicity channeled into it, the one small space between his palms. In a thrust motion pushing away from his chest he let the flammic ball out into the center of his enemies. The ball brightened and then burst out into a fan-like ray, flat as a dish and as wide as 30 meters, without affecting him or Denar'ka. Flammic rays, sharp and scorching, cut all who stood, beast and entan, at the lower torso. The fanned ray, once it reached its end, circled back just in time to catch the falling chunks of porcelan and impacted onto itself before vanishing entirely. Caladartian had sensed the danger and protected himself. By the end he had escaped the flash protected area and blinked out to safety.

Denar'ka and Razafon returned to Technomicon safely and Murmia-Sint was ordered in to escort them safely to the Omon Woods. None followed.

Chapter 5

AN AIR of disregard suited Ira's look when he was told of the bad news. He downplayed it with a few nods to show his understanding then paid their wages with a danger bonus and left it at that. At the end of handing out the zorn and as they were walking out of the secret room, Ira casually informed them that the two Arvinstrum pieces had been stolen by another party and Kalier-Sint was killed in the process. He said it so nonchalantly that they all confirmed that he was involved in some direct way but said nothing to ruin their upcoming vacation.

The vacation was long overdue. Two weeks on an adventure was like ten times that number in daily work. Their last trip equaled somewhere around five months of straight work and after working out the salaries – even with Ira's bonus and taking account of the number of near-death experiences – Boon suggested, very strongly, that their wages should be raised for any future scenarios that they might go on. It was Khan who reminded the thief of economics that it was Boon who first settled for much less and, if not for Khan, would be even poorer. That shut the thief up and prevented any complaining to Ira. They didn't succeed in their tasks and crying over the fact wasn't going to help. At least they were all still alive, but even that was close.

When they had reappeared from travel out of Seragorn's room, the three conscious party members felt queasy and ill from their milk being churned several times over while passing through infinite space. Within an hour, though they felt like dying, it passed and they decided to avoid long distance travel unless it was by talin. They had had an overdose of arvicity for the past three weeks and swore to stay off of it for some time. Alexan came to shortly after that though felt weak. He would end up feeling weak for an extended period of time from the arvic poisoning that he had received.

Paid and alive, the four of them scattered their own ways promising to see each other again soon enough without prospect of when that might be. Khan went about his business of tracing the significance of the Arvinstrum. He talked to older entans about the creation of Seranor. Rumors and stories were told to him without consistency or validity and it sent his head spinning for more reliable sources. The days passed quickly in research.

Locals were extremely interested in a new zorn making opportunity. It was Valuto, a game based on Seronian adventurers and risk takers. An initial list of thirty names were posted and two them included Khan and Griz for the rumors of them challenging two Sints and living to tell about it circulated quickly. Even the palpazine, Querist, had a feature on Khan. This helped to improve the image of his wind form and also attracted a number of fans eager to learn his style hoping to zorn in on the wealth of adventuring. Khan politely declined offers to teach his wind form.

Many of the younger Seronians, the Sub-Generation or Sub-G, asked him to open a school where Equists could be nurtured in the hopes of one day achieving Khan's status. Only a very small section of the Sub-G class could be interested in such a strenuous form of battle. Most of them, a credit to their name, were interested in technology as it substituted the traditional lifestyles their parents had grown accustomed to. Convenience was substituted in all areas of life from bathing to breathing thanks in large part to enicoys, the idealisms presented by Technomicon and its world-class engineers.

Valuto converted occasional players into addicts, a crypto-concept built into the game design by Zorath himself. Valuto players invested zorn in members of the list based on a preliminary value of *oracles* that rose or declined according to the success of the individual. Oracles would rise or fall depending on the actions that the adventurer in question took. Obviously, smart investors bought oracles that were low in value and sold when they jumped high. Positions changed daily and sometimes even hourly, and with its initial level of success the adventuring list would certainly grow.

Nibal, the cocky arvatist that Khan interviewed before the trip, was actually listed near the bottom at number 30. Rumor had it that he found an orange rod enchanted with gamma-level flamma and used it to bury two respected cerbors in the streets of Casus by liquefying their bodies. It was that and Nibal's escapade against the rich numularian Opopon, where he single-handedly wiped out his arsenal of troops and stole Z200,000 along with the plans to build a new type of artificial cerbus, that listed him. The riskier the adventurer the more likely that they were on this volatile Valuto exchange.

By week's end, and after Boon shared the story of his party's travels with the appropriate gossip channel, Alexan's name was added. Khan, for a reason that escaped him, was given the highest valuation. He replaced the last number one, Portica – an independent ventan luta who had been responsible for murdering two very high level government officials – with a high value, who was assassinated by Palindorn, a free for hire assassin wielding two translucent short batiers. Sometimes bounties earned more than investing in Valuto and the elimination trade had picked up.

DURING HIS research, Khan kept crossing the street where a crazy old entan; dirty and smelly like a mud ditch, who would repeatedly try to grab him speaking obscenities in quick pace. He avoided him, as best as he could, each time. Thrombus Street was unavoidable as it was the street where historical details about old Seranor could be found. Past knowledge remained and it had attracted the crazies, weirdos and the misguided. Khan adapted.

Today, he passed the crazy old entan again and what came from his dry lips stopped him dead in his path. The venerated Seronian pronounced the word "now" several times together with the word "ind". It stopped Khan because of its direct similarity to *Nao* and *wind*. He approached the dirty entan, hair messed all over and knotted in places where matter, mostly mud and bits of clay with some miscellaneous particles, had locked it together.

"Nao, do you know, Equist Nao?" asked Khan.

"Now, now, now," the crazy entan repeated endlessly.

"Do you know him? Have you seen, Nao? Have you seen him? Can you understand me?" He placed one hand on his dirty shoulder and asked in a desperate tone. The entan's eyes stared through him. "Equist Nao, where is he? Is he alive?" Nothing. Khan thought that his imagination had got the best of him and started to walk away and as he did the disturbed voice spoke again.

"Find, find, find…" the old entan said.

"Where? What?" Khan asked.

"Everywhere!" the old voice screamed then burst out in a laugh, running in circles. "Everywhere!"

"I am his student, Khan. Where can I find him?"

"Everywhere!" he spun his head around trying to dance but flailing more than anything. "Here. There. Everywhere. Round and round."

Khan left the crazy old entan flailing his arms stupidly in the street while he returned to his research. The experience left him with thoughts on his training and his near death with Denar'ka. He had to start training again, he reminded himself, not sure how to advance to the next level. He had to at least try. It had been three weeks without practice. Practitioners could not excel without practice.

The next morning, he found himself following his own bet and ended up in an isolated area just outside of the downtown. Some empty buildings were planted on three sides and an open road on the other. It was perfect because it allowed the wind to come and whirl away freely. He engaged his stance and took to the training seriously. The wind came and he moved with it much smoother than before and attributed that to the encounter with the icy Nivaton. Hours later while he was resting he felt a presence nearby. The crazy old entan appeared in his peripheral vision.

"How did you get here?" asked Khan surprised that he did not sense such an obvious thing until then.

"Get here, get there, get here, yes...get here," the stranger repeated.

"Get out of here," said Khan.

"Get here, out here."

"Go!"

"Trouble? Trouble? Trouble?"

"What?"

"Trouble?"

"What trouble?"

The old Seronian puckered his lips and blew a wind-like sound. It was dry and faulty. He blew again a couple of times.

"What is that you want?" Khan asked.

The smelly heap blew twice more and said: "Help."

"Help?"

"Help I, I help."

"Help to do what?"

"Every-thing. Every-where. Here. There. And maybe there."

"Yes, you told me already."

Khan grabbed the entan by both his shoulders and shook him. "Listen, go away! Go back to the street where you belong." He pushed him toward the open corridor. The entan walked away slowly looking left and right. One time he glanced backward with a familiar look in his eyes that Khan could not place.

He jumped back into his training.

Something pulled at Khan's cerbind for the days to follow. It tugged at him deeply. He knew that it was connected to Seranor but was not able to identify where. The temperature in Casus had dropped several degrees. Some sprinkles of snow fell onto the denizens and it gave opportunity to the numularian class as they introduced a new clothing line made of a cora fleece, thicker and softer than usual clothes. Cora was inherently temperature-balanced regardless of the weather conditions but the cold air called for extra protection.

Ira had contacted Khan by tard and arranged to meet with him at the Ice Scabbard. The tavern had become the only place to go for those in search of adventure. Anything and everything could happen there. It was unusual to see Ira still willing to go into the Ice Scabbard because rumors had it that an unknown assassin was hunting him. To Ira that news was probably outdated.

Chapter 6

SITA YOM-KELABRIMBA, gray skinned and beautiful with rounded black pearls for eyes and diagonally cut gray hair on all sides, was serving customers inside the tavern. She was new. Just come into Casus last month without zorn and was willing to accept what opportunities she could find. The new owner, Mocha, also a ventan with skin a shade darker than most, took her on. Not many were willing to work at the most famous tavern in Casus, on Seranor for that matter. She picked up the requisite skills quickly, as most Seronians can, and pleased the eyes of customers with her shapely body that moved in strokes rather than steps. There was a dance in her hips, a seductive dance that charmed all that looked.

Khan wasn't taken by her. Her perkiness reminded him of Calwin and also the trouble lutas brought to his free life. In his view, lutas were the death of a luto. Their corius was only filled with a well of wants and desires given to the luto to provide satisfaction without end.

A burly entan, thirty kilos heavier than Griz but more handsome and fat was staring at Sita all evening. They called him Gippo. The fat loof wouldn't stop shouting and annoying the others. Sita's smile was infectious to all and even Khan couldn't resist it, but Gippo began to prod and push her every chance he had. Ira still hadn't shown up. After ten minutes of harassment, Gippo got up and gave Sita an unwanted double-arm hug which she couldn't escape. The other customers encouraged it to continue.

Khan left his table and walked toward Gippo.

A few light pushes on Gippo had no effect. Khan considered. Then with split second effort and when Khan's defenses were down, Gippo released Sita and grabbed Khan trapping both his arms to his large chest. A second later Khan was flying head over feet into the wall. He landed and moved to strike the fat oaf who was ready with a bar stool. Out of the outskirts of his peripheral vision, Khan caught a cloaked figure leaping into the air with two hazing objects in his hands drawn then a flash and nothing. Gippo attacked and he engaged.

There was danger and he shifted his position slightly using his wind stance but one of the hazy objects, actually a short batier, pierced him through from back to front. He fell bleeding. The assassin had flashed directly behind him and would have killed him instantly had it been an average Seronian. Khan had been too careless with Gippo and hated himself for it.

A mere second after he was stabbed, the feet of Gippo wavered as another pair of armored feet landed heavily behind. A moment of strangulated silence and then Gippo's upper torso slid to the side. Milk gushed out profusely.

The assassin attacked again without wasting time. Khan's wind skills had recuperated dramatically and he moved with more fluidity.

Griz held his double clavus proudly, dripping with Gippo's milk. The alien compound that made up the sharpened edge of his clavus was unbreakable. As a consequence, it cut through porcelan and skeletal structures like virgin clay.

Two short batiers, held tightly by the assassin, came at Khan blindingly fast; he dodged, moved, countered and disoriented the hired killer. A final wind twist disarmed the masked warrior followed by a complex grapple and lock. The assassin was caught.

"Who hired you? Who did it?" Khan demanded. The other patrons in the tavern had all turned their attention to the number one on the Valuto list. They stood far enough back for Khan to do his work and close enough to see what he was doing. Investments were being made and sold as they fought. It was a zorn-making opportunity.

No response came from the assassin.

"Who hired you?"

No response. Griz took two heavy steps getting a firm grip on his clavus. Khan winked his eyes suggesting to only intimidate and not kill. He wasn't certain that Griz got the message. Griz stepped forward again and slung back his two handed chopper.

"The one you seek, Khan. And the one who seeks you," the assassin said in haste to save his life. He was well aware of Griz's reputation for body counts.

"What is your name? Tell me and I will set you free. You have my word," said Khan, serious about his offer.

"Is that Khan's word?"

"Yes. They have all heard."

"Palindorn," the assassin said finally, but not before scanning the crowd.

"You have failed, Palindorn," said Khan and freed him. Griz followed through anyway but missed as Palindorn flashed away. "He has failed."

"He will return," added Griz.

Sita stood there frozen by the nearest table holding onto the arm of a stranger. He, a married entan whose brother was an adventurer, was happy to have her touch, but she released her grip as soon as the danger flashed away.

Khan looked at her suspiciously. "Are you okay?'

"Yes, thank you," she said.

"Why did he grab you like that?" he pointed his chin at one of Gippo's halves.

"I don't know. One minute, he smiled, the next he grabbed me."

"Have you seen him before?"

"No, I mean, I saw him once but I'm not sure."

"You either saw him or you didn't."

"Yes, I said that I did."

"He told me that his name is Pollo."

"It's Gippo."

"Oh really."

"I think so, anyway."

Khan pulled Sita over to the cleaved body. Her hand was cold and smooth to the touch. Innocent. A puddle of milk surrounded Gippo's corpse. Griz had returned to the counter for a fresh drink. Khan, on the other hand, wasn't satisfied with the turn of events. It was too neat for his cerbind to accept. Gippo had set him up and was why he had grabbed him so easily. Palindorn was behind this little escapade with Gippo as the bait. The idea that Khan couldn't shake was the fact that if it hadn't been for the waitress then none of this would have happened.

Sita covered her mouth from the vileness of the dead and then threw up adding to the mess the janitor had to clean up. They were already complaining behind the counter as to whose turn it was.

"What is your name?" Khan asked after offering her a small towel to wipe her face with. He had to see how deeply involved she had been. Had she set him up? Who was this beautiful ventan?

"Sita," she said. "Thank you."
"Sita, there is something that I don't understand and maybe you can help."

"What is that? My time is limited. I still have to work."

"I know but this is important."

"Ask me tomorrow?"

"We must do it today."

"I do not feel very well—"

"I'll make it short."

"Okay—quick."

"You see these two pieces of entan flesh here." She wasn't looking so Khan grabbed her head and forced her to look at it. She resisted. He became angered that this ventan wanted him killed. "That's better. This chunky entan who held you was waiting…"

"I can't stand it!" she cried out, fighting to turn her face away from the milky body. By then the other customers had gone back to drinking and game-playing and the noise had resumed to its ear-deafening levels.

"…waiting for me to come," Khan added, raising his voice, "and as soon as I was where he wanted he executed his plan. Do you not find it strange, Sita?"

"What does it have to do with me?"

"Everything," Khan replied, thinking back to the crazy entan he had met with still no picture of what he wanted. "Tell me what really happened, won't you."

"You have seen it."

"What I have seen is that there were others involved in this plot. Care to explain?"

"What are you saying?"

"You were in on this."

"What are you talking about?"

"You, Gippo and the assassin. Together."

"How can you say that?!"

"You have been smiling at me for the past hour. Gippo happens to grab you without a struggle and then Palindorn comes in to do his work. You're a lousy actor. Why did you set me up?" It was the contained anger on her face, a humiliation that could not be shielded by her words.

"You!" she blurted out, confirming his suspicions.

"Yes, me. Why did you set me up?"

"I have nothing!" she cried. "Nothing!"

"Why? Tell me!"

"You have everything!" Tears had erupted. "Everyone plays you on the Valuto because they have zorn to play with. You have friends..."

"I want to know why?"

"They said that they would give me something. What do I have? What can I play with? I had nothing before and nothing now. You want to know why?"

"Yes."

"Because I had nothing to lose. Satisfied?"

"You have a life and that is worth something. As you can see my life sure is."

"They didn't tell me that they were going to kill you."

"Did you ask?"

"No."

"You know the difference between a stupid entan and a smart one?"

"Two shades of gray," said Griz, drunkenly from a distance. "What are you doing with the waitress? The primo is fresh tonight."

"It's fresh every night, you primoholic," muttered Khan. "Hold on! I'll meet up with you in a minute," Khan said to his brother. "The difference between a stupid entan and a smart entan is very simple. Smart ones ask questions."

"I'm not stupid," she replied.

"Yes you are because you are stupid to get involved in things you don't understand."

"You're more stupid!" she yelled back in defense.

"Why is that?" he asked, holding in a laugh.

"For one, no one asked you to help me. And, for two, you should have killed the assassin. That was really stupid."

Khan paused. "Killing is not a necessity for me. I certainly don't enjoy it, not as much as my friend over there."

"But he will come again."

"If not him, another. Assassins replace assassins," said Khan. "I will be waiting."

"Why do you accept it so easily?"

"It is the life I chose."

"And me?"

"And you? You should return to where you came from and don't be so stupid in the future because others will not overlook as many things as I have," Khan said, this time looking up near the front door. Ira had arrived. He waived Khan over.

Mocha finally came out, less afraid for his life. "Morbfarcker! Sita, this is coming out of your salary. Farck, this is your salary." He started to walk off. "And one more thing..."

"What is it?" she asked.

"You're fired!" Mocha had to yell over the noise.

"All endings find their own way," Khan said, turning to walk toward his waiting friends. Griz was already sitting with Ira.

Sita grabbed Khan's arms. "I have nowhere to go now," she said, sad tears quietly sliding down her beautiful skin. His chest pulled him towards her from the inside but his cerbus told him not to change direction. The resistance wasn't enough.

"Come. You can sit with us—but only for while," Khan said.

IRA ROTATED a slender goblet filled with high-class wanine, spun its contents and watched them in the light. Griz hunkered down on a cold Prime.

"The Prime is nice and cold today, Ira. You should try one. It's got a crazy kick to it," said Khan without introductions.

"I'm not the sort. This special batch of wanine is what I like," said Ira. "I see you have your own batch." He was referring to the lovely ventan under his arm.

"This is Sita and…"

"I heard. Have you ever heard of being low profile?"

"I didn't know that I even had a profile."

"My advice is to try it."

Three nicely-dressed Sub-G entans moved quickly outside from behind the two of them. They mumbled loudly in excitement with only two clear words: "We're rich!"

"Now that I've topped the list, doesn't make sense," said Khan. They all sat.

"Alexan has moved into my library. I can't seem to get him to leave it," said Ira. A new waitress, Olog, wholesome and heavy, served them.

"Any more drinks?" she touched Griz's right shoulder. He growled from behind his helm as if to eat her.

"What kind of beast are you, anyway?" she walked off fuming. "Mocha!" she cried into the kitchen.

"It's just a server," said Khan.

Mocha, out of obligation and respect, came out to defend Olog who had been working for him since he opened and was one of the few willing to put up with the dangers of the job. Nobody harassed her and the zorn was good. Ira apologized and gave Mocha a credit tard. It shut him up immediately and he returned to the kitchen. A new waitress, Wawaq, came out friendly, open and much prettier than Olog. She gave a snort to Sita. Jealousy.

"What is so important?" asked Khan.

"Codes," Ira said quickly, subduing the excitement that it gave him.

"Sita, why don't you gather your things and meet me two hours from now in the square," Khan said. She took a last bite and walked off without remark. "Sorry about that, Ira."

"New codes that we've never seen," Ira continued.

"Then I probably haven't seen them, either," said Khan.

"They're old, you can share the library with Alexan but this is important. Of course, we'll pay the usual for it."

Working salary for Ira had always been high for special tasks. Khan could earn thousands of zorn over a few days but it never had the excitement or the edge of an unpredictable mission. Since returning to Casus his life took on some predictability and he liked it without admitting it to himself. He knew that he couldn't remain in a stable position for long. His milk was not made for it. Some entans were born to settle, some born to act. Khan was an advanced form of the latter. After each death of his family he saw the decreasing importance of settling down. To be settled was to be in pain. It was against the natural order to stop the interaction. For now, life should flow peacefully.

"I thought most codes were discovered," said Khan.

"They were but new technology is coming in all the time. Arvic manipulation and embedding is going through a powerful change and devices are changing with it. Seragorn has shifted as has her energy. Arvicity is more vibrant. More alive. Soon – I predict – we will see an arvonic revolution. In fact, I am sure of it. Communications will be hit first."

Technology had evolved during the month they had been away. The tard was now two-faced, one side black and one side white, and used for both purchase transactions, as before, in addition to communications. A crystal was inset in the thick center that could send photon transmissions across short distances. Images could be viewed both inside the crystal or could be enlarged just above the tard for a larger view. And, from its successful market-oriented innovators, it was called a *tarc*.

"I did see some larger palp spheres," said the wind maker.

"They are *volas* for the extended of cerbind who wishes to learn. We have many at my library. When will you have time to start?"

Volas were the learning bibles that contained far more information than the palpazines though much less timely. They levitated above the hand so that they could be read for long periods without discomfort. Command glyphs operated them just as palpazines using the same elos.

"I will finish my business by late this afternoon."

"Then come immediately to the orange door. Be prepared to spend time there. It is important that we break it."

Chapter 7

WALKING HOME the wind blew on Khan's back, urging him forward to his next destination. A sheet of palp from his pack, a poem for Sita, slipped out and floated away out of his reach. It danced in the wind's song for several moments. He watched it, mesmerized by its elegance. An image of Equist Nao appeared in the crests and troughs of Nata's dance. A representation of his former teacher. The wind's gusty movements died down and Khan picked up the palp to the entan standing beside him. Equist Nao, he thought. The familiar smell of filth veiled his eyes. Could this crazed Seronian be Equist Nao? He looked up at his see-through gaze. Stared hard at his disfigured features.

"Every-where," laughed the delirious entan. "Every-where."

"Nao? What are you doing here? Who are you?" Khan asked, hoping that it was his teacher.

"Now, Nao, now, now, now," he repeated.

"Is it *you*, Equist Nao?"

"Now, Nao, now."

There were distinct similarities. Too distinct to be another. It was him. Khan was almost certain of it. "Come, come," Khan said leading the smelly Nao to his residence. He wasn't going to be late for Sita and then Ira's meeting so he left the crazed Equist inside hoping that he would still be there when he came back. He wanted to make sure that it wasn't him. A quick clay meal was prepared before leaving with plenty of aqua for the stranger to drink.

"I will come back. Stay. Okay? Stay. No problem," Khan said, reassuring his old teacher by smiling and nodding his head up and down or left to right. The crazed entan laughed and made strange noises. The smell was horrific.

Khan met with Sita, fed her and promised to meet with her on the following day after his evening of work. She was easily contented at this point.

The codes that stumbled the obscure leader of the Terium were multilayered and spread out in a rainbow formation indicating an absence of cohesion. Not many organic devices were capable of transmitting information beacons in such a manner. In each color, packets of unrecognizable and useless data were traced, and they only gathered meaning when a similar miscellaneous packet was added from another color. There were eighteen colors in total. By morning, Khan had determined the order and had joined four packets.

He returned to an empty room. Nao, or whoever it was, had gone. The food storage box was empty. "Stupid, stupid, stupid," Khan said to himself. He had to find him.

Denar'ka and Khan would face each other once more but without Nao's guidance the Nivaton would surely win.

The reeking old entan was found wandering the streets. Khan returned with him to his room, washed and fed him, and stayed the entire time. It was Nao. The physical resemblance and the eyes were his. Nao was incoherent, rambling in gibberish prose and, between takes, freezing into a dark stare from which he couldn't be disturbed. The cerbind had disassociated itself, Khan suspected. A detachment that Nao warned about. How to reconnect him? He said that it was impossible? But is it?

No Equist was capable of reaching this point, alive. Nao had. Khan owed his teacher his life, twice over, and determined to help the Equist to gain back his cerbind. He also hoped to get the training that he required. Without Nao he would die. And Nao surely wasn't going to come back on his own terms.

EQUIST NAO was allowed to rest and recuperate at Khan's residence. Khan would spend ten or twelve hours a day, when not working, caring for him and making sure that he received the basic physical needs. First, feed the body and build up the energy. After that he could consider other courses of action. The fresh pieces of clay and mineralized aqua did their job and his body began to strengthen. By the end of five days Nao was in perfect physical health thanks to a couple of potions from Ira's nameless healer friend.

Khan never mentioned Nao to Ira, and he didn't have to because there were enough Terium members around to ensure that Ira was well fed with updates. Ira stopped asking what Khan was up to during the times they didn't work together. There was no need. Khan persevered and mastered the coded language techniques of the Ice Timor. It wore him down especially on the difficult codes that would take ten or fifteen hours of concentrated effort to figure out. By the sixth day he had joined all the packets of data from the rainbow. The message:

> O. The first shipment of crystine pods have been consumed. Two pods leaked and damaged FP. Caution required. Start mass production on S3s by day nine. We require closely spaced shipments, each 48 hours and containing 1,000 kilos from Nn. Will advise later on transport safety. D.

Ira dropped his eyebrows and adjusted his head in concentration. He understood all the terms except for 'O', 'Nn' and 'D'. This cryptogram only confirmed his suspicions about an army under construction. Khan's puzzled face waited an answer.

"He is building an army," said Ira, dryly and still in thought.

"Zorath?"

"Zorath."

"And the S3s?"

"Zoldiers. A new form. A new model. I am not sure which. I am sure that they are an improvement over the ones we have in our streets."

"And what about the initials?"

"Any ideas Khan?"

"I do not know about the 'O' or 'Nn' but the 'D' would likely be 'Denar'ka'."

"The same one you met?"

"The same. What does he do for Zorath?"

"We are not sure. We have been unable to follow him outside of the main urbas. And in the urbas he has been restrained choosing to have his subordinates do the dirty work for him."

"If I may ask, where was this gram intercepted?"

"It wasn't intercepted. We monitored 200 different tas between Batall and Casus hours before I met you that night. That's why I was late. We found it odd and I had my specialists analyze for patterns. The 18 colors that you were given took integrated effort to assimilate. They've coded themselves very deep. Something is going on."

"They are using an inconspicuous form of communications," explained Khan. "Data packets are combined with random messages. On their own they have no meaning—Narcophalin!" said Khan.

"What?"

"That Nn!"

"Very good, Khan. So Narcophalin is behind this but how do you know of them?"

"I've been around for a while. We ripped them off a couple of times in the past. They were selling crystalloids..." Ira dropped into thought momentarily.

"You were saying about the data packets?"

"Their data packets have no meaning by themselves. They are just colors that brighten the beam. It is a very smart improvement in methods."

"How would they do it?"

"They must have some sort of collecting device – maybe it's built into a special tarc – to harmonize the colors and to sanctify the beacon containing the full message."

"This message can lead us to Denar'ka," said Ira, dipping his head in approval. After Khan had left, exhausted from his scrutinizing analysis, Ira lit his tarc and made a tata. The Nn became unmistakable as

Narcophalin. Boon had previously helped the company arrange for new licenses to move a new product. According to Ira's perfect recollection, the product consisted of a crystalline substance slated for use in jewelry. Boon's image remained inside the crystal. That way it could not be picked up by others. "I have a job for you."

SURELY HE should have seen the similarities. They were right in front of him. Khan felt dismissed about the delay. The idea of packets couldn't leave him. Was it possible that Nao's detachment had any relationship to misplaced data, spread out rather than concentrated and cohesive as it should have been?

Khan borrowed a transmission crystal from the Terium's stores and combined this with his own handheld tarc. Nao had sunk into a staring posture, shoulders dropped forward and head at a 45 degree angle toward the floor. Khan set the tarc in his right hand behind Nao's head and the spare crystal in front of the Equist's mouth. The entan cerbus exchanged information using flammic pathways, and Khan used the modern gadgets to peer into Nao's cerbind. Many of the beams passing through the infinite apertures inside his cerbus were being diffracted by tiny pockets of air or wind.

It surprised Khan that he knew what to do. Did Nao really find him for this? Khan put aside the technological tools and rubbed his hands together to generate a slimy wind. When a sufficient amount of wind slime was produced he created a dense bubble of it around Nao. It would help to attract what came out of Nao.

His hands were caught inside and it gave him just enough room to maneuver his next trick. A windy force was created and rushed into Nao's head and immediately upon entering was pulled out and dissipated.

This action was repeated several times in succession. Each time it was done, black specks of air came out of Nao's nose, eyes, mouth and ears, and became trapped on the slime bubble encircling his head. The action was repeated until no further specks came out. By the end of it all, Nao was left unconscious but alive.

It took Nao another 28 hours to recover and when he did he was back to a seemingly normal entity minus a long blank spot in his memory. Khan the cryptographer put together some of the last pieces of memory that Nao had shared and came to a startling conclusion: Equist Nao, upon achieving the ultimate stage of an Equist, threw himself back into the land and had returned to save Khan from imminent death while trapped in Escarotian's Tomb. Yet a third save. It brought tears to Khan's eyes when he learned that he was responsible for Nao's sacrifice, and his teacher had become a lost wind to reform as a crazed entan wandering for not or nothing. A slow cerbal death. And Khan had, by some fate, found him. Nao also found him.

Khan continued his wind training and as he did so Nao grew stronger of cerbind and often joined in Nata's dance. Soon enough he was able to masticate ideas and began sharing his secrets with his best loved pupil. Khan did not make mention of Denar'ka in the beginning.

Learning the wind was different this time around. The first time it was from desperation, loss and pain. These things fired Khan's need to learn something so that he could replace the emptiness his life offered. This time he was learning because he wanted to and that made him feel serene and whole again. His life was coming full circle.

Sita would join the two of them when they weren't in training. Nao liked Sita. She was of sweet innocence and she comforted him with the thought of his own lost love in his youth.

The venerated Equist taught Khan to let go of his physical weapon. He showed him that Equists had their own weapons. Khan was reluctant to stop using his beloved batier, or bastion, even though he more often than not broke it in battle.

"Subconsciously, you never wanted it," said Nao, holding Khan's batier in his hand. "This is not a weapon."

"It has saved my life many times, teacher, in both offense and defense," Khan said, defending his success in life.

"The wind is both your weapon and shield. It is why we Equists do not require a weapon. Have you ever seen me carry one?"

"No."

"It is also why you must learn to trust the wind and not ceramic."

"It is not easy to give up what I have had my whole life."

"No. It is not easy to find me. But you did."

"You helped me."

"I did not."

"How can I always be prepared for battle? Nata does not always come."

"The wind is all around you," said the Equist. "If you move, the wind moves first. When you strike the wind strikes first. When you defend, the wind defends first." Nao swung his arms and sent pocket forces of wind around Khan to illustrate his point. Khan had never thought about it but Nao was right. The wind always preceded the body. "Trust it and you will know its might. Once you command all of her she will shape any weapon you desire so it becomes an extension of yourself. But remind yourself of one thing."

"Yes, teacher."

"Remind yourself that the wind, Nata, is the balancer of life. She is not the terminator nor the healer. She is the balancer. You must remind yourself of this fact."

"Equist Nao, I have learned recently of the hollowing of the body and filling it with wind. It has saved my life in battle. But I am not able to capture this technique each time."

"Wind follows hollowness. Make the body hollow and the wind shall fill its path. It will flow through rather than against. Hollowness requires the emptying of the cerbind. It is why an assassin can never learn Nata's secrets."

"Why?"

"Their cerbind is full with rewards and strategies. Crave not these distractions, Khan. Crave them not."

"I am ready to learn more, teacher..."

"Before I continue, you must practice. For the next seven days you will train hollowness. Then we will see further. Come with me," said Nao.

"Equist Nao," started Khan, "you know of Zorath and the Ice Timor."

"Certainly."

"I have met one of his Nivatons. They follow him now."

"I have seen the signs in the street."

"The IceFist."

"It is run by one called V-Non, a Nivaton."

"I have not heard of him."

"He is a student to an entan, a Nivaton, who says that he knows you."

"Who is this entan?"

"Denar'ka."

Nao slowly sat down on the ground in contemplation. He remembered his seedhood friend and recalled how he had treated him when he was a careless seedling.

"Teacher, this Denar'ka tried to kill me in a duel because he said that he could not have his vengeance on you. He believed you to be dead."

"For all purposes I was dead, but…"

"He almost did finish me."

"You are alive from Denar'ka's fist?"

"Who is this Denar'ka? How do I fight such a Nivaton? I escaped him once but he will surely find me again. I am certain of this."

"He is a Nivaton? You are sure?"

"Yes. Why?"

"Denar'ka and I grew up together. He once wanted to become an Equist. He blames me for not letting him learn. In some ways, I did prevent him. I never liked him. There was an awful feeling about him and it put agitation into me then as does his name now. Agitation that he would cause my death."

"Why is that?"

"He hates life. Nata would not take kindly to his kind. She would have killed him and me along with him."

"He has gained other abilities."

"As a Nivaton he must have gained ice form. Did he achieve arkti? The naqui form?"

"Yes! His body changed to naqui and that was how he tried to kill me. He is with Zorath. Some have said that he was taught by the Nivian himself."

"You are right to fear this entan," said Equist Nao, recognizing the danger. Denar'ka had achieved arkti. It would be difficult to kill him in this form. "I was wrong to have pushed him away then but now it will not be so easy to disregard him. The ice thickens, Khan." Nao could not stop thinking about his own life and the danger he brought to the existence of wind. Khan was the only surviving wind follower left besides himself. He had to push Khan's training faster. The wind form needed to be propagated or it would vanish under the might of ice and order. "We must strengthen the wind, Khan. We must extend her reach once again or the balance on this planet will be doomed. You and I are all that is left."

WITH AN abundance of cryptographic work, Khan saved enough zorn to open a wind training school called WINDY PATH, and attracted students interested in following something other than arvicity which they deemed the pollutant of Seranor. Many of them had no idea what they were getting into it. Five in eighty students passed the first month of training and Khan spent more days with them, teaching them the basics. For the next batch he lowered the level of training until they could get used to this unique form of training. In his spare time, he worked on his own techniques with guidance from Nao. The Equist began sharing intimate knowledge of the higher level techniques.

Equist Nao wandered about the school, distanced at times, and Khan would sit and talk with him as often as he could. It was beneficial to both of them. Deep reaching sessions lasted more than four hours at a single sitting. During these discussions, Nao and Khan would talk openly about wind and other things on the planet.

Students at Windy Path were growing in numbers. Many of those who came decided on wind training because they grew disdainful of the ice and wanted nothing to do with such beliefs in structure and order. There was enough of that in the rules passed down from the government.

Classes increased in frequency and Khan became busy with training and teaching, as well as public performances to introduce the wind philosophy outside. Sita took a seat in the background and supported his work. His spare moments were spent together with her. She found a new job in administering the school and its activities.

At the same time, the IceFist grew and would on occasion attack students from Windy Path. Several deaths occurred from this but it had the opposite effect than intended. Seronians began to like Nata and her peaceful philosophies. It was not just about fighting and more about personal development. It was about finding peace within thyself. Windy Path satisfied consumers who were getting overloaded with mediamenta and technological gadgetry. Not Khan. He was still involved with Ira, supporting the Terium and their efforts to subvert the strengths of the Ice Timor.

Khan saw his other three friends, Griz, Alexan and Boon only on rare occasion. They would usually meet for dinner or drinks at the tavern. He became too busy to join the random adventures that came his way, and with zorn in his pocket and a beautiful luta on his side he didn't have the same interest in risk as before. Responsibility germinated in his milk. He enjoyed the sense of stability it provided him. He hadn't felt this calm since his seedhood in Ulaq when his parents and brother were alive.

A new birth had given Khan a new chance, and it was mostly due to Equist Nao. Once again, his old teacher had helped him to change his path and brought back a smile on his face.

So many had supported him over the tios. His life was protected by those who had loved him, and it felt good to have some result for their unrelenting love.

Seranor, he began to conclude, was really all about pure, unadulterated love. The kind of love that permeates all things and matter and does not stop until it has warmed everything through and through, and in so doing the love changes what has been loved, converts it into a giver of love that perpetuates itself onto all things that are touched. It was his turn now to give back what had been given to him. And it was this natural feeling that carried him through each arduous day and every testing moment. To give was to love, he decided, and incorporated it into his teachings. It was his turn to influence the future.

Chapter 8

THE FIRST night that Khan and Sita made love left him buried in slippery sweat from two hours of frolicking naked on the bed. She felt awkward afterwards as did he when he took her hand, slid her off the cora mattress gently, into his arms and out of the awkwardness. In some trance he led her first dance step to whispers of his breath. He reached with both arms around her smooth-skinned, protruding hips and felt her entire body vibrate from the shuffle of her feet to the sway of her neck. He pulled her closer.

Silhouettes of white and gray danced, passionately. A few steps here and few steps there. He could feel her soft abdomen sliding over his hard body. Massaging it with tenderness.

He breathed her scent, aromatic and natural. A basic smell suitable for a common luta who was, in some ways, elitist. The breath music continued to move them until their breaths became as one and the dance resolved itself into a long kiss.

Lovemaking was not a skill suitable for adventurers. It weakened the fight in lutos. Love made the warrior susceptible to the illness of gentility. Once the sickness began it was painful to remove. The host would not want it removed for fear of death.

Khan had taken ill. The illness spread into all parts of his body and his life. It softened his porcelan parts, beautifying them as would a potter's touch to a crude bowl.

During the time they enjoyed with one another, he often referred to himself as the last of the non-conformists. They were naked on the window sill that morning after an evening of pleasure. Her breasts shimmered like snow-capped mountains and reminded Khan of home. She did not understand about conformity. Society made the rules and she only existed within its bounds. So she asked him about what he said.

"The original entan has been morphed by social conventions. Lutos like me are fading," Khan said. "The planet is being restructured, this will one day push the remaining few of us into obscurity. Technology is hailed as our savior as if we needed to be saved. I'll be the first to admit to using technology to enhance my life, but I am saying that it is more than just using it. It about substituting the things that we were designed to do, and there are many to list, with things that will eventually do everything for us. Communications and entertainment. Machinery to drive our productions. Weapons to obliterate our enemies. Cerbi to think our new thoughts.

"The younger generation will manage it successfully. They are being born with tarcs by their bedsides and intrators in their homes. My class, the adventuring class, never cared for such conveniences. Some may have. Most did not.

"Everyday society runs faster than the day before. Faster to their deaths. I have lived the last stage of my life with death in my hand and a weapon at my side. I carried speed on my two legs. I earned my courage in battle and fought my enemy in close combat.

"Technology will consume our past methods. It will pressure us to believe that there is a better way to eat, talk, sleep and kill. But don't you believe all these lies. Technology is the greatest lie of all. I have seen it first hand. My father was one such liar. He was the best of them. He was the first.

"Conformity will follow the future trends. We'll give up the inefficiencies of our past for the prosperity of tomorrow. Fight against it and society will beat you. Conform and all will win in its glory. All will be slaves. We are surrendering our freedom to conformity, governments will dictate their whims, mediamenta will keep us smiling and battle will keep us dying so that none would have to endure such empty pain longer than is necessary.

"I will be the last standing non-conformist. What of me? They will hunt me and find elaborate ways to rid of me. Whether it is me or another who lives on it does not matter because society cannot all become slaves. It is a weapon coming against us. The greatest weapon ever created. Remove the will of an entan and the fight will fall out. Dull their cerbinds and their thoughts will whither away. What remains is a living statue that is easily manipulated to live the rest of its days in a meaningless life. Meaning was our gift. Isn't that why we are here?

"Meaning is the medium. Without it there is nothing to hang onto. There are no reasons to continue. We need to sharpen the cerbinds, make them willful and triumphant.

"It is a planetary curse cast by an invisible hand. Even if we survive against Zorath's purpose or Seranor's repercussions, we still will be weakened by the curse placed upon all of Seranor, porcelan and mud. We have to find a way to balance the mistakes we have and are making.

"I think it is time for myself to hang up my adventuring boots and divert my attention to making things right. It is about maturation, isn't it? I've tried to do good in my actions and it has always left me with the unexpected. She likes to surprise, our mother. She pushes me forward whilst I resisted to her subtle touch. Her love. It's not too late for me. I will try to do what is right for society. I have placed this burden on myself. My place is losing its value. I should not come before others. I want to teach them the other way to do things. To take action. The wind has shown me that in all of life's twists and turns the game is the same. Fundamentally we are on the same ship whether we choose to accept it or not. I only want to keep the keel in the water before it is too late for us all."

Sita had seen the world in a similar fashion as a seedling. But reality was the death blow. Society conformed and earned its name as a society rather than a group of misdirected independents. Khan was as much a part of society as anyone else as long as he existed in it. He did conform but there was an individualism about his character that refused the common choice over the greater or the harder.

On the surface, Khan seemed all wrong. But she had learned to understand his method of madness. It required attention. He refuted convention against his adventuring colleagues and pushed them to areas beyond their limits, and having returned intact they hailed him for his ingenuity in seeing what they did not see. He was respected for widening the boundaries of entans. That was what attracted Sita to him in the first place. He was calm and controlled with an intense emotional fire that burst when pushed and was softened by passion and a genuine character that did not lie about what was real and unreal. He had convinced himself so much that he himself was blind.

The next morning would be a special day. Their bonding had naturally progressed and without the shielding of clothes and an empty sheath, Khan did the unthinkable. He first took her hands, lightly into his, hugged her closely once and squeezed her tightly to his chest smelling the richness of her hair. Eating her scent. He relaxed. She eased back onto the surface of the bed.

"Sita, I have something to ask of you," he said.

"Yes, Khan," she replied.

"It is a most special thing that I ask for," he went on.

"Okay, what is it?" she asked, eager to know what it was, not suspecting anything.

"Are you ready for me to ask?"

"As ready as ever."

"Good."

"Okay."

"Then I will just say it."

"Go on."

"Will you be my bride, my wife and my partner in life?"

Her luscious mouth froze in its half-open state after the first five words came from his lips. Khan stopped breathing himself. Anticipation was replaced with rejection. Her eyes became glossed over in a reddish hue and then the subtle nodding came before she said: "Yes." He rushed in to grab her and held her in both arms until they gradually eased their strength.

Chapter 9

DEATH JUSTIFIED battle with creed as a warrior's vow and
they lived and died by their beliefs when armor, weapon
and creed met against their foe, said Teramon, the hero of
planet Seranor.

Marriage justified love. The vows between male and
female solidified their feelings. Sanctified the uniformed
couple. Brides wore gowns to accentuate their spiritual
status. Grooms wore armor to reveal their strengths.
Sita had worn a symphonic orange gown that unleashed
her ravishing neckline. A white necklace with a clear
crystal, a gift from Khan, glistened over her silvery skin.

The wedding received an unwelcome guest. All would
have went smoothly if V-Non and his followers hadn't
interrupted their wedding and threatened Khan to a
match. Khan declined to fight at his wedding and

promised to meet his opponent at a later date. It would never come. V·Non was called outside of Casus for unexpected business. Nevertheless, the whole event caused delays and inconvenience to the entire ceremony. Sita's impression changed.

Equist Nao had removed himself from the party during the commotion. He received a message, by ear, that Denar'ka knew that he was alive and wanted to see him.

He went to the empty street corner four blocks from the ceremony, whisked himself stealthily through darkness and remained in wind form, hovering over the corner of a two·story building. Minutes ticked by with no response from his old friend. A flash in the street caught his attention. When it subsided, a cloaked figure walking with two large stumps instead of legs materialized. Nao looked in all directions and found no one on the streets. The air was calm and warm. The figure stood briefly and began laughing, long and slow. It removed the dark hood. A disfigured embarrassment to his seedhood.

"So the wind does still blow, does it not, Nao?" said the cold voice. Denar'ka's skin had blued and Nao could see the fumes coming from his skin as a cold body and hot air met. "I see you there on top of that building. It has been some circle for us, hasn't it? You know what is true about this planet. For all the talk I hear of creation from the flamma beings and the inventors and the egotistical adventurers who think risk is worth something, there is a valid point that has been missed entirely. None of them can create! None! Do you know the only device of creation in the Versos? I will tell you. It is time. Time creates all things. Without it we would have nothing. It is the tool of creation that has been missed. Time is quantifiable and that is what gives it structure and strength.

"I have used time to create what I have missed, Nao. Time has given me a new body with new abilities. It has given me a reason. You know what I miss most about our seedhood? It wasn't the pain or the rejection. It wasn't the challenge. What I miss most was my father and how he would force me to do things that I did not like because in the end he was right. He was right. I did not know then. There are always those who know and those who don't and those who think they know. There are many things I know. I have earned them. I would have earned your place had you not rejected me. You see, you thought you knew but really you were wrong.

"In the end, I have returned a success. The question as to why you did it no longer disturbs me. The planet and all against us will fall under the ice. And I will have my goal. There is no life without goals. Nata does not teach that. She says that all things find their own path and earn their own name as long as the pursuit continues. She is wrong. Niva has shown me that. The ice is the purest power. Without structure what kind of world would we have. Wind can never offer that kind of stability."

"You have answered your own question, Denar'ka," said Nao and transformed into entan form as he landed noiselessly onto the ground.

"What question is that?" asked Denar'ka, sneeringly.

"Why I follow Nata and you do not. I shall give you the answer. I can at least do that much. Here it is: You were not fit to be an Equist. Purity is in freedom. That is what guides all life in the Versos. Freedom to do and be what it can. Unrestricted by any false laws. And in my own freedom I chose to serve rather than to take such as Niva has taught you. I have chosen whereas you have been coerced. By conformity to the laws of the ice. You are the slave to your master."

"My master would eliminate you with a single verse!"

"It does not change your relationship to him."

"I will have what you have taken from me, Nao. I will have my dignity when all is done. A test of ice and wind is to be made. I will give you one week to prepare. All the answers we will need will be made at our final match. I have fought your student and let him live, but if he is a reflection of you then your time is over. As is your freedom."

"Nothing has changed about you, Denar'ka," said Nao. Denar'ka could not be trusted. If Nao was able to initiate a fight here he would have a better chance than later. Nao did not need time to prepare, but Denar'ka did. That concerned the Equist. Prepare for what? Denar'ka would surely work the odds to his advantage. Here and now he had an even match. Even surprise was in his favor unless there was something, an assassin maybe, in the shadows ready to even those odds. He had to push his emotions. Let Denar'ka release that old anger. Emotion would be Denar'ka's undoing. "You are alive because of me. You owe me your life."

"I owe you nothing."

"Nata would have killed you had you entered. I, in truth, saved your life. You should be thanking me instead of challenging me."

Denar'ka burst out in laughter. "You are crazy to think that I would die where you have succeeded."

"You would have," said Nao, smiling at his grotesque face.

"You have not changed either," said Denar'ka.

"I am not deformed like you. A monster of the ice. Is that what you have become?"

"You are jealous!" His anger rose then he stepped back to calm himself down. Plans must be followed. His self control amazed Nao. "When you feel the strength of arkti you will be permanently dead. Not me. Theories are proven in battle."

"Then prove it here." The challenge was made.

"One week, Nao."

"No. Right here in this street."

"One week."

"Are you afraid of me still, Denar'ka?"

Swathes of condensation came off of Denar'ka's skin as it became colder. The anger was coming out. "Never! You will die a painful death for your words. As will your student, Khan."

"Kill me here. Are you capable to do that? Or are you afraid?"

"I am afraid of nothing. You!" he roared into an uncontrollable rage and hurled his naqui form at Nao who was fully prepared. The wind master dissipated into a wind and Denar'ka burned through the building coming out of the backside. He did not come around for a second attack.

Nao walked home slowly. The darkness hid his sullen face. He was thinking of a way to solve this conundrum. Khan was in greater danger. He was asking Nata for her advice. She only danced about his head. She was still angry at him for leaving her for his student. "I'm sorry, Nata. But you see, if I didn't come back who would be left to follow your footsteps?" She ignored him.

Chapter 10

THE BRIGHTNESS of morning arrived to lighten the sorrows and to surrender yesterday's memories into the past. Sita slept, half covered with the bed and half by Khan's upper body. Two serpents intertwined. He was wide awake. Cerbind clear. Thin cora bed sheets, common in all residences, covered the two figures. Sita stirred and was welcomed with a prolonged wet kiss.

"Good morning," said Khan to his new bride.

"You cannot imagine how much I love you," said Sita.

"And I love you," Khan replied. It felt good to hear himself say that without the need to consider or think of anything else. He attributed it to his wind training. While teaching the body to become hollow he was guiding his cerbind to remove unneeded thoughts. A cleansing of sorts had taken root. He calmed down and the world came into sharper focus. The residues in his head had cleared away and he felt freer.

The morning went by uneventfully. Windy Path was closed down for two days so that he might enjoy some extra time with Sita.

He should have realized, but didn't, that the excessive amount of time devoted to the school had taken away from his lovely bride, and she had some imperative topics that needed discussion. Khan welcomed them in his enlightened mood.

As she started expressing her concerns Khan's body crept back into a reclining position as the clarity in his head diminished under the assault from his new wife. He knew that her concerns would come but it so reminded him of Mareenth and what she wanted and needed in order to feel safe.

The meeting with V-Non last night didn't help the situation.

This time he would make a greater effort to listen and to understand. It was his failure with Mareenth to let her go in favor of himself. Selfish morb. He had no choice then. His cerbind was unclear, much different. He was willing to take part.

He didn't have it in his capacity with Mareenth and could still feel the pain of her leaving. She was right. The nonconformist. Right as a rectangle.

The risk takers: The adventurers who could wield a batier and strike down a Serag. Risk was their motto and pain their logo until it came to relationships, commitments and, ultimately, responsibility for others. Some of them grew into such things as a seedling grows into clothes when he is ready. Others remained and substituted risk for relationships. Steady relationships.

They could ingest a luto whole and once inside he would never venture off the beaten track evermore.

Fear kept adventurers adventuring. Fear of lutas and of families.

Boon, Ira had informed, was caught walking hand in hand with a luta of average beauty and innocent eyes. Even when pushed, Boon refused to say more and denied that it was serious. Number 51 and Griz became close. He spent nearly every night with her and after the first month back stopped paying for her services. Only Ira was never with a luta or a female of any kind. He did not desire one.

Khan had asked him about it without result.

"All males desire, yet you do not, Ira."

"I am already possessed," said Ira, referring to something oblivious to Khan.

SOME LUTOS were born to breed; others were born to rattle. Khan was walking the line between the two.

Indecision had become his friend when there was talk of relationships. And just as in life, friends changed and lutos were given chances to do the same. Decisions were hunting him down.

While in the hallway outside their front door he could hear the pattering of nervous footsteps. She had been thinking again. Waiting for him to return.

"You're late!" she cried out as soon as the door shut behind him. "You promised to pay attention to the time of your classes!"

"What? I'm only a twenty...twenty-five minutes late."

"Late is late. I don't keep you waiting."

"What is tormenting you today?"

"I have been wanting to tell you something. It is hard to predict your time of arrival. I wait around, teased by your false promises, ten minutes, twenty...It has to stop!"

"I will pay more attention to my tardiness."

She placed both hands on his shoulders and searched his eyes for the answer. "Do you love me?"

"Yes."

She continued to study the mannerisms of his face to test for visual confirmations to his words, past and present. Her profound look penetrated his thinly veiled masks.

"Did your students learn anything today?" she asked.

"Yes, we discussed decision-making from the perspective of the wind. I was quite impressed by their perceptions."

"What is the conclusion that you arrived at?" She sat down on the chair. Khan walked around a few paces then also sat.

"Decisions, even from Nata, come with responsibilities and it's by letting go of what could happen that allows us to make decisions with more fluidity. Quite often our decisions are muffled by our own precognitions of what hasn't happened."

He was on the right topic. She wanted to tell him that she was pregnant and had been excited the whole day unable to do anything constructive, but when she looked at his satisfied smile she could no longer bring herself to say it.

"What's going to happen to us?" she asked.

"What do you mean?"

"What will happen in the future, Khan?"

"We will continue. We will succeed, together." He leaned over to kiss her on the forehead.

"Then you have decided to keep the Windy Path?"

"Yes. Of course. I wouldn't open a school so that I could close it down. I want to build a chain of schools and bring Nata's lessons to all those who are interested in learning."

"And what of your friends, Griz, Alexan and Boon?"

"I still communicate with them on occasion. Lately, we have all gone our own way."

"What if they find a new mission for you or a special project?"

"I will consider it. I won't necessarily take it. I will decide for the both of us."

"Are you sure?"

"Definitely. My days of adventuring are limited. I have lost interest in it. What is really bothering you? I know it is something."

She was holding a drink with two hands cupped and the glass in the center, though she wasn't drinking. She watched him carefully, scrutinizing his every word with disbelieving eyes.

"Boon came by this afternoon—he was happy for the first time, not like his usual cautionary self," she casually said, "and he wanted to tell me that he was looking for you."

"I will catch up with him this week—"

"It sounded important," she interrupted him.

"It will have to wait. Nao has asked me to dedicate time for intensive training this whole week. I have waited for a chance like this for a long time."

"Training and more training. When will the training end? It seems to last forever."

"There is so much to learn."

"Life does have other things to offer."

"I know, but—" An answer didn't come to cerbind immediately.

"I have been thinking about our life and what will come of it. The armies of Zorath invade the urbas in all directions."

"There are counter armies to stop them. We are not part of that."

"But you are with Ira—"

"Is that what this is about—Ira?"

"I like Ira. That is not the trouble. Well..."

"I have known Ira for many tios. He is like an older brother to me. I have earned good zorn working with him. I know he's a little over-the-top but anyone else would be worse under his conditions."

"It's his profession."

"House Levin?"

"No. Zorath. Ira is focused on Zorath and if Zorath continues to grow so will Ira and sooner or later it will involve you."

"We can decide on that when we—"

"How imperceptive you all are, you lutos! Can you not understand that marriage means family and a family needs stability," she said, getting excited at his failure to show responsibility. "With you and Ira still maintaining close ties and the ice chilling our urbas by the day it is inevitable that he will involve you in something. What will happen to us then? What will I do if you are dead?" she said. "You have given me no insurances. How do I know that you won't change your thinking next week?"

"Please stop right there! Stop! I have told you what I plan to do with all my honesty. Is it not enough?"

"Yes."

"Then why are you pushing me for something that I cannot give you? I cannot give you a tomorrow that is free from death or variability. Anything can happen. I can only do my best. That I can guarantee! But the world is changing. You are right. It is clearer to me since I have partaken in some of its recent history. The ice king will come and I will not lie to you. If Zorath invades and puts our lives in danger I will extend my reach to hurt him or his armies in any way that I can."

Sita's solemn face said it all in a glance. His response was not what she wanted to hear. Not enough to calm her in her nervousness. His words were words of the luto designed for lutos. Lutas spoke another language altogether that he had yet to fully grasp. When she mentioned Zorath a paralysis came over her sweet face and captured her beauty. He looked at her as a leader would protect his troops, noticing that having asked them to defend had made them vulnerable to attack. And in the midst of this impassioned discussion he knew that she would not retreat on his advance but feared that she could hamper his movements under times of heavy attack when he would need her support most, and because of his love for her there was no way to prevent this.

"Very well, Khan. I know that you will keep us safe," Sita said. "I wouldn't be with you if I didn't feel that way." She wrapped her arms wide around his midriff and buried her head in his chest. "You promise?"

"I promise. Let's stay calm until the need arises."

She squeezed her arms tightly as if hanging on for dear life on the edge of a cliff. He could not understand what motivated such a reaction. She dropped a tear as she looked at her belly. The family was on the way.

Chapter 11

WIND TRAINING increased in so much intensity that days passed without seeing anyone but Equist Nao. Haze in the cerbind. An exhausted body got the best sleep. Thinking time was automatically removed, replaced by instinct. Dreams of Sita washed away like milk in the ocean.

Khan pushed his body to flex in the wind, to twist in its force and to dance in its steps. Techniques were refined, flow came to movements, and his speed of attack and defense trebled. Soon the force of attack improved sending strikes easily through walls, ground, and blocks of ice even without touch. The wind blade movement formed as his second weapon.

Nao sat back mostly calling out phrases like "Wind is water insecure" or "Bend cerbind become sublime". The more Khan improved in skill the more Nao came back to his former self. He also trained by running backwards around Khan's wind stance. Rewinding back to his former self. It was Khan who had saved him from imminent death. The most horrible death. Splitting of the cerbus.

Nao's brief discussions to help where he didn't understand brought with them only more questions.

"Your arm is hollow," Equist Nao said.

"Hollow?" Khan asked.

"Hollow like the pack you bring."

"Hollow? You mean that my arm should be hollow."

"Your body is supple. Your kol is centered. But..."

"What master?"

"Wind is hollow. My cup is hollow. Life is hollow. Remember this."

"How can I make my arm hollow?"

"Body hollow makes arm hollow."

"I'll remember that." As much as Nao had improved, Khan thought, he had not yet reached himself. It did not matter. What presided over all else was that Nao was not going to die. That provided a strong sense of comfort. A sense of family.

Khan continued. He established his stance in the wind, raises himself up and puts Nao's fresh ideas to use. Make the body hollow.

The evenings were reserved for either discussion or rest. It depended on the success of the training during the day. One dark night was put aside for training the wind without sight, reference or familiarity. A snapped leg bone along with many bruises were the result. As if Nao somehow expected this, the Equist warped the wind around Khan's injured leg and reformed the porcelan tissue. Then master taught healing to the disciple.

This fifth straight day of training really exhausted Khan and Nao told him to stop. They had pushed the limits of their time constraints. The Equist also knew that deeper questions formed in his student's cerbind.

"What is the final form?" Khan asked, sitting at the edge of a cliff overlooking a small canyon not far from Casus. The urba was now his home and staying away for nearly the past week gave him feelings of loneliness when he thought about it. Calm eyes and soft words came from his mouth.

"Becoming."

"Becoming what, master?"

"There are many steps before it."

"Have I achieved the steps yet?"

"You will know this yourself when you are ready. It will fill you and carry you."

"Will my skills continue to grow? I have learned so much. Is there so much more to learn from Nata?"

"Nata is everything. Learn her...follow the storm and..."

"The storm will be my form?"

"Storm is form."

"Storm is the final form?"

"Storm is storm; form is form."

"But you just said that the storm is the form."

"Form is storm."

"Stop it! Stop it! I am serious. You haven't improved much in your thinking..."

"Form is improved in you."

"Well...you are right...you, you...where are you, master?"

"Everywhere."

"Come back to me. I need you here."

"Need...needing...needy."

"I must learn."

"Learn...learning...learned."

"You're not making any sense today—I know, let me guess; sense, sensing, sensed."

Nao smiled. He spoke breezily. "Everywhere."

"What is it, this everywhere?"

"Everywhere, everything. Parts, pieces, abilities, skills are...not you."

"They are what makes me."

"Wrong. Nothing makes. All is. Form is one, not many. It is the disease."

"Form is one."

"Everywhere."

"Everywhere..."

The tarc illuminated. Ira's face appeared in the crystal. Urgent.

Nao continued. "Just like batier. I do not carry batier. You do not need batier. Everything is here already." He circled his pointed finger around Khan's body.

The tarc illuminated again. Khan couldn't resist. Ira's image was projected up from the tarc over Khan's palm.

Nao was still talking to Khan. "Acceptance is the hardest."

EQUIST NAO had, up until that day, been reserved in words, action, and thought. Khan understood this to be part of the new character from his transformation while immersed in the wind for such a long time. This was not true and had been misinterpreted by even Nao himself.

"Equist Nao, I fear that the wind has distorted your cerbind for all your days to come," said Khan concerned about his master, his second father.

"I, too, feared such young Khan but we must thank Nata rather than distrust her for what words she doesn't use to communicate have intertwined within them a

message of essential understandings. When I became the
wind and entered Nata's domain I became afraid..."

"You were afraid of Nata? Nao, you are an Equist,
master of the wind, teacher of her ways."

"Very afraid of Nata and her power. I failed her and
she cast me out. She could not accept me as I was not
able to accept her. I failed, young Equist. And where I
failed, you will succeed."

"How may I succeed over you?"

"It is in the capacity of beings to be afraid of what they
do not know, but fear is not without pain and regret. It
was the pain of my failure to be lost, Nata had nothing to
do with it for, had I stayed as the wind form, I would have
stopped existing. She saved my life and I, no longer able
to accept my own failure, hid in my own insanity that I
could not find a way out until your kol reached inside and
reminded me of who I was. Your love brought me back,
Khan." A red tear swelled and rolled quickly down the
Equist's face. It felt good for it to roll down his cheek.

"Will this happen to me, Equist Nao? Will my life face
such fate?"

"No."

"How can you be so sure?"

A muted laugh. "Experience, Khan. Look at your
experience and all things are made clear."

"My life has been full of loss and misdirection."

"This will continue until you see your life for what it
is."

"What is my life? To fight and to lose?"

"No."

"It is all I've ever known, master. Nothing can ever
stay around me."

"Look at yourself without such harsh judgment.
Imagine that you are someone else and you will see the

richness contained in it. All life is rich. It is our eyes which are desperate and hungry."

"You ask a difficult task. Finding oneself is a lifetime's work."

"Try to find and you will forever look. Try to accept and you will always have."

"How can I accept what I cannot find?"

"Life is not about finding yourself as much as it is about accepting yourself. You already know who you are, but you have not accepted it, Khan. Acceptance precedes decision. Acceptance makes decision. You destroy your life because you cannot accept it. What you have lost has been related to your connection to it. Your hold on it. Your lack of acceptance of who you are."

Khan's head was down, silver hair hung still over his entire face. His right hand holding the sleeve came up to wipe his face. A red smudge was on the sleeve as the hand returned. "What have you accepted in your life?"

"Simply the fact that my path was chosen before acceptance. In that mistake, I was on the wrong path."

"And now?"

"I have accepted who I am and therefore chosen the right path."

"Then it is not by error that we are chosen to go after Denar'ka."

"Ira knows much more than he reveals. It is what makes him an excellent and strategic leader. If Denar'ka succeeds, opus will lose as will soon go our freedom. Ora is the permanent. It is our weakness to be permanent and our strength to be free."

"The Nivaton—"

"Denar'ka will prey on you. He has despised me ever since I would not allow him to become an Equist. His cerbind is fixed with ora and could never follow the wind's ways."

"How do I beat him? How do I overcome a Nivaton?"

"This is for you to know. I have taught you what I could in the time we have spent together. Your training remains your entire life. Remember the strength of Nata. She is free, unrestrained as you can be if you let your cerbind fall. Make yourself hollow and he cannot hurt you. When you have learned how to be hollow you will be ready for the storm. Then all shall be clear."

"I will try."

"Do not try. Do."

He considered. "I will do."

"Are you ready, my young Equist?"

"Always willing master. Not always ready."

"We are like the wind, constantly changing, but always there."

Chapter 12

THE MARKET for tarcs proved profitable for the industrious
Boon and his mechanical mouth when it came to terms
and agreements of sales contracts. Casus had become an
economic certainty, one which Boon found pleasure in its
business adversity.

He had arranged a first shipment of 23,000 tarcs to be
distributed across the urba through organized outlets of
sales. Ira's tata earlier in the day disturbed him from
strategizing his next round of shipments, 50,000 units
this time, to accommodate the rapid number of users in
Casus.

Penetration was reaching 30% and climbing every
month, and as new technologies were built into the
communication devices, users upgraded and used them
more freely. It was a revolution in mobility and social
protocols that beckoned Seronians to indulge their audible

sensibilities and visual banalities. Boon dug his niche into the technological arm of Technomicon. The company's aggressive expansion plans were filling his storage devices full of premium zorn. From Casus he had access to Zahara and Batall and had reached far north, as far as Storh. The demand for enicoys was also on the rise and Boon was in the midst of preparing the contracts with his assistant, Korso, when Ira's impatience materialized.

"Leave this room," said Ira to the assistant. "Return next week to finish your business." Korso looked at Boon for an answer. The thief of verse closed his eyes in approval and the assistant left disappointed at the delay that would come.

"I was just in the middle of my biggest transaction and—"

"Calm yourself before it upsets me. I am drawn of all my patience this day," said Ira. "I am vacant and will accept no refusal from you." Ira had managed his temperament in all his affairs of business and battle but his Kozotian shell could not contain the urgency inside him, and it was certain to Boon that any rebuttal would end his life where it stood. He convinced himself that business could wait, delays should be expected in economic matters. As he quickly drew his conclusions he hoped that Ira had a profitable project for him. Before speaking plainly, Ira touched his bracelet.

"Have you heard of Narcophalin?" Ira asked.

"Yes. It's a trading company that ships crystalloids. I'm not sure where. It's led by a very strange entan named Omnitacus whose taste for emotions are as dry as hardened clay." He breathed deeply, filled with bored. "The company earns generous zorn for its operations which I think now process the crystalloids in small factories. I've never seen the crystalloids used but I had a couple of run-ins with their operations when the founder was in charge, he's dead, of course, but top management changes often can cause that," explained Boon.

"Good. You are familiar enough that I will share no more than what I want you to do. I want to know what the product is made out of, what it does, and where it is shipped."

"That should be straightforward."

"I want details, Boon. I want proof – transactional, scientific and logistics! Fail to bring me any of these and you will not be able to hide from my reach, thief."

Boon was beginning to feel that his profession was not appreciated. He had solved disputes, replaced valuable relics, saved companies from trouble, as well as many personal issues too many to list, but it came down to this unappreciative fact. "And what about—"

"Zorn?"

"You have seen my thoughts."

"Worry first to accomplish this task in five days and, if you succeed, I will stuff your pocket full of zorn."

Boon wanted to knock down the monetary details before heading out. There was no indirect way to say this. "But I would prefer—"

Ira's batier reached Boon's neck, not even the thief's agility could avoid his blazing speed. The batier hummed. Boon revised his proposal and continued: "I was just going to say that I prefer to leave right away."

"Good. You have five days at most. Don't get yourself killed," said Ira.

THE MORE Boon thought about it the more inconvenienced he felt and he was bothered that he wouldn't make his quota this month. He was on a personal mission – early retirement. Ira was sure to pay him without satisfaction of his own under-handed dealings where he netted far more in his convoluted partnerships and side deals. The last transfer of tarcs were sold to three different dealers at three different prices and then he negotiated for a cut in each unit sold to the public. Static projects such as Ira's were both dangerous and non-negotiable, and they were strokes to his ego that he often missed. The escapades with Khan were his most memorable and dangerous. Some nights he dreamed of escaping the boredom of business; being a numularian wasn't what inspired him. The zorn was great but it made him feel stale and statuesque.

Boon scaled the curved walls of the serpentine building made of a marbled stone three days after Ira's demands. It took him a day and a half to monitor the security and test it, and another day and a half he waited to reduce suspicions and prepare his equipment. With five days at hand there was no need to rush into it.

The stone was mixed with a crystalline material that gave it a sparkling outward appearance, and it acted as a security system that served the entire building. Boon's scaling equipment, zero-friction pads fitted to his joints that eliminated friction and enabled arvicity to read through the attached object without detection, were custom made by Special P, an expert designer and producer of specialized items.

Once inside the fifth story window he would only have to climb another three stories to the main office, using the shadows as cover and another activated device that negated his presence completely, attuned to the arvic frequency of the current spectrum. He moved quickly to acquire his information. When he reached the main office at the top it took him four twists of his hand to open the door, disarm two traps before entering inside unnoticed.

The storage device was shaped into a fifty-centimeter statue and his tarc add-on device surfed for the data he needed. All of the data was visualized through the crystal and could be stored as he wanted. He hadn't anticipated any serious resistance to a corporate office; nothing was evident in his analysis of the building or the security procedures at the start, and still he was unnerved more than usual. He was here and was getting what he needed.

Narcophalin was controlled by Technomicon and run locally by Omnitacus in conjunction with Denar'ka. It did not register at first but then he recalled the adventure to retrieve the Arvinstrum pieces and of the malkar and of the ice being who called himself Denar'ka before challenging Khan to a fight of death. His cerbind reminded him of Sints and the immense danger he may be in. He worked faster, sifting through information, watching cautiously all around him. Information came up about crystalloids which were reprocessed into concentrated pods of crystine and shipped to an anonymous place outside of Maffin, an area labeled only with a strange string of numbers which he put into memory. Crystine was being used to generate enormous amounts of arvicity and fed into arvicular machines to form zoldiers. Intrigued, he read on and on and did not pay attention to his discovery by the enemy through the networked device with which he played.

He exited just as he had entered and didn't make it three meters down the hallway when he was blocked by four armed zoldiers intent on killing him. He dashed to the rear and ran into half a dozen more. The last sound he heard before it went dark was a familiar laugh.

When he awoke, some hours later, he was facing the floor from the ceiling in a horizontal position. The room was empty except for light that emitted from the walls.

His hands and feet and waste were tied by ceramic cuffs and chained to the ceiling. Only his head was free.

The monstrous thundering of unnatural footsteps trembled inside of his body. Each step vibrated into the ceiling and into him. He tensed in expectation and felt a chill on his body. His clothes and his items had been removed.

Denar'ka entered with a tall cerbor by his side. Boon could only see the tops of their heads. The Nivaton's was the easiest to recognize, not only because it was bald but also because of the warped ear.

"You owe me a favor, thief. I have helped to find your niche, but it isn't on the ground or in a cave. No—it is on the ceiling," said Denar'ka without looking up at any time. "Speak and I will consider your release. I could have further use for your tricks. You are good, are you not? None would miss your absence."

"There is nothing to say," said Boon. "I'm a numularian and not a thief as you have said. I was considering getting involved in the crystalloid business and wanted some free competitive information. You caught me. I'm guilty."

"You're caught and you will be dead if I don't hear words to soothe my irritation! Do not bring bother to my ear with your falseness and your talk of being a numularian. A thief can only be a thief without the conscience needed to be more, and such a thing are you. There are only two kinds of thieves – the well-paid and the dead. Since you are still alive, thief, you have been well-paid to come here and to invade our privacy and for that I should have removed your existence but for upsetting me, you will divulge all that you know or you will become a dead thief and I will suck the information from your cerbind." The cerbor rotated a short scepter in his hands. "This is Crispier. I will return in ten minutes to gather what you have given. If I am not satisfied, I will freeze your body centimeter by centimeter until you are thoroughly dead." Denar'ka left.

Crispier waved his hands and swung his scepter as he worked to probe Boon's cerbind. Why use manual techniques when spells simplified things? Boon felt the spell reach inside of him. He had had the fortune to spend many tios learning how to fool spells such as this and had been caught enough times to have perfected his technique. They all worked on the same principle. There were some painful lessons in his training. He did the usual struggle and resist motion before getting emotional and letting slip the false thoughts slowly at first then quicker and quicker. Crispier did not notice.

"I was hired by Jicama, the director...Technomicon has lost trust in Narcophalin and has paid me Z200,000 to investigate the business operations of this company. No, no! I was to get the data and report it as soon as possible. Once that was done Technomicon would take its own action against the company if there was a discrepancy in what it had recorded. There is also fear that Omnitacus has contracted an information virus and could harm the operations. Stop, stop, no! Denar'ka was going to face any of the blame – I don't know why – along with those who had aided him like you..."

By the time he reached this point of his lies, Boon had unlocked his inverted entanglement and was waiting for the satisfied cerbor to move more directly under him. He would only get and need one strike. When the time was right and with four minutes to spare before Denar'ka returned, Boon dropped onto the back of Crispier's neck and snapped him face first into the ground without a chance to yell out. Strike two, the follow-up, came from the cerbor's own scepter and then silence came again and he could only hear his soft breath. Not even a sweat bead dripped from his face. Time was short and had to suffice, he thought to himself and spent a minute to adjust his skin color to that of the far wall until his image and the wall's became one and the same.

Denar'ka returned to the room, picked up his stunned servant and, infuriated, sent out zoldiers to hunt Boon down. It was easy to sneak out under the commotion and the distraction.

He wondered why many hated the thief. How could society advance without thieves? It was a most useful profession in a corrupt economy filling with greed and blind ambition. That title wouldn't suit him in the long run. When he retired, and now he saw the possibility coming, he wanted to retire not as a thief but as a catalyst for great change.

Chapter 13

IRA'S RESEARCH and development laboratory carried rare
machines and devices that were capable of quixotic arvic
manipulations. The rooms that housed all of the
equipment and the hand-picked staff were loaded with
advanced technologies that if in the hands of the
consumer world could potentially do massive damage in
the wrong hands. This was the place of Levin and was
devoted to the proliferation of technological and scientific
knowledge for the protection of Seranor. It was also why
Alexan decided to stay in here day after day without want
of leave or rest.

The young arvician indulged himself, with Ira's
permission, and studied all manners of spells and lists,
most of which were custom and not available or shared
outside of the upper circle in the Terium. It was one of

the reasons why Ira had an advantage in spell combat as his opponent would have never seen such spells before and would have trouble defending against their effects. It was rumored by the staff that Ira had created unique lists for himself and retained them all in his head with perfect clarity.

Alexan's own spell casting had become more succinct from his travels and he was really enjoying delving in arvicity. That was not the most challenging thing for him lately. It was what had been enhanced in his ability that struck him as very dramatic, and it all happened after touching Seragorn and being sick for some time, near to death. Once the sickness had passed, his body accepted and allowed arvicity to flow more freely through him and with such an ease that his chances of failing to cast higher level spells dropped to almost zero. He continued to improve his arvic manipulations even impressing Ira and Int, the creative inventor who ran the R&D laboratory. Int was a seedling who had lost the ability to become a luto, and in his dilemma found that his creativity was unmatched on Seranor, and this led to rapid technological advancements at the Terium.

The staff were heavily devoted to the protection of Seranor and it was this extreme level of dedication that was siphoned off into Alexan, a Kozotian who was dedicated to nothing and no one.

Dreams came into Alexan's sleep after the first couple of months. It may have been due to his lack of rest or his unhealed illness but Alexan knew that it was more than that. He had wielded two of the Arvinstrum devices and they had left their impression in him. The visions came as usual in his sleep and it motivated him to sleep less and less. In his dreams there were seven Kozotalians, crystal-like and awesome in every facet, and they urged him, pushed him to find them as they ran about hiding in the oddest of places. Alexan would try to track them down and would be eluded by their tricks and skill so he would tire and rest. One of the Kozotal would come out and prod him to try again and again. By the end of the dream, Alexan was so exhausted that he could not try anymore.

The dreams motivated him to satisfy an urge to find out more about the Arvinstrum. It made him feel at ease just by starting his search. As he found information in Ira's storage libraries he was encouraged to find more about the Arvinstrum. It was later he began to sense the connection to the Kozotal.

Originally the Kozotal created seven tools to stabilize the planet but the power embedded in each tool was so great that it became unstable and dangerous. This was what led seven elected Kozotal to insert their kols into a device so that their energy could stabilize the relics and they could be used safely for all time. He hit upon something that he found relevant to Ira's campaigns and ran out to find the revolutionary leader. He found Ira playing with a cylindrical device that displayed visual images from one long port on the side.

"Are you busy?" asked Alexan.

"No."

"I have been researching the Arvinstrum and have found some important facts."

"What is it?"

"The kols of the Kozotal are held within them."

"Is that all you have found?"

"There is more. The Arvinstrum was used to trace and seal Seragorn—I'm sure you knew that."

"And?"

"The relics have the power to release Seragorn."

"There is nothing new so far..."

"Once released, Seragorn's arvic stores can be transplanted to another location by the devices. But it requires another object called Orbis Inigra."

Ira stopped playing. "Where is Orbis Inigra?"

"It was said to be given to Escarotian, stolen by a Kozotal named Kozo."

"Then that is what he found." Ira muttered. "Alexan, do you have a picture of this Orbis Inigra?"

"Yes, just give me a minute to put it up onto a PT." Alexan worked several devices at once before an image of a bright sphere appeared. "This is it."

"What does it do?"

"It stores energy. It does not make anything else clear. The history is very vague at that time. From what I have gathered the device stores masses of arvicity and was used in the creation of this very planet."

"Then the box must contain the Orbis..."

"What box?" asked Alexan.

"Khan mentioned a box that he had found in the tomb of Escarotian and it was stolen some time ago by the Ice Timor. If the box contained the Orbis, protected somehow from accidental use, then the Orbis is in the hands of Zorath."

"Then he has the ability to drain Seragorn of his total energy."

"He has been doing this to Seranor already but with the Orbis he can take all of his power also. The Arvinstrum will help to accomplish that."

"The planet will die!"

"Yes. It will, but it hasn't yet because he doesn't have all the pieces or maybe he hasn't figured out how to use them or it's the Orbis that he can't use..."

"Perhaps he cannot use it as a Nivian."

"Yes. Or what if he cannot open the box as a Nivian..."

"It is dangerous in his hands."

"I am waiting on some vital information that will need your participation, Alexan, for it concerns the Arvinstrum." Ira stroked his hands.

"I am only working on this right now and can make time."

"Be ready. I shall know soon."

Soon arrived one hour later after Boon had relayed the information he had found. The coded location was being used to produce mass zoldiers for Zorath. Oddly enough, two Arvinstrum relics remained there and with Khan's decoding and Ira's tracking devices they located the area and had detailed outer perimeter maps by the end of the day. Ira had called in Alexan once more.

"I have a mission for you," said Ira. "There is a place called Vatu, located north of Maffin, and it is producing zoldiers for Zorath's army. You will go with the others and you will ensure that Vatu is destroyed before you leave at any cost but the others must not know about this so I will send you there as an expert on the Arvinstrum."

"Who are the others?"

"Your colleagues Khan, Griz and Boon. I will arrange for a meeting in two days' time. Start preparing yourself now as I inform the others."

"Back to adventure."

"This is no longer adventure for you, Alexan. These are orders that must be done. Zoldiers infest our urbas and fight against us. I can only guess in saying that Zorath is building an army of synthetic beings bent on one purpose. To destroy us and this planet."

"He already gains the pieces that he needs. It is all fitting together more clearly. Stopping his zoldiers will hurt him."

"It will not permanently stop him."

"That is the next challenge that I will absorb myself with after I have understood his technology—Here, take a look at this." Ira threw Alexan the cylindrical object.

"What is it?" Alexan rotated carefully and studied it.

"A device that can think."

"A cerbus?"

"Not exactly. It processes information based on mathematical formulas."

"So it is possible to construct a mathematical processor."

"It seems so. Zorath did not make it. It was a half-entan who did."

"Why does it darken your forehead, Ira?"

"I have just found out that Zorath's minions have improved it. They have created malleable cerbi. We have yet to even understand this basic unit."

"It is starting then," said Alexan.

"What is that you speak of?" said Ira.

"Technological war."

"It has already begun. The Ice Timor moves to unify its strategy."

"When the pieces are all put together he will have us cornered and vulnerable," said Alexan.

"That is why we must succeed on this next mission," said Ira. "I will hold you responsible for your part. Your days of adventure have ended. It is the time for thinking beyond us and what we need. Seranor calls and there are very few who can help her."

"A few good can make change."

"The right few could. The greater society falls into the hands of mediamenta and drowns in its falseness."

"And the Terium?"

"Let us send out the signal. Even Zorath must move forward step-by-step. We will follow his steps until we are ready to cut off his path."

Chapter 14

TO BE sexual was to be Seronian. Sex was encouraged in Seronian life to stimulate the body like no other activity could; caress and sexuality wrapped together under the warmth of two kols. It was not uncommon for entan and ventan to indulge in paid sexual activities especially in areas of public prostitution. The sex trade was sterile and trustworthy. It was a respected area the general ceramination accepted as part of everyday life.

There were two areas in Casus where one could find sexual satisfaction. The Pad, a private area where sex was done behind closed doors, and the Oviata, the public pornography area. With official areas marked, masturbation was not allowed. Self-satisfaction was deemed unnecessary and one could be jailed for performing a lone sex act. An abundance of partners were available. There were even free love-making partners that could be found, but one had to go to Oviata for those.

Of course, the Pad and Oviata were last choices for the average Seronian; practically everyone had or could easily find a sexual partner with similar interest. Lutos and lutas had physical commonalities. The Karulis enjoyed sex the most. All Karuli females were nymphomaniacs. This inherent chemical trait encouraged them to work in the sex industry. They mixed with any of the races without pride or prejudice.

Entan and Kozoty did not mix for reasons of appearance rather than those related to sexual inability. Kozoty considered entans to be physically unappealing. It was the color of their porcelan skin. It just wasn't white enough and in areas of pleasure, where kozotians had a translucence sexuality, entans maintained an opaque whiteness.

Griz spent his wealth on two things: number 51 and cases of freshly made Prime. He indulged in both to an extreme. Number 51 had risen above that of a figure in a numerical list of prostitutes. She had grace, class and perception; features not found in others, but at an early age she was invited to surrender her body, to live in daily bliss as a living sex object. She loved it now, as then, though preferred to share her bliss with Griz. She was listed as Number 51, it was illegal to disclose names to patrons, and she brought feeling to his life. A feeling of warmth and of purpose.

It was the first night together that attracted her to him. He was strong then, a face like that of a clay embankment that the ocean had hit for fifty tios. A raw, elemental beauty about him, ugliness to the point of simplicity and naturalness. The beauty of nature when you stripped away the illusion.

Griz never removed his armor for sex. He didn't even change his new armor into a suit form. The extra weight of armor had given her a lot of pain for the first two months after they met. Following that initiation period she adjusted fine and took even more joy in it. That was five tios ago; before he could speak, before he could share and before he could feel. It was Khan's fault for awakening his emotions. Khan was responsible for many many things.

Killing, travel, murder and drunkenness had fulfilled his youthful desires. Griz longed for meaning to his life. Longed to smell the native charm life once had; the way things smelled when he was born, before he realized his deformities and the torture his father brought upon him. Scarred for his entire existence from his family, he reached inside of himself for a family of his own.

"Marry me and we will leave," said Griz without his helm, the softest voice he had ever pronounced. It was genuine, she felt that. Griz hugged 51 and held her close enough to smell the fragrance in her hair. One whiff and he drifted away on a cloud of love. "I could float forever on your scent."

"Marry you?" Number 51 asked, thinking she might have misheard. She struggled to get out from his embrace. Finally, he let her go and she turned to face him. Her eyes scanned his and were met with an honesty that scared her. There had been other clients who took interest in her and wanted a relationship. She had tried some of them. It resulted in the same misconceptions and led her to keep her corius to herself and only her body to her clients. Griz and her had a romantic chemistry that attracted her to him as much as he was attracted to her. Marriage was another thing entirely left for two kols ready to join in life as one. She was not capable of making such a decision. Prostitution was not a job. It was a long-term career.

"Marry me," he repeated. "We could be happy together."

"I cannot do that," she said. "There are so many things."

"You can."

"You don't understand."

"What is there to understand?"

"I'm a prostitute. I'm paid for sex."

"I'm a mercenary. I'm paid to kill," he replied and picked up two pieces of equipment. "We are like a batier and a shield. I strike and you protect. Your love has protected me in all my adventures and in my moments of pain."

"Griz, I cannot."

"Without your love I would have died long ago. What reason is there for a mercenary to exist? None, I tell you. We are killers, paid to kill or be killed. Where is there pleasure in that, I ask you? I have only known this reality. Killing gave me a reason to live before...before you and your love came to save me."

"I cannot," she said, shaking her head and looking away from his face.

"Why? Tell me why?"

A sobbing pause.

She blurted out a laugh. "Once a prostitute, always a prostitute," she said. "I do not know anything else and I do not care for anything else. It is hard to explain to you."

"I care not for what you are today nor yesterday nor tomorrow," he said. "I only care that we are together."

"And the day after tomorrow?"

"That will be the day you will be my wife," he answered, assuring as could be. His plated armor rubbed together as he moved in expression.

"I am a prostitute," she said with conviction. "I will always be a prostitute." She knew with certainty that her career gave her the satisfaction needed to continue. It was what she enjoyed doing.

"You are the shield. You protect the sexually weak and the needy. I know. I was once like that. Your shielding protected me."

"It also shields me, Griz."

"Leave this profession as I will soon leave mine. I grow tired of killing. Tired of wearing this armor to hide my love inside. Is that not what armor was created for?"

"It is not so easy, this change. I have tried. There have been others before you who pulled me away. Yet, see me still here."

"I care not. We will try together," he said.

"After, I will be different," she added.

"After, you and I will remain together and no longer need the comforts of our weapons."

"Your life purpose is to kill."

"My killing must end," he said, revealing his future goal.

"Mine is to pleasure. It is why we have been together."

"Then you understand why we must marry."

"No."

"Why?" he asked.

"There are reasons for your violence. Reasons beyond our knowledge. Seranor needs you. She needs your clavus, Griz." She loved Griz and in another way she did not know how to love him. She had learned to love as her profession dictated. Griz truly loved her, she said to herself, trying to convince herself that he would not let her fall by the wayside. Could she love him the same? The answer eluded her.

"Then I will give it to her. I will toss it into her bosom along with my armor to be with you."

"Do not be so blind to what is in front of you. The clavus is you and you are the clavus. Talk of marriage is a dream we both have, but is nothing more."

"I speak openly about this. I grow tired of killing. Tired of the paid murder upon which my reputation is built. We could be together starting all things fresh and new. Surrender from this life!" He grabbed her hands and was pulling her gently forward as she resisted. "Take me into your corius and we will live forever!" She wrestled away her hands.

"We have been together for some time...It is difficult for me to..." Tears rolled gently down her face. Her sobbing was quiet and, embarrassed, she turned her head away.

"Will you not accept my proposal?"

"You must leave me now," she said. Her voice was dim and distant.

"Will you not accept my proposal?" In his desperation for an answer his temper flared. "Will you accept?!" He repeated.

"I cannot," she muttered, afraid to let the sound out far from her lips.

"What?" He grabbed and shook her. She bit her lip. It bled milk and it mixed with the red tears streaming from her eyes. Griz saw it, unsatisfied.

"Answer me! Will you accept?"

After a tense two minutes, a sound came out. It was intended to answer all of the questions at once and was why it was so loud and painful. "I cannot. I cannot! I cannot! Leave me, leave me, leave me!—Leave me." He let her down gently. She huddled her legs and arms together into an entan wrapping.

Griz, hurt and distanced, obeyed her demand not wholly accepting it. The portal tugged hard at his corius, drew him fast to the exit in one slow suction that he could not resist.

"Leave me! Come back nevermore!" she yelled as she slammed the portal shut behind him then fell to the floor and tasted tears she had never known.

All of that stored warmth in his chest was fading fast as he wallowed in anaprimo at the Ice Scabbard at a large table to himself. Those who knew his temper did not bother him. Those who did not know learned of the results from his rage by evidence of a dead ventan, arms twisted back and chest caved in, on the far side of the table. At closing hour, when he was completely disassociated with the physical matter around him, Alexan arose from the back of the tavern. He had been watching for the last couple of hours. The young Kozoty slipped on a device around Griz's ceramic wrist. His weight changed to a 10 kg mass and his arvician friend carried him out.

Chapter 15

TAVERNS WERE abundant, serving fresh brews of average anaprimo. The highly popular, Prime, made with a mixture of elemental ingredients had saturated the market, especially in Casus. Adventurers took to the liquid drug as their first choice of intoxication. Wanna-be adventurers, usually just average workers loaded up on mediamenta, drank Prime hoping to turn into a real hero and to be listed on Valuto. Since Khan's calming, or what others called his point of domestication, his value of oracles had fallen 82%, but his name still remained in the top 30, actually 29. Riches were being made playing Valuto and, in exchange for such wealth poverty was rising from the losers.

Khan, not caring about his oracles recently, considered what Nao had been teaching him over the past week. His teacher had wandered off as he often did and Khan was left alone to train.

His life was turning from the work of a mercenary to that of a common citizen of Seranor. This was reflected in his lowered Valuto price. Yet with Nao back, he was once again aiming to become some sort of champion for Seranor, a Seranor he did not love. And as he looked back upon his previous missions something truthful stared at him, straight in the eyes. All that he had done was to serve Zorath or Seranor. He was already a servant to either of them, but if Zorath succeeded the planet would die and all Seronians would go along with it. Despite his choices, his path had already been laid bare and it was clear which was the next step for Seranor could not die, not if he could have a chance to protect her. How would Sita view his revised decision?

With time on his hands he contacted his three friends and arranged for the four of them to meet at a tavern. They had all been busy with their lives. Griz had become distanced as once before.

Boon recommended a new tavern and Khan was easy to agree. TECH, a technological tavern with invisible seats except for a bright yellow stripe around the round seating portion, was the choice of the day. It was half-filled with patrons. Most young and upcoming adventurer types who had something to prove. Khan, Griz, Alexan and Boon looked old sitting around but their spirit was the same. Experience colored their cheeks.

They chatted away about their trials and tribulations. Khan shared some of his classroom discussions with his students at Windy Path. Several of them sat at the other side of the tavern. Boon bragged on about nothing in particular while Alexan tried to impress the others with his advanced thinking and scientific terminology. It was Griz who sat drinking and withdrawn from the others and

Khan knew it best to let him have his time. Time moved in conversation.

A muscular, thick-bodied entan angrily walked into the tavern and sat at the bar, ordering a drink. He began to drink heavily. Boon glanced in his direction. "Ugly morbfarcker," he commented in the midst of telling a funny story.

The over-sized entan, Jod, after drinking six jugs of expensive anaprimo in only forty minutes, cleared a table of two young adventurers and started taunting two bulky entans in a wrestling match.

Jod called out, "Any brave warrior who is capable of lifting me and throwing me more than ten paces will receive my credit tard with a value of Z10,000. Who will try first?"

"I will," said a voice in the back. "I'll throw you out the door."

"Maybe, but now hear the other bargain and tell us if you are still able. If you cannot you must kill someone immediately or I will kill you." There was a short silence in the room after the fat entan's statement. "Still want to try, brave one?"

"I'll knock your morb ass out the farcking entrance so far that you'll forget which plane that you are on!" yelled Julubu, a young confident mercenary type, a reflection of his father who was killed fighting a cerbor.

"Then try," said the muscular Jod. The young entan came up, grabbed one leg and one arm and lifted. The heavy set Jod was relaxed and happy. The mercenary yelled out and lifted with minimal effort. As he had Jod high above his head his knees buckled.

Boon was watching and saw Jod make some motion with his head. He told Griz: "You see, it's a trick Griz. This guy's going down. Watch."

Just as he finished, the legs completely buckled and he dropped Jod whose body cracked the tiled floor all around him. Jod didn't seem to be affected by the fall.

Julubu, still down on one knee, said, "I had you. I had you! What happened...what the farck are you?"

Then Jod stood laughing, but its that little too familiar laugh that Khan took notice even from the back of the room. He thought about it briefly. Griz, on the other hand, walked up. Jod said, "Kill someone!" The young mercenary sat still for a few seconds, then jumped up, grabbed a short batier and pointed it at a younger entan's throat. Julubu held it out crying.

"Kill him!" said Jod.

Julubu started to shake violently then fell to the floor crying.

"Die entan!" yelled Jod all the while laughing.

Khan realized that the laugh was a un-entan laugh and started moving to the center of action. "Be prepared," he quickly and quietly said to Alexan. Griz was already there and just as Jod raised his hand for the death blow, Griz stopped him with his right arm and said, "It's Griz time!"

"So the armored entan wants to try. Will you pay for the life of this porcelan penis?"

"What is your price?"

"Throw me out the front portal or face death." The front portal was more than eight meters away. Griz glanced up at the portal.

"The front portal it is."

Griz lifted him up without effort or time wasted, then something strange happened. Jod's weight increased five-fold and even Griz was caught by surprise but his alien strength fed to him by his girdle proved a match and added to that was Griz's own primal ferocity and only moments before his legs would buckle, Griz focused, yelled out and threw Jod far out through the front wall and heard him crash outside in the street. A luta screamed. Then there were sounds of other screams.

Khan arrived to the center of the room with verse ready to burst from his lips. The pungent smell was much more evident now and Khan was certain of his guess: a malkar in disguise. Griz recovered, confident. "Griz is strongest."

"Griz, what happened?"

"I win his game. I am strongest. Heavy shat."

"Griz, there is something wrong with him...he is not entan...the smell is the same as a malkar."

"Malkar?"

Jod calmly walked back into the tavern. His body gave off a really bad odor now.

"You owe me, smelly."

"But you won't have a chance to use it," Jod threw the tard toward Griz but it fell short and landed on the floor. Griz didn't move to reach it. Jod kept walking but began to lose his shape. His height doubled as did his width. A brown malkar, round and fat, four feet in any direction with two over-sized arms and mace-like fists took shape.

"M-a-l-k-a-r." Khan muttered to confirm his earlier suspicion. Other patrons froze like statues in sight of this. Some were afraid to miss the action. Others were afraid to die. Griz smiled from beneath his helm. "Morb farcker."

GRIZ GRABBED his clavus. Jod ran into the first bystander, grabbed him and threw him through the roof, killing him instantly as he landed as a corpse on the roof outside. All heard the thud of a limp body.

Then Jod grabbed another, the bartender, and threw him at the rushing Griz. The bartender's body got spiked onto Griz's sharp clavus and as Griz tried to shake him off and recover, Jod attacked with his flail-like fists. The first hit, knocked Griz back two meters and he dropped his weapon with bartender and all. The slightly stunned warrior unsheathed a broad batier off of a stunned mercenary. He swung hitting a fist, the batier snapped in two. He was not prepared for the second flailing fist which landed squarely on Griz's left shoulder and cracked the bone inside. Griz dropped to one knee, stunned. Jod prepared again but was attacked by Khan at his backside. Khan's rapid strikes with his curved bastion, more than six in all in a blink of an eye, prove non-damaging to the beast's impenetrable hide. Khan questioned his choice of weapon.

Khan's momentary disappointment gave Jod a slight edge but his speed was impressive and three fists of the malkar couldn't touch him, only to destroy furniture and kill a stander by. Khan leapt onto the bar to safety. Jod prepared a spell. A line of white arvicity came out from the back of the tavern to cancel the malkar's blue spell. A quick burst and Jod's spell failed. Finally, Alexan stood on the table for a better view. Jod focused his already shifty eyes and dissipated Alexan's second arvic spell.

As he turned back to Khan, Griz was there with a large invisible stool which he smashed the malkar with. That followed with a powerful right fist to the back of the head which had a small effect. Khan noticed that and chopped the legs off a full-sized table, called his strength and lifted it high.

Jod turned to Griz, picked him up and pile drove his head into the ground, also putting a hole in the floor. If not for Griz's helm and thick neck, he would have died instantly. Griz lay motionless.

"Helmhead. I am Raknajod. You are floor now," Jod said, just before a full-sized hard lutium-based table top of three inches thick came smashing down on his head. Raknajod went down. Alexan yelled out. "Give me your bastion! Give me your bastion!"

"But it's useless against his body."

"I will correct that." Khan tossed it over, Alexan cast a spell on it which required him extra time to prepare. Jod came around and threw Khan to the wall and cast a wall of life-sucking mud at him, encasing him in black mud. Alexan dropped Khan's weapon and cast a number of fiery missiles at Jod which damaged him slightly. Then a couple of stander-bys jumped in to hurt the malkar with broken furniture and after a massive beating that would have killed any mortal, Jod flailed one entan to death and hugged another so that his was encased in his mud body suffocating him. Alexan cast a noxy spell on the wall of mud on Khan. The white fire hardened the mud and Khan was able to break free, coughing and spitting mud.

Finally, Khan retrieved his bastion and thrust it clear through Raknajod several times cutting up large chunks of soft brown lutium. The malkar's mood raged as he regenerated. "This isn't working, Alexan!" he yelled. Jod moved in on him, dispelling another one of Alexan's arvic balls but one escaped him and a noxy ball exploded near his leg removing most of the clay meat. Then the leg snapped under the pressure from his excess weight.

Khan shifted into wind form, rising above the downed foe, and shaped a drilling weapon from the air. The air drill hit Jod and bore a large hole through his chest. But he did not die. No. Jod got up, coughing black mud, and stood on one thick leg this time. When the drill came again, the malkar jettisoned a massive amount of black mud into it just after reversing the effects of the air drill. Khan was sent back reeling under the pressure.

Jod turned on Alexan, wielding an arvic spell, and released it on the arvician. Alexan failed to deflect it and the spell impacted him square on, holding him in perfect stance for Jod to strike. Khan saw this, then saw too his friend Griz – no sign of Boon – but with no time to think he reacted quickly. He called the wind, not from Nata, from himself. The wind came and he unleashed its potency upon the malkar, finishing Jod for good. Khan collapsed breathing heavily.

Extensive damage to the tavern was seen from holes in floors, walls, broken furniture, dead bodies and large ones filled with unnatural blackened mud.

Griz lived.

"Why couldn't we strike it?" Khan asked Alexan.

"It's a malkar. Mystical and elemental beings are not always affected by terrestrial weapons."

"What is it doing here?"

"Something is amiss."

"What happened to Boon?" Khan looked around to find his head pop up from behind the bar. He came out. Khan noticed a heavy bag of tarcs and tards at his waist.

"That's shared four ways."

"What is?"

"That!" he pointed.

"They're mine."

"I'm not going to argue again. Anything we do together is for us all."

"But its mine."

"Pay up."

"I hate this. We have to change this."

"Yeah, next time you fight the farcking malkar."

"Okay, okay. Take it easy. Can it wait?"

Griz stumbled over to the bar with Alexan's help. He ordered a drink but no bartender was there. "Boon, I want a drink of cold prime."

"What am I a bartender?"

"Shut up and get it."

Boon grabbed him a nice bottle of Prime and a drinking cup and put in front of him. Griz indulged.

"It must have been here for a reason," Khan said.

"Maybe. Not sure what it is," Alexan answered. "We're lucky that it wasn't a pure malkar."

"Why? Is there a difference?"

"The average malkar has only about 30% of the power of a pure one. My guess was that this pool of black mud was very average."

"Must be a good reason for it being here. We should be more careful. Including you, Griz." No response.

"C'mon, grab your things and let's go. Quick."

"Let's use the back."

"Who chose this place anyway?" asked Alexan.

Just before leaving, the party arvician decided to manipulate the arvic field around Jod's body in an effort to obtain some information.

"Farcking mud ass," Griz finally said as he left together with the rest.

The Seronian guard came shortly after. Tech was closed for a week with a sign that read: UNDER NEW MANAGEMENT.

Chapter 16

BY THE next morning, when everything at Tech was more or less cleaned up, the Querist filled its headlines with the story of Khan, Griz, and Alexan and how they, in their attempts to rid a malkar on the rampage, destroyed a tavern along with the deaths of six Seronians.

The details of the article highlighted Khan's use of extreme wind force to subdue the concealed beast; live moving pictures, captured at the event, were provided by those who hid on the peripheral and used their adapted tarcs to record the event, all the images were skewed to the brutality from the trio. Spots of details was made about Windy Path, a manipulative school. Boon was curiously absent from the incident. He had a couple of good clients at the palpazine who owed him some favors.

Considering Sita's intimate understanding of her husband, and her willingness to marry an adventuring luto by her own free will, she did not anticipate at any level that the contrived palpazine article would affect her so dramatically. On reading the entire coverage of the event twice, first a gloss over and then a detailed check, she couldn't fathom the ring that was attached to her finger. The bridge that she had so carefully built shattered beneath her.

He will never change, and the fight in him is not over, she said to herself; stroking her distended torso as a hand supported her on the wall. Closing her eyes to stop the tears from coming out, she held her breath and forced her eyes further trying to remove the sight from them.

Do I know his goals, his dreams, his will? The voice came from nowhere and asked in whispers. She wiped her eyes on the backs of her fist, and her thoughts solidified. Fear invaded her – fear for her unborn family.

What if he goes back on an adventure? What if he dies? What is he is incapable of giving the love that I need? she asked herself. He may have already realized after last night that he can't be fixed to a family and its responsibilities.

She became furious at herself for not having shared her news with him before. It might have altered the course of events. May have prevented him. But now it was too late to just tell him such news.

Sita stood up straight as a tree and calmed her breathing to normal. I must leave him, she said to herself. When he returns I will tell him and make him understand. It will be easier for him if he is free. No – it will be easier for me.

Khan returned to the residence as the beauty of Seranor's day opened in the middle of the afternoon. He was anxious and racing ideas through his head about Nata and used his body to confirm his own suspicions.

"I think I've had a breakthrough," he said, all excited with emotion, when he saw her. "Nao is incredible. If I didn't find him – I – I'm not sure where I would have ended up..."

"You've been saved," she said, staring plainly at the chair.

"Has something happened?" he asked, noticing the Querist on the chair and her heavy expression pulling the air down in the room, and was held in shame for not having told her about the encounter with the malkar.

"Khan – I'm in my last desperate breath! I cannot carry it alone," she said in a strangulated voice. She stood rigidly in front of him probing his face delicately, sympathetically. She could see the pride of his own exacerbated skill and the love that she knew would keep intact no matter what became of them, but she had to continue for her own sake. It was no longer about Khan. Her unborn preceded personal issues. "I have to tell you something. Two things actually. I'm pregnant and I'm leaving."

"When? What? You can't! You can't leave me! What has happened to you?"

"What I have most feared has happened – you cannot become what I need! You are not made of such things. You must let me go. I have made a serious mistake to have thought that we could raise a family. It would be difficult to...impossible to live with such a luto. I have lived my whole life running from the disease of family separations. I will not bring it to my family—"

"Our family, Sita, now that I am aware of this important matter. It is our family since our joining," Khan added.

"You are still careless in your obligations. Still seedish in your thoughts."

"I do not pretend to understand a luta's needs and how a seedling complicates and confuses the situation," he said, somewhat frightened. "I may act in a manner unfamiliar to you, but I am not a luta and my method of life is not the same. It does not lessen my actions to be responsible, and I have not faltered in that basic premise."

"But last night, Khan, last night was out of madness to have thought such actions."

"Do not believe all that you view in a palpazine," he said. Many believed that the information in the Querist was false, especially at the start, but as Seronians came to rely on it as the only source of news it was inevitable that more and more actually thought the lies were truth. "Our view of the world is different. It is a dangerous world. The Ice Timor seizes the planet and all of us together in a hand of bitter ice and we have only one way forward—"

"Fighting!"

"Yes. Without resistance, we, and life, are dead. Everything draws our resistance. The malkar is just a vile representation of all of that combined. Fight, yes. Would you prefer that I surrender my life?"

"Still a luto of extremes. Why not choose a peaceful life?"

"I cannot be less than what I am. What more does a luto have than the chance to be what he was made to be. I only choose that path. If that is what you fear most then I more clearly understand your desperation. I even—" Khan could not finish his conclusion. She would keep her plans to leave and with his now obvious support from what he has haphazardly expressed. As he realized this and felt Sita's head burying itself into his chest and his clothes wet in her tears, he knew that he must not let her go.

"I don't want you to go. It is not right to separate our love like this."

She continued to cry and then while still sobbing pushed herself upright, and looking down at his feet said: "I have already packed."

"You do not accept my love for you? Do not leave. I will protect you and all of our family, today and tomorrow."

"It's too late, Khan. I've packed and I must go. Please let me go this way. Please…"

He could feel his own world slipping off of him like an old set of clothes. She only needed his support. His affirmation to the thing he least desired. He could not stop the increase in hatred for Zorath. As for Sita, there was nothing more he could say except the words that gurgled up into his mouth. "If that is what you want…then…that is what…I…want." Turning abruptly away from her, he walked out, head stooped low in thought searching for answers that were not there.

Chapter 17

IT WAS a cold and lonely morning in the decrepitude of his corius. The sorrow had moved in and replaced the better part of his cycle of moods, and had rectified their variabilities. Khan missed his usual breakfast and training routine that had become a piece of his daily existence. No longer did he wish to exist in the chilled hollowness of his lone self. He continually tried to convince his cerbind that she hadn't indeed gone and would return soon enough. Love, the potentiality of it, was that strong for him. That mesmerizing.

He found himself in Ceramin's Square half-way between the earliest part of the day and the middle, much like his own internal state. Where once there was an unoccupied spot, at once a pair of feet appeared in front of his. The boots were brushed clean with no markings as was expected from a brush, free of lint or signs of long travel. Khan recognized that they were of his teacher, at least his eyes recognized them but his cerbus was far too retracted to be of any use.

"Do not enjoy your unhappiness," said Nao. "There can be worse things to occupy your thoughts." His eyes blinked and paused in the closed state. That hadn't happened before. Khan failed to see it but it was the only real warning that Nao would give of his departure. "Keep the hollow and unleash the storm. It is inside you." Nao was gone as quick as he had arrived. To Khan it was the space of the time during one of his own sullen blinks.

The tarc lit up on his belt. Ira was ricking him. An urgent meeting required his attendance.

EQUIST NAO took the speediest route to the edge of the urba and to the arranged spot the two enemies had agreed to meet. He had communed with Nata during his travel over, reassured her that all would be smooth and in place, and asked her to show his student the way when he was not around. The week had gone by faster than he had expected but he welcomed this day. The last of the dying breed of elemental practitioners walked across the snow-covered plains. He reached an area of well-cropped cora trees in a semi-circle that faced Casus. The large area was thick with snow, thicker than the other areas and would hamper ground maneuverability. The fight must take place in the air. Nao's domain. Nao would have no patience for the ice Nivaton, the element of the dead cold.

From a distance at the fulcrum of trees on the other side a figure appeared. Bluish skin glistened as it flowed around his body. The ground beneath Denar'ka froze to ice as he moved ahead, carried forward by his two stumps.

When he had passed the hundred meter mark he started shouting. "You are the last and the end!" he said and continued, body determined to destroy. "Welcome to your funeral, Nao. Khan and his students will join you soon enough." Nao never trusted Denar'ka to keep his promise and intended to remove the ice master this very day.

As soon as the 50 meter mark was breached, Denar'ka struck forth his spray of naqui. It seared the snowy floor and sent up billowing steam. Nao floated effortlessly above. His body massaged the windy air. Denar'ka leapt up, stretching out long tentacles of liquid ice at the wind master and as Nao shifted, the tentacles opened into a liquid web that encircled Nao and froze parts of his solid body. He wind shifted ripping the web apart and immediately swallowed the Nivaton in a whirlwind. He spun blazingly fast miniature cyclones that began to separate the naqui form from its pathways. Denar'ka fought without success then he began to freeze outward and the wind slowed then stopped, captured by the ice.

By the time that Denar'ka had removed his own body from within its grasp, the frozen whirlwind cracked and tore apart in a fierce wind storm that sent Nivaton and snow flying away until he became a speck in the distance. Nao was there once again as Denar'ka survived and; instead of doing more of the same, he sliced his hand twice in the air sending invisible but dreadfully sharp blades of winds at his opponent. Denar'ka survived the first which nearly removed his upper body. It reached the front line of trees and cut down half a dozen tree trunks. The second wind blade caught the Nivaton across his upper thighs and severed two legs off completely before chopping down several more cora trees. Denar'ka's torso fell back as masses of circulating naqui sprayed in all directions. He gasped for breath choking in a pool of blue liquid.

DURING THE time that the Equist watched the dying
Nivaton, fastened to the floor by his own frigid milk, Nao's
body was struck through by a white fingerless hand
almost killing him instantly. The snow that had once
been on the ground, peaceful and neutral, came alive and
reformed into a hideous ice malkar.

Nao was injured – but because of his automatic
defenses that allowed body parts to shift from wind to
ceramic without notice – he was not dead. Another large
hand followed the first and it was much easier for Nao to
avoid, just in time to face his new opponent. His tranquil
halation irritated the malkar all that much more.

"I am Raskavron, ruler of ice! I command the ice!
Command it!" screamed the malkar. Its voice drowned
out all sound, stunning the Wind Equist. The air
thickened and became difficult to breathe. "The wind is
born to freeze! To chill until it is no longer the wind. And
the windseed will so perish. Perish!"

Raskavron trudged ahead and each step it took it grew
by twenty-five percent. By the time that it had reached
Nao, who by now was shaking off the last of the stunned
effect, the malkar was a small hill of ice more than 8
meters tall. It stared down at what it considered the
pitiful entan and his pathetic reality.

Denar'ka's upper-half had gone silent and both pieces
lay in a puddle of naqui. A cloud a billowing white oozed
off of his body and was wooshed away as Nao's form
affected it.

"Mortal is born to die." Raskavron outstretched its
huge arms and froze solid the air around them as Nao
assumed wind form.

The wind blew hard on the small mountain without effect but as Raskavron brought together his arms he congealed the Equist into a frozen ball of wind, and the malkar could not stop laughing as it considered how it would putrify the planet once more. It tossed the ball between its fingerless hands as it considered what to destroy next before returning to Zorath. It wanted to delay its return for as long as possible – without destructive playtime a malkar's moods softened to dangerous levels – and there was opportunity.

Wind is Nata and one who attains all the powers of the wind shall be born into it and digested by it until they are part of Nata and part of nature. It is the wind who is free, always free. Nothing can keep the wind, not even the strength of a pure malkar can remove the wind's effect. Nata is the free.

The ball of wind, so happily kept in Raskavron's grasp, exploded and removed the entire right hand which so held it. The force grew into a ferocious storm, dense as rock and fluid as aqua, and it wrapped its arms around the elemental beast and squeezed with the might of a tornado.

The windstorm squeezed so hard that it penetrated the very molecules of the malkar's hide – and once inside the screaming Raskavron – became a turbulent force that lashed out flake to flake and atom to atom. The small ice mountain expanded more to accommodate the wind's spacing. It grew and grew until it could grow no more at which point the malkar and ice and wind detonated and blew out into a snowy blizzard of ice bits that filled every visible space from snow to tree.

By the time that the storm died down, a wind still blew carrying bits here and there and slowly rebuilt itself into the greatest Equist that ever walked on the planet. Wind cannot be kept against its will. Nao was the wind. He was Nata reborn. It was why he was given the responsibility for Khan.

Soon after his return, Nao noticed Denar'ka and his regenerated lower limbs, no longer stumps but fashioned legs and feet. He hadn't died as he had hoped. It was Denar'ka's laugh that confused Nao.

"You have lost, Nao," said Denar'ka, still laughing. "You are bitten by malkarian ice."

Then Nao noticed it, too. Both his forearms were frozen solid along with part of his face and chest. Raskavron had sealed his fate. He stumbled in pain trying to remove the frozen body parts that were continuing to freeze the rest of him.

"Ice cannot be beaten, nor stopped, nor altered. Ice is the doom of this planet. You can see that. There is no resistance to the greatest attraction. Ice will subdue this planet as it has you," said Denar'ka walking closer to the dying Equist. "I was lucky to have been denied by Nata. Her denial was my destiny."

"You have betrayed yourself," said Nao, struggling with words. Frozen chunks of his face fell out followed by his forearms and a large chunk of his chest dropped to the ground. Milk poured out and he was unable to stop it. "You have been betrayed. Do not follow the ice. It has no remorse. Denar'ka...I live or die does not matter...Nata will never stop..." He was calming himself and trying to reach wind state once again, but was prevented by the ice that chewed his ceramic flesh.

Denar'ka reached the disoriented Equist, grabbed him with his left, straightened him, and then let two naqui fists fly.

"Betrayed? No—I have won," said Denar'ka as he injected Nao's body with naqui and froze him from head to toe. A small gust of wind left Nao's body and vanished into the air. "The ice is purity. It is the supreme master of control and in it we can be made eternal."

Denar'ka picked up the statue of Nao, petrified in permanent ice, the last of the great Equists. He walked toward Casus.

Balance and the order of things were in transition. Once again the wind had brought the revolving future and the revolutions were speeding faster and faster.

Chapter 18

NO SOUND would escape, no spell would pierce its walls. If detected by device the room would reveal itself as a solid piece of rock with trace elements, common as common could be.

Ira, silver streaks in his hair and with a smooth pitch, pronounced his verse with resoluteness to his bedraggled bunch as they took their seats in the protected underground room. Facial expressions were Ira's low points as were the emotions that preceded them. His controlled presentation covered the tenseness under his breath and concern in his brow, and the participants were so occupied by their own thoughts that they did not notice anything extraordinary about their secretive meeting between the five of them.

"This meeting regards an urgent matter that needs doing and the four of you are needed. Our enemies – whom you all know – grow in strength and strategy. They have broken our defenses and entered our urbas. That, I could tolerate to a point, but now a significant play has been made and this cannot continue lest we sacrifice all that we are."

"Why all the precautions, Ira?" asked Boon.

"Zorath watches from his ice mountain. There are few places that I trust are clean. This room, I trust."

"Khan, can you decipher this message?" Ira tossed Khan a tarc that illuminated as he caught it. Khan studied the encrypted message inside.

"It's a location," said Khan.

"As I suspected."

"It is called Vatu and it has the exact coordinates. Do you want me to read them out?"

"Not necessary."

"It sits north, close to Maffin."

"We traced a shipment of crystine pods from Narcophalin to this uncharted area – this Vatu," said Ira. "There is no urba called Vatu. It must be in reference to a location or a base. I am not sure." Ira wiped his hand across the table's edge and three seconds later a fully armored guard entered.

"Take that device and have it analyzed."

"Yes, sir," said the guard and exited with the tarc from Khan's hands.

"Narcophalin used to be a trading company but it has expanded its operations to process crystalloids that make these pods of crystine." His eyes glossed over Boon and went on. "My sources tell me that the crystine pods contain arvicity that is used in arvicular machines. Concentrated arvicity derived from crystals buried in ice lakes. The machines, in turn, raise Zorath's armies of zoldiers – Army of Naquior – that move against us. We can fight the zoldiers with our batiers and our tactics, but there are some things that even our most experienced cannot do battle with. You are all familiar with the Arvinstrum?

"If you have forgotten, I'll remind you. The pieces that you unearthed on your last escapade for the Terium were Septana and Lavo, and they were stolen by Denar'ka and his guards; Kalia-Sint and Kalier-Sint. As you know, Kalier-Sint was killed, the pieces stolen by others then once again put into the hands of the Ice Timor.

"Septana is a relic of protection and Lavo is a cleanser of the earth, both of them are part of the ancient seven piece set of the Arvinstrum designed to seal the seragon, Seragorn; and it is the same set that Zorath has collected.

"I say collected because Septana and Lavo were the last two that he did not have until recently. With these, he completes the ancient set." Ira crossed his arms and eyed them all sparingly displeased with what he saw. Only Alexan sat with any interest and he was already familiar with the primary objective. Griz drank heavily while Khan studied his hands over the table. Boon waited anxiously for the terms of agreement. He had little interest in historical details. Ira prevented a disgusted laugh from fully forming and became more serious.

"Why is this relevant to us?" asked Boon, by now bored with the introduction.

"It is important," said Ira, "because we have traced those two pieces to Vatu. Zorath has not yet joined them with the others in his ice mountain and we have a chance to prevent this from happening." Ira raised the volume in his voice. "With the Arvinstrum in his hands and the Sints to wield them he holds life and death at his command. He aims to remove Seragorn from her seat and us along with him."

"Is that even possible, Ira? He is cosmic and immovable," said Khan clasping his nervous hands together.

"Cosmic he is. Movable also. Oh yes—Seragorn lives under the surface. You have seen him, some of you. Without his presence the entire planet will fold." Ira wanted to explain about Orbis Inigra. He did not want to hide it from Khan or the others. Only Alexan knew. He avoided looking at Khan's eyes. "The same two Sints return to retrieve the items."

"Return to Vatu?" asked Boon.

"Yes. Denar'ka remains with his staff and guards at an above-ground location. We are processing the details of that location as we speak and will have maps and drawings by early tomorrow."

"Is this place far from Maffin?"

"About 18 kilometers in my initial estimate but it will not affect you."

"Why?"

"Do not concern yourself with travel. Time is short and we must improvise. Instead, I want a commitment from the four of you, especially you Khan." Ira found out shortly before the meeting that Equist Nao had died but did not want Khan to know. It could hurt the mission. He debated whether or not to inform him.

"Ira, why is it that you have brought *me* here?" asked Khan. "I am busy with my school and my students. Sita has left me with only that. I only wish to train with my teacher and to stay in Casus."

"Are these the words of Shev'la Khan?" said Ira. "No, I do not think so. The name Khan would not know such verse nor would it dare to speak it in front of me now!"

"These are my words."

"I am saddened by the inequities you feel but there are other threats that we cannot forget."

"I have come to show my support and nothing more. Send another team member instead of me; one who is interested in such things."

"Before you reject my proposal, know this, Khan the Reformed. Your teacher is dead."

"Never!"

"Yes. I do not lie."

"How can he have died? He is the greatest Equist in all of the planet!"

"He was killed in battle by Denar'ka and a malkar. Not just any malkar, but one of pure ice called Raskavron." Khan's emotions were lost. They did not know whether to cry or jump in anger, and so he just sat there perplexed and clasping his hands tightly to reduce the hurt. "Denar'ka has crafted an ice statue of him. See for yourself," said Ira and beamed an image of Nao's frozen body on a rooftop above the table. "This was stored an hour before this meeting began by one of our members."

"It cannot be, it cannot be like this," said Khan, shaking his head and wiping his eyes with his empty palm, stroking away the vision he had seen.

"I am sorry that this has happened to your teacher. It is the same entan that waits up north that killed him."

"And now waits to take my life. Is that it, Ira? You want to send me to my death?" Khan said staring directly at Ira. His head turned away in contemplation. "If he has killed Equist Nao, I have no chance against his strength."

"He was aided by a pure malkar, Khan. They are the most powerful of all malkars and Nao conquered it while doing battle with Denar'ka."

"He is still dead. Neither you nor I can change that. It is the second time that I have lost him and I could not bear any more loss. My skin melts from loss."

"I must tell you more and you will want to hear what I have to say."

"What more is there to tell?"

"The world is far more complex than you or I could ever imagine. We are simple objects in the game of the Versos. It is unwise to think that we are anything more than objects with a purpose, and there is more to tell. Some time ago a white box, or case if you can call it that, was taken from you. Am I correct?"

"How did you know? I told no one."

"I just knew. I had hired three cerbors to steal it from you so that I might have examined it's strange source of power, but my plan was foiled by that of another and my hirelings were killed for what they had succeeded in."

"You? Why would you want it? How did you know that I even had this item?"

"I detected its strangeness on your person and needed more information. These are days of information."

"You needed more information…"

"Excuse me," said Boon, "but can we continue on the topic and not get too sidetracked. I've got business waiting and every minute we waste here I lose zorn. Time is zorn. What's this box have to do with what we are talking about?"

"The box holds a key to power. A large orb called Orbis Inigra," said Ira.

"The final box is not opened," added Khan.

"Correct, the box has not been opened for when it opens I will surely know as will many others," said the Levin.

"I still do not understand why you wanted to steal it from me. Why didn't you ask to see it?"

"Would you have allowed me to see it?"

"No."

"I considered it important enough to take alternative action. I would have returned it to you unharmed a day later."

"I had opened the first two seals but the third remains shut."

"What's this got to do with us?" asked Boon impatiently.

"The Orbis is a key that Zorath wants and, along with the relics, can allow him to control Seragorn and his primal energy. This will give him all the arvicity on the planet and along with his Army of Naquior he will control Seranor with an ice grip. This cannot happen and I have sworn to prevent this.

"There is more. Because of its high street value, it has attracted others. The rich cerborian numularian, Werewul, hired three mercenaries to retrieve it two weeks ago. And it is you four who must venture out to return the Arvinstrum relics and take back that box."

"Wouldn't the other mercenaries have reached it by then?"

"No."

"Why not?"

"I followed them as far as the location and then lost their trace. I assume that they do not have them yet."

"You assume that they don't have it? What if they are dead?"

"That is also an assumption, is it not?" Ira threw back at him. "Listen to me. The three hired hands ahead of you work in our favor."

"How is that?"

"They provide cover for your steps. Denar'ka would not suspect two parties to come. He would be surprised at one."

"Or maybe he waiting for us—for me," said Khan, bitterly.

"It's suicide," agreed Boon.

"It is not suicide," defended Ira, confident of his conviction.

"It is suicide," said Khan, agreeing for once. "The last time we met with them we were lucky to escape alive. My teacher is dead because of him! I am sure he wants to kill me."

"You are all much more capable now," the noble Kozoty added.

"Ira, why don't you do it?" asked Khan.

"The demand for me here is of vital importance. I cannot. There is no other group with a measurable chance of success on such short notice."

"What are you measuring it with? Palp?" said Boon. "By the way, how much does it pay?"

"How short?" asked Khan.

"Eighteen hours," replied Ira.

"Seranor must be protected, Ira, but we surely are not the most suitable for this mission. It would mean the death of at least one," said Alexan. He had sat quiet throughout during which he reconsidered the statistics and voiced his opinion. He would certainly go no matter what was decided but it would be better if the four of them went together. "Besides that, the time is too short to cover such a distance even by spells of transport."

"I will take care of that. Limited physical travel, I promise," said Ira, smiling to the audience. "And I will equip you with what you need plus some of the most advanced technologies available. You will have all that you would need."

Griz sat drinking heavily from the free bar.

"Judging by the armored interest at the table, I would venture a guess and say that it's not a good idea," Boon's attempt at sarcasm didn't come off funny.

"I'm sure you have the equipment but I would agree with the others. If it means our death, it also means our failure and a waste of time. Send another team," said Khan. "Our team, as you can see, is not interested."

"Maybe it is you who is not interested," said Ira, looking directly into Khan's eyes. Khan turned away from his stare.

"I will not speak for the others, but I do not wish to go," said Khan. "I wish to pay tribute to my teacher and stay in the urba. Good day." With that Khan got up and left the room.

"I agree," said Boon. "Send Teramon and his friends."

"He is already on another mission. Griz, what do you think?" asked Ira.

"I'm already on a mission," Griz said.

"It's helmhead's drinking mission," said Boon.

"Your only use thief is to be the mud under my foot," Griz remarked. "Keep pushing." He jugged another round of Ira's special anaprimo. The anaprimo had been processed under exact temperatures that derived the purest form and cleanest taste. The dreamlike buzz soothed Griz under his armor.

"If the four of you do not go, it will mean the upper hand of Zorath. It will mean war. Do you realize the consequences of that?" said Ira. Alexan's eyes remained fixed on the door that Khan had passed through. Without Khan there would be no mission and no chance of success.

Boon left. Griz fell into a drunken sleep that he would not awake from for several hours. Afterwards, he would wish it was longer.

"What will we do, Ira?"

"Zorath cannot be allowed such an initiative. I will not allow it!" cried Ira. He flashed away and left Alexan alone with the slumbering luto.

IRA FOUND Khan by his teacher's statue on a rooftop overlooking Ceramin's Square. The vivid death of his father came to his thoughts as Khan touched the petrified Nao. Both forearms (and the accompanying hands that were once joined to them), pieces of his face and a chunk of his chest were missing and in all of that pain Nao held a neutral gaze on his face. Acceptance, Khan said to himself. He could no longer feel the cold. All pain was blocked by the pain in his chest that ached in every centimeter of his body.

"You have left me as all have left me. I am without end," said Khan out loud.

"This is only the beginning," said a voice from behind. It was Ira. "Death is coming. Many more will die."

"Death?" snickered Khan. "To you, life is a military campaign that you must strategize your way through to stay alive. To be the first! To me, life is but a place of ultimate self expression in peace and tranquility. I am not the luto of my youth who cared only for adventure, stealing and energetic waste. I mature in the minutes that join the minutes of the past."

"I am asking you to do what you have always done."

"You are asking me to die," said Khan. "What waits for me up north will kill me. Why do you ask for my life like this?"

"Because death, mass death, can be prevented."

"Or delayed."

"You can prevent it, Khan."

"At the expense of four lives and four futures. Ira, we are not martyrs. Most of us are mercenaries. That means that under normal circumstances we get paid for going on missions that we have a chance at succeeding in," explained Khan.

"Mercenaries who have helped Seranor before. Mercenaries who have stood against Zorath and are alive to say so. You are not mercenaries any longer." Ira waved his hand outward and pointed to the mountains in the distance. "That is what you are."

"I have decided to retire as a mercenary."

"You cannot. Your team is the best choice. It is all we have."

"I do not stop the others from making their own decisions. I think you have Alexan who is eager to go. Griz and Boon may need some convincing."

"You may run from fate but she will find you," said Ira.

"Sorry, Ira."

"You are the unlabeled leader. You must go and convince the others or it will be too late. Your father would approve of this."

"Do not talk of my father as if you knew him."

"But I did." Khan raised his eyebrows to Ira's false words. "Oh yes. My father, Amid Levin, knew of your father since the time that he awakened Anativo and released the infection upon the land. Zorath has prospered faster than anyone could have predicted. My father was wrong to let Tulai have his way."

"What could your father have done?"

"We came to visit your father. I do not know if you remember me when I was very young."

"No. I was very sick then and cannot remember much."

"My father brought me along on his secret mission to kill Anativo while he was still powerless. When we arrived and he looked upon Tulai's seedish eyes he too believed that Anativo would bring benefit to the land, and we left without finishing our deed. The deed I chase after now and it absorbs my entire persistence."

"You too are responsible for Zorath."

"I am and I am doing my part to stop him. I will not mix words with you, Khan. Nivians are gifted with

purpose and unlimited power on Seranor. Zorath cares
not for entan nor Kozoty nor cerbor. He cares for his own
plans, one of which will cause our demise. Do your part
then, Khan."

"I have chased the Nivian for many tios. The chase is
gone. The fire is quelled."

"Do not let Sita shape your thinking so. Think of what
was done to your town. Do you want this to happen to
every urba? With the power of the Arvinstrum, Zorath
will crush all Seronians. Then where will you and your
seeds hide? His synthetic troops already invade urbas
and cast their oratic ways upon us. Will you not consider
it further? They need you, Khan.

"You can bring them together and they will listen.
They respect you. Respect yourself for what you are and
you can be more. Your purpose is far greater than you
realize. Remove the dead from your thoughts or they
alone will destroy a luto. The future is toward the
mountain. Rise up that mountain and strike it for all that
is in your chest, and the world shall be yours."

Khan laughed.

"Why do you laugh?" asked Ira.

"My purpose was to raise a family," said Khan then
plopped himself uneasily onto the snowy roof. "A
household that I could love and now all of that dream is
thrown to the wind as seeds without hope. Seeds of
wind." He tossed up a handful of snow and it blew off the
roof and out of sight. "That is what we have become. Ha!
You ask us with resolution to sacrifice our lives." He
pointed both hands at Nao's body.

"To embrace it."

"How can we give so much to Seranor? What has she
given to us—to me? She knows only to take and not to
give!" Khan was piling together snow with his hands and

forming a roughly shaped luta with a noticeable pregnant torso on her. "She cannot take my thoughts."

"I know that much has been taken from you." Ira helped Khan up to a standing position while contemplating how much more he could safely divulge. "Without Seranor, there is no life. Nothing. Zorath wants to remove the existence of Seragorn, to suck his energy so that he may seek revenge for what others had done to him. He cares for the lives of Seronians as he does for the morb whom he feeds to our soldiers and their batiers."

"How can *we* succeed against such a monstrosity?"

"Success is made on sincere attempts." Ira placed a firm hand on each of Khan's shoulders. "Maybe your dream of a purpose was not your reality."

"Then I have forgotten my dream."

"These are the moments we cherish, not the empty dreams in our sleep that fade away as fast as we open our eyes in the morning light. Here is your chance to find out if it's true." Ira shook Khan's collar before turning his head to face the mountains. "Live your dream! Become it. Taste it before it eats you alive."

"I will consider it because you ask it, but I can make no promise of what that will be."

"That is all that I ask," said Ira.

"The others are on their own."

The face of Equist Nao captured Khan's gaze once again. It even mirrored Ira as he flashed off of the roof into some other secret place to strategize and invent. Khan could not shake Nao's expression of acceptance. He wondered to himself what it would take to reach the level of his master. Was death the answer? Or had he accomplished what he was made to accomplish and died as a result of that? Khan juggled the alternatives in his cerbind and the more he juggled the more alternatives that were created, minor alterations on the originals. My family and my teacher are dead, Khan thought. They have died before me. Maybe for me.

One week before, Khan would not have believed he could strongly resist the temptation for adventure as he had just done to one of his oldest and most trusted friends. Living a life dedicated to family and structure, which for that matter was against his basic character, and then having found out that his second wife (pregnant with his second seed) and his father-like teacher (actually he did consider Nao like his second father) who now stood frozen in death beside him—he would never have believed that he would no longer crave adventure. But under the influence of confusion, misdirection and the hopelessness that he felt he kept the answer he had given to Ira. He kept it because it was something that he could keep.

Chapter 19

DREAMS WERE cosmic reality unrealized. A dream could absorb the wholeness of a luto's attention and once the luto was blind and empty, the dream would recede away along with all that the luto held dear. Consumption of the kol.

Khan felt his kol twisting in the fate of his paths. Should he go against Denar'ka? To refuse, that would mark him. To accept, would scar him. It happened quite by accident that he met up with Jaspron, his old friend. The art teacher had been busy with his lectures and did not care so much that fewer students attended. His skin had become smoother and his eyes more brilliant in his teachings. The same could not be said about Khan.

"You have become bent and worn since last we met," said Jaspron.

"Old, you mean," replied Khan.

"Perhaps that is what I mean." Jaspron was distracted as usual by the vivacity of colors around him. The green hue from a small stone block looked at him.

"It never seems to lose its attraction, does it?" asked Khan.

"Color is all that I need."

"If only life could be so simple. I remember a time when my life was simple and now I am faced with decisions that have no right answer."

"Was there ever a right answer? You talk as if your existence, if I may use this word, were a complex mathematical formula. I think that my talks with you about math and art may have confused you more than helped you. Forget math. That is what the Kozotal have tried to teach us for a millennia. Math is only theory. Why do you think that they hid it so well from our eyes and in its place filled our world with splendor. Math is the complication upon which our world sits."

"Is it splendor that my Sita has left me with my unborn? Should we rejoice now that my teacher is murdered? Are these not the results of math?"

"I did not know of this news. You have my sympathies, my friend."

"But I have lost my love from her and it burns my corius through and through."

"I am sure that her reason was valid."

"Yes. She could not accept me."

"I do not understand."

"Sita could not accustom to the life of an adventurer even though I promised to bring steadiness to her life. She could not trust me with that," said Khan.

"Why are you so selfish sometimes?" Jaspron questioned him. "Sita did not trust you? She had her own thoughts and dreams. She was free, was she not?"

"Of course, I would not force her to stay."

"So she chose willingly. Maybe it had nothing to do with you. Maybe it was to satisfy herself and not specifically to reject you. It is funny."

"What is?"

"You."

"Why?"

"You remind me of an old student I used to know. This student took life very seriously and calculated all of his decisions before making them. He became so good that he saw the results before they even happened. Many offered to pay him for his future sight but he did not value his sight so much. No, he valued his ability to protect himself from hurt. His decisions prevented things from happening. Things that he feared would hurt him as others had hurt him before when he made poor decisions."

"What happened to this luto?"

"He came to a point in his life where he had to make a new realization. He looked back on his life and saw that each calculated decision still brought turmoil and pain to his life. Even his expertise was not able to prevent it. It made him reconsider his way of thinking. It changed him. He decided on that very day that choices always brought new choices, and that there were no right choices. Life was not so clear. Choices were made right in action and reaction. Choice makes choice."

"And have you met him since his changes? Was he satisfied with his choices?"

"Yes, I think that he was."

"How can you be sure? Maybe he made all the wrong choices and condemned his life."

"I would not agree."

"How can you be so sure about his decisions?" asked Khan.

"Because his decisions were my decisions," Jaspron replied.

"What?"

"He was me," said Jaspron. "I enjoy every part of my life now and could see it no other way but I arrived here, at this place, by making the oddest and most senseless decisions that I couldn't imagine before."

"What drove you to do it?"

"Frustration. I became very frustrated at the results of my decisions. My life receded every step I took forward until I had no life left to live. I did not tell you but I was married once to a lovely luta named Pillana. We had a seedling together and then one day they were killed in the street by a drunken mercenary by accident. I attacked him but could not kill him myself and then I did something that I will always remember. I hired an assassin, paid with my milk, to kill that mercenary. When the job was done I became assistant to the assassin and he taught me to kill for one tio as our original contract was made. Made in milk that I honored."

"You were an assassin?"

"I have murdered 23 entans with my hands. Entans with families and jobs. You cannot see the painted milk any longer, but I feel it as a hardened coat of clay.

"After that I moved across many urbas until I reached this island and Casus. From the time of my wife's death until then I had carefully carved my own path with more consideration than there is aqua in the sea. That was what brought me to art. The color was my savior. I have been healing ever since."

"You never thought that your decisions were wrong?"

"You still don't understand," said Jaspron. "No decision is right or wrong. It is only a step and means very little when taken as a whole. Are we not free to decide at any time and at any moment?—Yes, I tell you!

You teach the wind and still do not know its freedoms.
You prevent yourself from becoming the true form."

"I had forgotten until you reminded me. Again there is
always much to learn from your speeches."

"Learn from yourself and it will serve you longer."

"In good time, my friend. If you will excuse me, I must
prepare for my next step."

"Do not take it as serious. When you combine all the
steps you will have created a dance. A most beautiful
dance for all the world to see. They will envy you. Dance
now and you will learn how to dance."

"I will leave you to your dancing and I to mine." Khan
shuffled his feet and danced away back to the orange door.

He visited Ira to tell him that he would go to retrieve
the relics and he would convince his friends to do the
same. That was the easy part of the whole affair. By the
time Khan left, a sad smile had appeared on Ira's face.

IRA WAS certain, as certain as the aqua was wet, that
Khan would eventually succeed. His assistant, Loria, did
not not understand the depth of the decisions that had
been made. She looked upon them as one would upon a
fresh slab of clay taken from the nearest shoreline, naked
and pure. Clay was the material of rejuvenation on
Seranor. Its opulence provided sustenance to entans and
morb alike. She thought of Khan and his party as chunks
of clay born to feed.

Her Kozotian hair was rolled tight into one shoulder-
length strand at the back and all was perfectly held
together. A protective suit matched her hair in style and
compromise.

"Lord Ira, I have little optimism for achieving our dire
objectives with this team," she said.

"Why is that, Loria?" said Ira.

"They are as opposed as the elements. How can they cooperate and win over the Blue God?"

"Extreme circumstances require extreme actions. Should we send a team – an efficient, trained team – into Vatu, they would fail."

"They would fail?"

"Yes. Fail. Why? You ask."

"I was—"

"Pressure. Pressure turns matter into better matter, turns being into a better being. Think of it like clay subjected to flamma and with the right heat you get ceramic. Take black lutium and fire it up and what do you get if not a translucent material far stronger than any individual piece of the original.

"Seronians have lived in comfort until now and do not have the element of pressure. That is what reveals the native character inside of us. Training and skills are ineffectual without pressure. It is the secret ingredient that we need but most Seronians lack it.

"Zorath may suspect of our plans—in fact, he probably is aware to some extent—but he will underestimate our team. He will not know pressure. And they will become better because of the pressure they give to each other in addition to the environment in which they travel."

"And if they go against one another?"

"Then they will die. I believe that the thought of death will provide greater intensity and need for their cooperation. They will live and become better for it. And we will have the upper hand against Zorath. Right now, we need to surpass his advantage or even the Terium will be lost. We need those artifacts. Our best hope are those four."

"They failed last time. Why not use Teramon and the others?"

"They did not fail. I knew that the Sints would come to stop them. My intention was not for them to get the artifacts."

Loria gave Ira a confused look.

"Then what? I do not understand."

"Of course, you don't," said Ira. He paused to detect and analyse the external situation. When he confirmed that his information was safe he continued. "Zorath played his hand upon mine. We succeeded at the first step. Now they must succeed in order to reap its full benefits. I never intended for the four of them to escape with the Arvinstrum pieces. But if Denar'ka and the Sints had arrived first then they would have entered the underground chambers and found the ancient portal to Nivata. Upon finding it they would have destroyed it. Zorath is not yet aware that it exists for he has been busy with other immediate demands."

"So you sent them to avoid the destruction of the portal?"

"Not only that but more. To Zorath, the Arvinstrum is useless without the Orbis, and he cannot open it without Khan's help for Khan was the one to open its first two seals. Only he or a Kozotal can open the device now and there has not been a Kozotal on Seranor for hundreds of tios.

"Zorath wants the Orbis and knows that Khan will come to Vatu. He waits, I am sure. Can you see?—No Orbis, no Arvinstrum. Khan must go. And he must go willingly."

"Teramon could do the same thing and he could bring Khan along. Even you could go."

But he didn't agree with what she was saying.

"Sending such force against a Nivian will cause tremendous opposition. He would unleash all the he can to stop them and would succeed. The Terium is not ready for this. My leaving – should I go also – would leave the Terium itself vulnerable and this cannot be left alone. Do not worry about these four. They look as adventurers to you but they are not."

"They're just crazy mercenaries like the rest," said Loria. "Vatu will eat them alive."

"No. They are – despite their masks – the ones who will rescue us from all of this. It will get worse before it gets better. It must do so in order for us to win. We need more pressure and Zorath will provide all of that in time to come. If I have made my estimations correct, Zorath may become our savior."

"I find this hard to imagine as much as I try."

"Wait and watch," said Ira with a smile.

This was not one of his confident looks, it was the sadistic look of a pressured and tormented Kozotian luto that appeared in his eyes as he spoke those quiet words.

Loria caught this look and mistook its meaning. To her, the idea of things getting worse meant about the same as military engagement where many would die so that many more would live.

Ira did not clarify. He instructed her to make preparations for the next mission, assured her that he knew what he was doing, because he saw that she was felt uncomfortable with it; he did not do so in words as much as in knowledge and execution. She acknowledged what needed to be done and returned to her duties at the Terium. By the next morning, everything was prepared as ordered.

Chapter 20

IRA LEVIN'S tailored two-piece green suit was in fact made of a flexible fine gray lutium mesh. The disguised armor, named "Zagna," was impervious to all normal missiles (ones not embedded with arvicity). It left the sound of a cool breeze when he moved rigorously about during the presentation on the strategic infiltration and acquisition of the three items. "Quel," his black lutium batier, was quiet at his side, fed for the time being. A hexagonally-shaped bracelet on his left arm, an advanced communications device, which he called "Ack", rotated as his forearm did. Ack did not reflect flamma, it absorbed it. The arvic ring, "Keeper," on his right hand did shine. Ira enjoyed his favorite four and was never without them.

The presentation was aided by strong visuals projected from a wide PT, shaped like the side of a long curved shield, emitting a three dimensional image that changed as he demanded. Khan, Griz, Alexan, and Boon were present.

"Vatu is a Battlekeep under the Ice Realm of Zorath (IRZ) buried in the southern ice mountain. It lies several kilometers below a solid lake of ice and is completely housed inside an enormous cavern. Seca, the cutter piece, was used to carve it. The Battlekeep, you can see, is surrounded by a liquid.

"Zorath's domain has grown and stretched itself outward encompassing the entire Rim of Nivata down to Maffin and including Nivata Lake, the place he was found. The IRZ expands and soon enough the entire planet will be frozen by the ice at the current rate of growth."

"Naqui," said Alexan in reference to the liquid.

"That is correct. It's naqui. The purest kind."

"What is this Battlekeep?"

"A Battlekeep was so named because it resembled a ship designed for stationary military battle. We believe it be of Nivian architecture. Best intelligence gave indication that the top side of the Battlekeep was loaded with armaments, watch towers, and communication systems. The lower levels consist of quarters, storage areas and energy generation cells among other areas such as production."

"These are detailed descriptions. Has someone been there?" asked Boon sarcastically.

"Good equipment," Ira said. "Quality counts in times of technology."

"It had better be good to get these visuals," Boon added, studying the plans.

"Can I go on?"

"Sorry."

"Back to the Battlekeep. You see the bridge and a corridor. We weren't able to map all of the corridors outside but they run nearly five kilometers to the mouth of the cave outside. It shouldn't be heavily guarded as less than a handful in all of Seranor could make the high climb. The inside is far more complex." The 3D image displayed a side view of the surface layer of the keep and five lower levels. "The surface is well guarded by morb and cerbors with some naqui zoldiers as far as we could tell, but there aren't many of those. What is important about the top level is this circular area here. This is where they mass transport soldiers, the destination is still unknown.

"You must reach the third lower level through this portal either in the living quarters or in this building here between the quarters and the transport area. All flash transport is done here directly to a secure location close to Zorath. That will be heavily guarded."

"Can the flashport be used to travel back?" asked Boon.

"No. It is a fixed radiation device, much larger than normal, used exclusively for flashing large numbers to a fixed location. I am sure you would not want to travel there."

"Then how do we get back?"

"We will get to that. Now, you must pass through the armor and equipment level first to get to the military warehouse then to Level Three where the Arvinstrum pieces are kept. There may be one piece locked on Level Two, if so, you must go up to retrieve it. But first go to Level Three. Levels One and Two are heavily guarded. The Arvinstrum, because they are so powerful, are difficult to hide completely, so they are in this area here. Denar'ka's chambers are also on this level as may be that of other commanding officers.

"According to recent information, Level Four is the factory where zoldiers are produced and the lowest level we are still not sure what is there. I suspect a small lab or crystalloid storage or I am not certain and you should not be traveling there in the first place. As you know, crystalloids and crystine pods are stored arvicity."

"Are the pods or crystalloids sensitive to certain spells?" asked Alexan.

"Yes. If they melt they become extremely explosive but the entire area is extremely cold so that cannot happen by circumstance. You must be careful when around them. Consider them volatile."

"How deep does the complex go?"

"Fifty meters, maybe more."

"Are there any secret entrances?"

"We haven't found any but our technology is not designed to find small secret entrances. Any other questions?"

"Any Sints?" asked Griz.

"No. Any more?"

"Those empty areas along both sides. What are they?" asked Boon.

"Those are for airing ventilation."

"They may provide a way in or out..."

"Listen, you must follow the plan closely or all will be lost. Denar'ka is no fool and ice is his domain. There is no mistake about it. You are on his home territory but you have the advantage. He doesn't know that you are coming. I cannot stress this enough. That is our only chance. You must move in and out quickly. Forget your differences and focus as a team." He stared at Boon.

"What's that got to do with me?" defended Boon after feeling he was the perpetrator of group problems.

"You said that it is approximately 8,000 meters up the mountain. The temperature and air will not be livable. How can we survive this?" said Khan.

"The morb use special rings which we were unable to take back safely even so they might not work on entans." He pulled two small vials from his jacket pocket. "You will each have a pair of these. There is sufficient protection for the body against cold and air differences including all of their bad effects for about 18 hours. At that height you could get sick and die from air damage to your body or freeze from the cold, so be aware of the time. Some of you will be given a vial of naqui protection as well. It's still under testing so there are only two available. Once ingested it should offer complete naqui protection for twenty to forty minutes."

"So we could go swimming in the naqui?" asked Khan.

"Yes. Naked. Don't drink the naqui and you will live."

"Too bad my luta can't come," said Boon. "Any more equipment? I mean, a thief cannot live on maps alone."

"We'll get to more of the equipment in just a moment. Now, because of time restrictions we are going to flash the four of you directly there. The entire inside area is guarded by an encrypted flash shield so we will flash you here, about one kilometer into the cave. It's a one-way trip in. You must travel to the bridge on foot, enter and secure the items. You will have to search for the white box on your own, we could not fix the location."

"How do we get out?" inquired Khan.

"This ceramic can holds enough flamma-laced lutium spray paint to enable six entans plus equipment to flash through. It is only useful with this large floor ring which must be placed on the floor and kept together to keep the connection. Keep it outside of the flash shield, here. Spray the paint on any wall or floor and jump through. The flamma paint changes the metabolism of the material so that it equals the low level flamma of the flashport device."

"Does it take a long time to apply?"

"About two to three minutes. It will completely dry after eight minutes after which time it is completely unusable. Only one at a time. What you carry will come through with you. Listen to me carefully, if the return port is disconnected and one of you walks through your kol will be ripped out of your live body."

"Great. And you want us to use it?" said Boon.

"If you've got something better, no. You should really use it when left with few options."

"Can they track it?"

"If the paint is still wet, it's quite possible. But when it dries it no longer has any flamma or other properties. I invented it that way."

"It gets us out but how do we get down 8,000 meters?"

"This flat card that each of you will get is a chute that will allow you to safely land from any height. Twist the card and a pyramid cora chute will come out. Do this after you jump. We will meet you at the bottom with fresh talins twelve hours after you leave. Because we will flash in, we cannot wait more than thirty minutes or risk danger ourselves. So mark your time and don't be late. Remember – twelve hours.

"There is more. Pay attention. I'll go through this once. These special tarcs have a number of extra features including data storage, encrypted locaters, personal health scanners and timers set for our rendezvous.

"These white eye covers are similar to what Boon had used before but have no frame, unlike the glasses. Arvic suction keeps them safely on the eyes. They will protect your vision from height damage, bright flamma is seen through clearly, as well as night vision. Even works under aqua. Tears and moisture can escape but other things cannot enter. Khan, yours are blue in color because we have added cryptographic translation features for anything visual. You will need it.

"And I'm giving you one of our latest *arvigun* prototypes." Ira pulled out a small device that curved down into a long grip with a hole on the other end and strange markings along its short, straight barrel. An arvic projectile device.

"It's the first version of a *vig* – that's what they are called. Simply aim and call the command glyph to release the contents which are balls of arvicity embedded into the device. They each have one gamma, two noxy and three oxy balls which will explode in a radius effect. Khan or Alexan will help you translate the glyphs.

"You must pronounce the type of attack command first. So, after you identify the type of attack then you can lock and load using 'Nak-Dak', while you are holding it. Aim at your opponent before calling the last command 'La' or it will explode upon you. The minimum safe distance is 5 meters.

"Even we are not sure of the exact size of the radius of effect as it is too difficult to control. We are working on an improved model currently but it won't be ready for a couple of weeks. Do not be surprised if Denar'ka also possesses such devices for our first plans were stolen some time ago."

He placed it on the table and Boon was the first to slide it over to himself.

Ira continued: "You'll all have standard healing potions—"

"Hey, what happens if you are locked and loaded but the chance to fire is gone?" asked Boon, intrigued by this arvic weapon. "I mean, do you have to fire after you start?"

"No. Just call out the commands again to cancel them. Here—" Ira snapped back the vig and said: "Kal-Nak-dak." The vig made some strange sounds like air being squeezed into a small space. He pointed it around the room as if targeting someone then finished on Boon.

"I don't think that you have 5 meters," said Boon. Ira didn't move. "You want to evaporate me don't you?" Khan smiled as he watched the thief put into an uncomfortable situation.

"Next time, don't interrupt me when I am speaking," said Ira, stern and stable. Boon got the message. "Nak-Dak." And he placed the unloaded vig down on the table once more. Kal was the command for gamma, a deadly orange fire.

"As I was saying, you all have standard healing potions, enough to heal light to serious injuries. There's sustenance gel that replaces your daily meal. You've got enough for two days including mini ice-melting kits for purified aqua.

"And finally this small pack is for Boon. It's an advanced thieving unit that other thieves dream of having. Int, our top creator, developed it with you in mind. You'll have to thank him when you come back."

"Put that to good use," said Khan.

"Melt me." Boon reached for the pack. Ira pulled it back just before his hand touched it.

"Relax," said Ira. He opened the thieving kit and pulled out a 20 cm long cylinder. "This unique device is only in the preliminary stages on the planet – you are getting some of my best stuff. It's a borrowed design of the *Ratio I*. Boon, this individual Ratio – we'll call it 'IR' for short – will enable you to work on advanced locking mechanisms, download information, and even generate data based on selected inputs. It's still limited but can help. We detected a system of intelligence built into the architecture of Battlekeep Vatu. Take a few hours to study the IR carefully before you go. He handed Boon the kit.

"You all have maps of the area stored in your tarcs, as well as some things that I have said. Hold your tarcs with both hands for one minute to attenuate it to your AW. After that, none other can use it. If there are no questions, you will leave in four hours. Prepare your equipment in the empty cells over there. You can wash and eat. Meet me here when you are ready." Ira walked out, a breezy sound followed.

"He's got to learn to relax," said Boon.

"You've got to work harder, thief." Griz made his comment.

"Alright helmhead—"

"Don't call me that."

"Ira is right! We're going into Zorath's domain with surprise as the only advantage. So every little thing in our favor counts. But we can't succeed unless we work together," said Khan.

"I don't want to sound negative, but Zorath has never been surprised," said Alexan. "Every military move against him has been responded to and matched."

"If he knows we're coming then we're naqui," said Boon.

"He won't know. We keep our advantage for now and we will succeed no matter what. Are we not here to win?" said Khan.

Collectively. "Yes."

"To win or to lose?"

"To win!" All roared together.

"Then prepare yourselves to infiltrate Vatu. Prepare yourselves to win!"

If there was fault that could be spliced open, dissected and pulled out like a cancerous disease then it was optimism. Feeling that all things would work out was life's gamble. Striking a win assured massive rewards to the psyche and to one's life, with the chance of winning nearly to the bone. It was the will of opus to be optimistic and the will of ora to be practical. The battle of opus and ora at infinity could not be solved, and it was the tension from their result that activated life on the planet and stimulated the Versos.

Chapter 21

ZOLDIERS INHABITED the main urbas across the land and
had been allowed in with full political support. Seronians
as a whole could not accept these naqui-milked soldiers of
Zorath but had been left with little choice. It was better
to have them exposed and visible than to have them
hiding in forgotten warehouses. Should something go
wrong the resistance forces would have a chance at
success. The minor skirmishes between the Army of
Naquior and the Terium of Seranor had been just that –
minor.   Both sides had been testing the opposition with
both afraid or unable to make a significant move.

Even House Levin and House Draconus had supported
the Terium to little effect. Most success was obtained
from the underground societies tightly held together and

run by Ira Levin and his close circle. Assassins were still in high demand as the equalizers in the war of espionage.

The race was on full ahead to produce, train and equip armies in sufficient size to wipe out those of the opponent's. Up until this point both sides fighting for opus and ora were evenly matched. And Zorath considered himself steps ahead as he masterminded his even greater task of recovering all of the Arvinstrum pieces and removing the artus locks. In his brilliance of play, he had distracted the home resistance with his artificial armies made of naqui milk, and had pursued the categorical strike in his aim.

Zorath knew that the resistance had developed new military technologies and thousands of new recruits were being trained as he now stood in the lowest chamber of Battlekeep Vatu. The S3 series zoldiers would not suffice in his battle to overtake the planet but they had an effect in large numbers. Vatu was not just for battle preparation, more importantly it was used to manufacture zoldiers in mass quantities as it was situated in the middle of a deep naqui lake that was used to transfuse the zoldier body with naqui milk of the purest kind. This cut down production time from one hundred and eighty days to less than thirty. Eighty percent of production had been shifted to Vatu.

In the experimental laboratory a new development had reached the final stage. Zorath had come to see first hand the product of his investments. He had come to see the fate of Seranor.

Standing at the front of four zoldiers was the self-proclaimed Ice King of Seranor; and his rightful hand, Denar'ka. Zorath inspected the new S4 zoldiers. The S4s were taller by 25 cm than the S3s. Behind the short row of S4 zoldiers were differently-sized devices placed neatly on tables and along the walls. At the rear of the chamber, in the east wing, about twenty-five meters away, were six upright cases nearly three meters in height, filled with an odd-colored naqui. Inside the last two were naked and headless zoldiers hooked into some cabling devices. Their heads had been placed on the table to the side. Both of the skull caps had been opened. Inside the top a small black gel could be seen.

Zorath stood face to face with the nearest zoldier to the end.

"WHAT IS YOUR NAME?"

"IRZ101559, Series A, Zoldier S4," it replied clearly and succinctly. No trace of emotion filled its intelligence.

"WHAT IS YOUR CAPACITY?"

The zoldier stepped back two steps then walked over to an open area, the rader unsheathed with a sharp and short twang. The zoldier faced Zorath.

"I am ready to be tested."

Zorath telekinetically catapulted eight hand-sized objects, taken randomly from the tables, toward the zoldier. Its weapon danced, hit and deflected all objects.

His black hand waved its three long fingers and from the floor two ice beings of entan height and shape morphed into tall and featureless, wielding batiers of ice, fixed to their hand. The zoldier blocked the first wave of attacks and couldn't avoid two cuts, instantly regenerating the damage. His rader swung in response to the danger cutting the nearest ice creature in two, pieces crashed to the floor and broke. Weapons clashed momentarily with the last enemy before the zoldier pierced the ice being completely through leaving a large hole in its mid-section. It spun about and fell. As it fell, the zoldier moved in for another swing, lopping off its ice head in a crisp whip of the quattro-blade. A head flew. The ice body crashed. Zorath caught the icy blue head in his hand and evaporated it. The mist cleared slowly revealing a small grin.

"WHAT ARE ITS FEATURES?"

"Enhanced cool vision sees detailed images," Denar'ka said. He threw a small writing instrument into some tools. "Zoldier, retrieve the object." Denar'ka faced the Nivian King as the synthetic fighter went to accomplish its simple task. "The new eyesight is modeled after my own. They can see the variations in small objects, distinguish colors and texture by sight."

"CAN THEY READ?"

"Only the larger elos, but that can be fixed with some work." The zoldier returned with the object that was thrown. "Join the line."

Zorath walked up to it again. "WHO IS THE OWNER OF THE LAND?"

"You, King Zorath. You are King of Aquanomicus and we serve all your needs."

"WHAT ARE MY CODES?"

"The four codes: Do not kill, harm, or go against the creators; eliminate Seronians against Zorath and all against his cause; protect oneself and Domain Zorath at any self sacrifice; and do not possess any object, identity or emotion beyond what is necessary."

"WHAT IS THE PRICE OF FAILING THE CODE?"

"Extinction."

"KILL ME!"

The zoldier unsheathed his rader, swung back and in early swing collapsed into a pile of snow. Denar'ka scooped up a handful of what once was a zoldier.

"This new series is without bugs," said Denar'ka. "Flawless. The S3s must be networked in order to be controlled. Networks make us vulnerable, but the S4 is an individual fighting module. A genetic creation perfectly designed to wipe out the enemy – whoever that may be. And they are difficult to track because of their ice structures.

"We have found a way to implant those mathematical cerbi taken from Technomicon. It gives the S4 reasonable thinking capacity. The one that you just tested used a mock up of that cerbus technology. Two of the three remaining have the prototype intelligence. The third is another mock up. My scientists are currently working on the other intelligence and individuality module over there. The S4s are nearing perfection and can be superior to entans and kozotians."

"DO NOT BE SO CONFIDENT ABOUT PERFECTION. OPUS STILL EXISTS."

"Its days are numbered."

"START MASS PRODUCTION AT THE EARLIEST."

"The factory is not equipped to mass produce the S4s."

"MAKE IT SO, NIVATON."

"It shall be arranged immediately. More funds will be needed."

"INFORM KALORIAN. HE IS RESPONSIBLE FOR SUCH MATTERS."

"The new batch of S3s will be shipped according to the schedule."

"SEND THE S3S TO THE ASSIGNED LOCATION. OUR SECOND STRIKE ON SERANOR BEGINS IN TWO DAYS. THIS WILL HURT THE RESISTANCE AND WEAKEN ANY ATTEMPT TO STOP OUR ACTIONS.

"THE MAIN CERAMINATION IS SWOONED BY MEDIAMENTA. THE ENTAN CERBIND RESEMBLES A SOFT PIECE OF ICE, FRESHLY PICKED FROM THE EARTH, AND QUIETLY NESTLED IN MY GRASP." A roughly shaped ball of ice formed in Zorath's black hand. He rolled it finger to finger. Played with it. "ALL THAT IS NECESSARY IS A GENTLE TWIST, AND A STEADY FORCE." He blew warm air onto the ball melting its form. Changed into the shape of a headless entan figure. "AND IN THEIR OWN THOUGHTS THEY WILL DROWN. THEIR CERBINDS WILL DULL UNTIL THEIR HEADS BECOME SO EMPTY AS IF IT DIDN'T EVER EXIST BEFORE. OUR ZOLDIERS SHALL DISTRACT THEM LONG ENOUGH SO AS TO ENSURE THE DULLIFICATION IS MADE IRREVERSABLE." His dark hand closed and white snow squeezed out.

"HAVE THE S4S READY FOR THE THIRD STAGE. I WILL TAKE THESE THREE WITH ME. I TRUST YOU NOT TO FAIL."

"It will be done."

"THE THREE MERCENARY-THIEVES, WHAT OF THEM?"

"They were caught as they crossed the bridge. We are scanning their cerbi now. All relevant information will be retrieved."

"PUT IT ON A STORAGE TARC AND GIVE IT TO ME BEFORE I LEAVE. ALL OF THOSE ASSOCIATED WITH THEM WILL BE WIPED CLEAN. SEND THE TWO RELICS WITH THE NEXT S3 SHIPMENT. HOLD ON TO THE WHITE BOX."

"Yes, my King."

"LET THE NEXT PARTY IN WITH LITTLE INTERFERENCE."

"There is another party coming?"

"I WANT THEM TO HAVE SOME APPRECIATION FOR THEIR FEAT BEFORE WE CATCH THEM AND REMOVE THEIR TRACE. SEE TO IT THAT THEY ARE NOT KILLED. I WILL RETURN IN DUE TIME. KHAN HAS ONE MORE TASK TO DO BEFORE HE IS DONE BY YOUR HAND."

"All your wishes will be served."

The Kium King walked around the room. Denar'ka was left to smile of the news, especially after the freezing his old nemesis, but he couldn't help staring at the extra zoldier brains on the table. After Khan was dead and the S3s produced, what would he do? He had to be ready to expand himself in some aspect or he himself would be replaced by technology. The technology that he helped to create in the first place.

Chapter 22

FOUR FULLY equipped figures materialized in the center of a smoothly cut ice corridor deep within the southern ice mountain. The roughly put together retrieval team inspected the environment. For the normal eye, all was pitch dark. Synthetic eyes made all things clear. An unending corridor measuring more than 8 meters wide and 5 meters high stretched out front to back. Deathly silent was the thick blue ice, but when listened to closely enough, one could hear the hum of life deeper within, as if pregnant and readying for birth.

Four hot breaths exhaled in turbulent excitement.

A large area covering all sides of the wall and containing deeply engraved glyphs cover the next 2 meters in front of them.

Khan stepped closer with his cryptographic eyes and understood. "It's the flash shield—Alexan."

The quasi-arrogant arvician took his time moving up. He held his bracelet out. Their relationship was good, but Alexan loathed to listen to take commands from others.

"Boon, place the temporary flashport in that alcove there," said Khan. "Make sure it can't be found easily and that there is a good connection. Everyone take note of where it is for we may indeed use it." Alexan waved his left hand signaling okay. "Let's move. Eleven hours and 58 minutes."

The four of them jogged stealthily along the corridor, Boon slightly ahead holding a pen-like device out in his left hand monitoring for anti-welcoming devices. All was bright. All was clear.

Excessive cold emanated from all sides, enough to drop a naked entan in minutes. They continued on as comfortable as a warm night on one of the southern islands. Griz jogged freely in his flexible suit to keep pace. Four morb patrol guards led by a cerborian arvicerer were held at a distance by Alexan's spells. Boon and Khan struck to remove them. Not a step was missed. Long distance scouts. A single tarc was pocketed by the thief.

Two kilometers later, they arrived at another corridor opening. Under Boon's recommendation they went to inspect the possibility of a secret passage. Inside the room they encountered three icy-blue snake beasts, long singular claws on three slender arms followed by 5 meter tails, breathing blue fire. A tail surprised Griz who became coiled up in it and was winded by asphyxiation. Alexan's fire spells proved useful as did the first noxy ball from the vig though it scorched Khan's clothes because the radius was larger than Boon had estimated. Other than that he was untouchable jumping around hitting

high and low with relative ease. Khan still preferred solid
weapons over windy ones.

Griz was released and the blast gave him enough time
to chop through scale and bone with his clavus. Three
snakes slain with only a few bruises and burns to the
party. Griz's armor un-dented itself centimeter by
centimeter.

Boon detected a passage. He checked it out cautiously.
A wide naqui lake 30 meters across blocked their path.
Using his own tarc, he captured the image of guards on
the bridge and tower. Could be useful in the future. The
central crystal on the patrol guard's tarc glimmered.

"Bridge station 2359-768 here. Contacting long patrol
901-22. Report." The transmission was repeated two
more times.

Onto the bridge.

So far, so good.

The bridge was already lowered. Six morb guards and
two zoldiers. Minimal reinforcements. Perfect for a
surprise entrance. Boon snuck up, crawling underneath
the bridge feeling the chill of the naqui lake on his
exposed back, passed the guards while Alexan weaved a
spell to take out the zoldiers. Khan noticed the marks of a
previous battle on the bridge. It was recent. He motioned
to Griz who had already seen it.

A spell wrapped itself around the zoldiers and seared
off two heads. Boon then signaled them to pass. Poisoned
morb lay dead as they remained in the standing position
they originally had. Poison. Visually effective. Very
expensive. Ira was paying.

Inside the compound they moved fast. Griz's noisy
armor was silenced by one of Alexan's spell. He didn't like
it. They moved past the quarters, cautious and quiet.
Morb and cerbors walked about, mostly unarmed, some

slept. Beaks and natural body armor. How ugly they were.

One by one, the four mysterious kols entered the stairwell as Ira had showed them, Boon ahead again checking for traps. Some advanced warning devices were disarmed. Nothing serious. He liked the thieving kit. It made him even more efficient.

They reached the Basement just above Level One. Two morb guards and a cerbor were avoided. Building and construction materials were neatly stacked in a warehousing area. A special room labeled CRYSTALLOID STORAGE was nestled across an open central area, about 12 meters wide, that ran down to the lower levels. Boon estimated two-30 meter wide areas running about 50 meters deep, six to eight meter ceilings. At the very center a 4 meter disc hovered next to Level Two then after two morb guards got on the disc it carried them down to Level Four.

"Arvic travel disc," said Alexan. "It must accept basic commands or run by thought."

Vatu was perfectly crafted out of ice. The air was fresh to breathe. Floors were polished ice but not slippery or noisy. Dual stairs, one on each side, lined all the levels. It was all well lit. The entire area creaked and moaned occasionally but they soon got used to it. An unmusical hum came from the lower level.

Too late. Six guards, four morb and two zoldiers rounded the corner. The party moved to strike. It was quick and dirty. No mercy. The zoldiers were taken out first before they could contact the network. Alexan's idea. Two morb lay in pieces from Griz's clavus. He had a reputation to keep. A third knocked down his clavus and Griz, undeterred by a rader that glanced off of his armor, thrust a fist and forearm through the morb's chest. It jerked in all directions then stopped dead. Spilled milk.

THE BODIES were left where they were. There were several odd-sized pools of milk on the floor. Too much to bother with.

"That must be the factory level down below," said Alexan interpreting the sound. "It's unusually quiet."

"Whoever built this must be far more powerful than Ira mentioned," said Boon. He pulled out the IR. It lit up. He interpreted. "An intelligence is scanning the entire complex. Don't lose your tarcs or we're dead."

"It is the day of death," said Griz and meant it.

"Let's move. Time is short already. You can take pictures later," said Khan, trying to lighten Griz's cumbersome stare.

Level One turned to Level Two. Everything was going as planned. No reaction yet.

The third level was illustriously built, hand-crafted by the power of an ancient relic. They went through the rooms in the area that Ira suggested. Khan decided to split up to find the box which was definitely separated from the two items. He went to the uncharted end.

Two locked portals were easy for Boon. Too easy.

Septana was quietly resting on an ornately carved mantelpiece of ice waiting instructions of execution, protected by two spells and an alerting mechanism. Alexan and Boon cooperated, successfully. He wasn't happy to work so closely with the thief, but Boon was efficient and that made it bearable.

Khan walked into three rooms. Signs of clothes were scattered without care. Ceramic weapons hung on the wall. He avoided a patrol by lifting himself up to the ceiling alcove. There he noticed an inset crystal in the ceiling and threw on some spit mixed with boot dirt with it. They were watching. Back to the search. No sign of the box or a safe to hide it. He rejoined the party at the foot of the stairs.

"No box," said Khan. "Denar'ka must have it."

"We found one piece," said Alexan. Khan looked at it and knew its design – Septana the Protector.

Khan dared not touch it. The memories of his father and of Anativo, Zorath's first incarnation, filled his head as he glanced at it. Much death surrounded him after the Nivian was uncovered and the first rod, Seca, revealed her true power. What if they hadn't found it? What if Anativo was not awakened? There was something more to his involvement with Zorath and the war against him. Reasons for all things.

"The other piece must be on Level Two. We must move quickly to retrieve it. I will get the box after," said Khan. He suspected that the Nivaton had hidden the box well or was probably carrying it with him. But why? No matter. It might just require a personal mission.

Alexan, Khan, Griz and Boon moved at fast pace to Level Two. Boon led them to the special storage area after checking his IR. Narrow corridors led them to three locked vaults preceded by a sealed frosted-ice portal, thick as Griz's body.

"Stop," whispered Boon, but he couldn't stop the heat from inside coming out his mouth. It billowed like white smoke. No reaction. He removed a sharp device from his kit and stuck it into the wall near the portal. A flicker of flamma then nothing. "Okay."

"What is it?" Khan asked.

"A flamma detection ray, sub-eye level. Whoever engineered this place is smart, but…"

"But what?"

"It's strange…the system seems to be only on minimal function."

"They're not expecting us."

"It's not right."

"Open it already, will you," said Griz impatiently.

"Why don't you open it, helmhead."

"I'm going to use your head in a minute—"

"Okay—Can you open it?" Khan interjected.

"Give me a few minutes." Boon pulled out some special tools for the job.

"Alexan, see if you can help—Griz, what's wrong?" He pulled Griz to the side.

"This place. This place is wrong. There is death in the cold air. I smell it. When I smell death, rivers of milk will flow. The stink is strong here."

"We are moving quickly enough. Time is on our side."

"Optimism is your gift, Khan, but survival is mine."

"There is something that you are not telling me."

"...She declined me..."

"Who? Number 51?"

Griz nodded once.

"Farck."

"If battle is all that is left then..."

"Khan, up here," whispered Alexan. He moved up.

Griz's voice faded into his helmet. "...then there is nothing left but death. And so I have come..." Eyes cold.

At the center of the frosted ice portal was a large round blue dial carved out of the same singular piece of frigid matter. Glyphs were carved into the eighteen checkered dial.

"A hidden mechanism in a tangled web of connections behind. I have no direct contact with the lock. Maybe Alexan should take a look at these glyphs," said Boon.

Alexan couldn't translate the glyphs. "Not related to spells."

Khan studied them.

"They're not glyphs."

"Then what?"

"They're codes." Khan looked closer. The glyphs reflected in his synthetic blue suction eye shields.

Chapter 23

CRISPIER, RED trimmed cerbor wielding a long spear, walked briskly down the stairs to Level Five, the experimental lab. He walked over the foyer adjoining the fourth and fifth levels then reached an oval portal with a small transparent window in the center. A pass of his hand opened it.

Inside a lit chamber housed the complicated equipment used for experimentation. Zorath and Denar'ka watched three zoldiers, Series 4, demonstrate their abilities. Crispier signaled Denar'ka's attention.

"Sir, we have detected the second group as you had warned. They have continued their mission under the guise of our low level security," said Crispier.

"Where are they now?" said Denar'ka.

"On Level Two."

"Have they suspected anything?"

"They continue their movements unaware of the trap set before them."

"Good. King Zorath, the prey is trapped."

"Not yet. Let them take Septana and Lavo first."

"But—" Denar'ka was afraid that the relics might be used against them. Zorath didn't have this fear. He was certain that they wouldn't live beyond their capture. It was over-insightful.

"Prepare the morb on Level Three and line the zoldiers on Level Four. Do not attack any of them unless I command it. We need the wind disciple alive or this play is wasted and heads will melt. He will not leave without it. Keep them tracked. I want to be informed."

"Yes, my King," replied Denar'ka. "Crispier, get the zoldiers in place."

"Yes, sir." The cerbor climbed up and out.

"What of the IceFist school?"

"The schools are under construction now. V-Non is overseeing it. The Windy Path is proliferating despite the resistance from the politicians. Seronians flock to it. Pray that it will restore freedom to their measured lives. They do not see the end coming."

"The Windy Path students must be eliminated one by one as soon as we are done here. Alert V-Non and make it so. The Seronian Guard must not interfere. The young Equist and the hope of Seranor will die today. His disciples will follow if they do not obey."

"It will be done. And of this box?" Denar'ka pulled out a small white box from a small fitted pack on his rear hip. It came to Zorath's hand as if invited then spun silently as it hovered above his hand.

"This box contains the ancient Orbis, lost for all time and found by a seed's demise. The Kozotal are

BELIEVERS OF FATE AND SO HAVE CONSTRUCTED SUCH
EVENTS. CONSTRUCTION SHOULD BE RESERVED FOR LESS
ROMANTIC NOTIONS."

"What does the Orbis contain, my king?"

"THE KEY, DENAR'KA. THE KEY THAT WILL SPELL THE
END OF THIS PLANET."

"Then Seranor is finished."

"SERANOR — IN HER DEATHFUL STANCE — IS NO LONGER A
THREAT. ONCE I HAVE THE ORBIS, I WILL REMOVE ALL OF
THE ARTUS LOCKS." The box froze in the midst of a spin.
"AND ALL OF SERAGORN'S POWER WILL BE ABSORBED INTO
ME."

"We can open the box. We do not need, Khan."

"SHEV'LA IS NEEDED ONCE MORE. YOU HAVE FAILED AT
YOUR ATTEMPTS OR HAVE YOU FORGOTTEN."

"I had the chance to kill him in Casus only two weeks
ago. No matter, I have claimed the life of his teacher and
lured him closer to me."

"YOU ARE TOO ANXIOUS TO MEET HIM AGAIN, DENAR'KA.
YOU WILL HAVE YOUR CHANCE SOON ENOUGH BUT IT WILL BE
AFTER HE HAS FULFILLED HIS FATE. THIS BOX CAN ONLY BE
OPENED BY THE ONE WHO FOUND IT, THE ONE WHO IS
DESTINED TO OPEN IT — HE WILL SOME PRODDING FIRST —
THEN YOU WILL HAVE HIM. PREPARE TO WELCOME OUR
GUESTS FOR THEIR FUNERAL. I GROW TIRED OF TALK WITH
YOU."

"Yes."

SEVERAL MINUTES passed, still nothing. Griz paced while
Khan worked the translation. Arvic glyphs with physical
connections wired at every angle and possibility. A
hidden pattern behind the ice mask.

"We're short on time, have you figured it out?" asked Boon.

No response.

Another minute passed.

"Why aren't you complaining now, helmhead?"

"Don't use that name to call me," replied Griz, stopping his pacing.

"What? Helmhead? You're always wearing a helm. You're always wearing a full suit of armor. Don't you ever get sweaty?"

Alexan was staring at Griz. "If you're looking for a date, lonely luto, you're looking at the wrong tree—and you, mud for muscle, shut your tongue or I will pull it out completely," said the tempered warrior.

"Come on and try, helmhead."

"That's enough!" Griz turned from his rear guard position and held his clavus firmly in his hands ready for action.

"Griz!" Khan called out. He stopped. "And you two, we don't have time to argue—Quick, I've solved it." Griz let the clavus head fly into the wall. Ice chipped after a sharp cracking sound. Khan cringed, ready for anything. The others followed suit.

"Shat," Khan muttered.

Complete silence followed rapid anxiety.

A security unit passed by uneventfully. Boon's anger at Griz distracted him just enough to miss the dull crystal lodged into the ceiling above them. It flickered briefly.

Back to work.

"Boon. Each code on the dial is related to a lock. I will call and hold the glyph open, you must then find the exposed lock and disarm it. No mistakes. You'll have about twenty seconds for each, after that it's over."

The expert thief checked for himself. "I'm on it."

Khan spoke the glyph while Boon picked the exposed lock. One by one a smooth shuffling noise, polished ice on polished ice, slid across and unlocked the portal. Once complete, Boon and Alexan checked again before moving on. Though none of them said it, there was an obvious tension in the air around them as the time to open the portal was too long. The thief wrestled with the possibility of a delay trap where items were stored in a location that, should something go wrong, would enable those being intruded on time to prepare and to catch the unwelcome guests. No time to consider it, thought Boon. Move quicker. In his focus to prevent detection he failed to see that they had already been detected. He was considering ways to exit should something go wrong. That narrow passage across the naqui lake came to cerbind.

A second portal, much simpler in structure, was opened by Alexan and Boon in less than a minute. Inside, the second Arvinstrum piece, Lavo the Cleanser, was found.

Boon found extra time to open a second portal before Khan said something. Inside he found a large crystine pod which he packed and strapped to the back of his hips, and when he came out he threw Griz a long rod-like device with twin barrels at the end. "No bad feelings."

Griz caught it in one hand. It was nearly a meter long, 3 centimeters in diameter and had several embedded glyphs on the end of a long stock than ran downwards in an arch about a hand-and-a-half to a rounded point. The lutium shell was beautifully engraved depicting an image of two serpents, one on each side.

"Alexan?" said Griz.

Alexan waved his hand to identify its properties. "It's a double-barreled vig. *Drakgun* is inscribed on the bottom. You've got six noxy balls, two ice slugs, and four ice shard sprays. Here, here and here. Most are fairly damaging, about lower-middle level. Just aim and press one of these firing buttons. Maximum range is about fifty meters. And this is an extra cartridge, in case you need to kill some more."

Griz twirled it around already familiar with it. He had mastered nearly every imaginable weapon though preferred the clavus to any other, and took a liking to his new long-range weapon. "My new Rak," he said. A black holster contained it. The stock was bothersome but livable.

Boon and Khan covered the exit as Alexan handled the relic and Griz kept quiet in the middle. The quiet muffles before they entered had turned to total silence. The only sound came from the machines now distinctly heard on Level Four. It was not a good sign.

Khan pulled out his tarc. At first glance the indicator appeared to show that their encryption system was still in force. He examined further looking for structural weakness in the flamma frequencies and after tracing the photon response line he noticed two beveled drops. This was marked with about the time they entered the last sealed area.

"We've been tracked. When we entered the area we must have missed an alarm or an imaging device. They have known our presence for more than half an hour," said Khan.

"Or maybe even longer," said Boon. "It's been too easy. We should evacuate the area. Get out while we are still alive."

"They haven't acted," commented Alexan. "Yet."

"Right, why haven't they?" said Boon.

"They'll block our escape. We have to surrender the box, Khan."

"We need that box! Seranor needs it. Without it, this trip has only a small effect," said Khan. "Our only insurance now are these two relics."

"It's a trap," said Boon getting excited at his conclusion. "What was I thinking? I should work alone. Why did I ever listen to Ira? Fool a thief and the trip is over..."

"Death is around us," Griz said. The area inside his helm seemed to darken.

Chapter 24

ICE GROANED. Without emotion. No compassion.
Four warm breaths billowed out in the stillness of the
large underground ice complex. Exposed. Visible.

"How did they know we were coming?" said Alexan.

Khan held his breath before speaking. "I don't know
but we still have to get the box before finding a way out –
alive. Boon, any ideas."

Boon grabbed the ceramic spray can. "I've got a great
idea. Let's get the farck out now!"

"Boon! We stay until we get the box. Keep that clear
in your cerbind. I'll ask you again, and don't farck
around. Any more ideas on how to exit?"

"...Let me work on it."

"Alexan, can you provide some kind of arvic diversion so that they can't trace us for ten minutes?"

"Should be able to," Alexan replied.

"Good, when I give you the signal throw your spell then I want all of you to give me access to your tarcs. I'm going to recalibrate your tarc frequencies so that they can't find us but I'm not going to activate it yet. If we run into a situation where we can lose them, I want you to activate the new signal and they will only be able to track us visually. If they try to locate us again it will be extremely difficult because I'm looping the current AW frequency so they won't be able to change it. Ready yourselves..."

"YOU ARE CAUGHT, SURRENDER AND YOU MAY LIVE. CONTINUE AND ALL OF YOU WILL BE EXTERMINATED, PERMANENTLY," a deep voice spoke from within the area, unrecognizable. "YOU HAVE TWENTY MINUTES TO CONSIDER YOUR OPTIONS, SHEV'LA. AGREE TO SURRENDER AND FOLLOW THE DISC PLATFORM TO LEVEL FOUR."

It had been ten tios since he was called by his first name and Khan did not need to guess any further who was waiting below. Zorath himself had come. Why didn't Ira warn him? All of their lives were in serious danger.

"Go Alexan," whispered Khan. An arvic envelope surrounded the area just outside of them. Khan moved quickly from tarc to tarc. He looped a steady transmitting signal then, using his bastion's blade, recalibrated their AW modifying it with that of lutium so that it was outside the normal range. Even if they were capable of breaking the loop they would never consider looking so far outside the normal AW range.

"YOU CANNOT HIDE FOR LONG IN HERE. SHEV'LA, SURRENDER AND THERE IS CHANCE FOR YOU AND YOUR FRIENDS."

During the twenty minute wait, Boon had out the his IR trying to tap into the intelligence network to find a weakness.

"I found it," Boon said. "There are several fresh air ducts leading to the upper areas. Each level has two main access points but are trapped against intrusion."

"Can you break the traps?" asked Khan.

"I'll need a couple of minutes. The air shafts have a number of branches and if this information is right we can find refuge there."

"Whatever happens, let Boon go ahead so that he can work his hands first. Now, we still need the box. Denar'ka is certain to have it. Our time is nearly up."

"You talk as if you are not coming with us."

"The box is a key to the fight for Seranor. I must try to get it. If I fail at least we will have the Arvinstrum pieces."

"But Zorath will kill you."

"Zorath wants something or he would have killed us all by now."

"What does he want so badly?"

"Me," said Shev'la Khan.

"It's even more insane then," replied Boon.

"Yes."

"Why?"

"I do not know but it is our chance."

"Khan, come with us and forget the box. Let Ira obtain it at his own risk," said Alexan.

"If the box disappears again, it may never be found and I will never know my connection to it."

"I agree," said Griz. "I smell death here."

"What will you do?"

"I will show my surrender."

"You'll surrender?" asked Alexan.

"I'll play his game for the moment and give you time enough to exit. Use the arvic flash paint when you have entered the shaft. You must all leave and return the relics to Ira. Get out, now!"

Alexan, Griz and Boon stood there dumbfounded. They couldn't let him die. As much as the young Equist was confident he was also ignorant as a piece of dried clay.

"Go! I will find my own way out. Wind in your steps! Make speed."

KHAN WALKED over to the disc platform at the center of the underground complex. The 70 meter drop swallowed the range of color at every level until all was a deep cold blue. He descended slowly. Three friends, possibly his only friends, stood side by side, faces riddled with both the anger and the fear of his stubbornness. Starting from the feet up, their bodies were erased centimeter by centimeter from the rising floor as Khan descended into the icy domain of Zorath.

The hum of factory devices around him were more apparent as he approached the factory level. Drum-like pounding, stamping of artificial bone, came from a machine near the far wall.

The clothes of the self-proclaimed hero against Zorath fluttered behind him as the disc came down. On Level Three, thirty morb, three cerbors and a dozen zoldiers waited on both edges. Waited for an order to kill. Khan tensed.

After passing the third level flooring he caught sight of Denar'ka's unfamiliar disfigured body and bald head. Beside him stood a two and a half meter high glossy black figure wearing a golden ice chain girdle around his waist.

Long arms ended in three extended fingers on each side, with a ring wrapped nicely, one finger on each side. An amulet of blue and white was embedded at the base of his neck with the ice strike in the center, lined with the tiny sparkles of pure crystal. Orange eyes glared at the wind maker.

Khan was numbed. Zorath was the curse of his family and was responsible for the death of his brother and father. It had been more than five tios that he had seen him. His body had been completely replaced with an animated, flexible kium structure. Artificial.

The platform stopped at the fourth level. Behind the black figure were two scores of zoldiers. Three taller zoldiers, whiter skin tone, were lined neatly along the wall. On the west side, stood forty-five zoldiers and two cerbors.

"YOUNG SHEV'LA," started Zorath, his voice now the synthetic construct of the ice body he had wrapped himself in. "I AM IMPRESSED AT YOUR ABILITY TO REMAIN ALIVE IN THESE TIMES OF OPPRESSION."

"Maybe I am like you and can never die."

"YOU ARE ONLY AN ENTAN. A SIMPLE SEED WHO BECAME A LUTO. BUT I AM A KING, BY MY BIRTH, WHO WILL SOON BECOME A GOD AND RULE THE ENTIRE VERSOS."

"A god that my father rescued. A god that my father gave secrets. Without him you would still be frozen in the ice."

"GET THE OTHERS." Zorath commanded to Denar'ka.

"They are gone," said Khan.

An invisible hand pulled Khan to the shiny black chest. He couldn't move away.

"DO NOT WORRY AS I WILL NOT KILL THE SEED OF MY FOUNDER. YOU WILL SOON UNDERSTAND YOUR FEEBLENESS. DENAR'KA WILL NOT LET YOU GET AWAY ALIVE THIS TIME."

"I hope that he's improved."

"ALL THINGS NEED CONTROL, SHEV'LA. YOUR FRIENDS
WILL BE CAUGHT AND MURDERED IN FRONT OF YOUR EYES AS
WILL THE ONES WHO PRECEDED YOU. BRING THEM."

Three beaten and bruised mercenaries were thrown
out to the front. Their nude bodies revealed well shaped
limbs with minimal imperfections in the skin. Probably of
a noble house trying to make an independent name for
themselves. Even the wealthy had the dreams of the
average. They were worn out like cora rags used for
washing floors. Red smudged tears covered their faces.
They would be defenseless against any attack.

"THESE ARE THE BRAVE KOLS WHO PRECEDED YOU. IRA
THOUGHT WELL TO USE THEM AS A DISTRACTION. LEVIN
OVERESTIMATES HIS INTELLIGENCE AND UNDERESTIMATES
MINE." He turned to the first rank of zoldiers choosing
randomly. "YOU THREE—ELIMINATE THEM."

"They are defenseless! Stop!" He pushed himself to
move but couldn't.

Four zoldiers marched up in unison, raders drawn.
"Stop!"

Milk started dripping down to the next level as the
helpless bodies were ripped and pierced ruthlessly.
Zorath prided his technological construction.

"Murderer! Why is it that the black god murders?
Why is he afraid of the weak? They shall give you a
name. God of Murder."

"I WILL ANSWER YOUR FOLLY ONLY BECAUSE THAT IS
WHAT IT IS—FOLLY. IT IS THE WILL OF SERANOR TO MAKE
THE WEAK—STRONG. BUT IT IS FEAR THAT KEEPS
SERONIANS WEAK. FEAR AND DISTRACTION, YOUNG
SHEV'LA. MURDER IS A DEMONSTRATION OF FEAR, NOTHING
MORE. IT TEACHES."

"Murderers will die! Wind in your eye!"

Khan twisted his body and forced the wind form. The
flowing milk turned to a whitish haze as wind digested it,

distracting the others including Zorath while Khan lifted himself up. He looked back to see Zorath and it was then that a giant invisible hand swatted him, he fell helplessly back to the black murderer.

Boon, Griz and Alexan heard Khan's voice while listening intently. They had made it safely to the nearest air shaft and ran deep within the tunnels until they stalled with indecision. Their activated tarcs erased every trace of them from the system. They were safe unlike the fourth member. Silent forms listened to what was happening down below.

Chapter 25

KHAN AWOKE, the numbness going out of the side of his body. He shook the sleep out of his head and felt wet underneath. Milk. The milk of the three young mercenaries.

He felt Zorath's presence close and wasted no time. The wind came to him quickly and easily. "Wind in your eye!" he yelled out. The wind flowed under his body and took him to a point behind the black figure. One easy wave. Three successive strikes caught the Nivian by surprise but without effect. Zorath rotated a finger and an arvic envelope gelled with naqui came around Khan. He swooshed away to avoid it. The next round the wind came stronger and it sliced through Zorath's clothes. Again, the Nivian cast a spell and Khan deftly pulled himself out of harm's way. Breathing heavily and expending excessive amounts of energy, Khan circled and returned with a greater force as he twisted into a whirlwind catching the entire body of Zorath inside. The wind howled and caused pain but Zorath reached out both arms to the side and the whirlwind stopped dead. Khan dropped hard onto the ice, gasping for breath. Several twists of his artificial fingers and the Equist's body flipped about as would a soft porcelan doll, helpless by all effort against his oppressor.

Khan landed crumpled. Broken like a tree snapped in a storm. Milk ran out of his mouth. He spit it out in front of Zorath's feet.

"YOUR WIND SKILL HAS IMPROVED," said Zorath, showing no emotion or sign of a strain. "THE WIND, WHICH CANNOT BE CAUGHT—IS CAUGHT. DENAR'KA IS PLEASED."

"The wind is constantly changing," Khan managed a sentence without gasping in-between.

"Not this time," said Denar'ka, standing to the side, looking down upon the Equist Nao's disciple.

"WIND AND CHANGE," Zorath started. A heavy "Ha" sound came out of his mouth, his attempt at a laugh. "IT IS THE SERONIAN WEAKNESS TO BELIEVE IN CHANGE."

"Change is the balancer," Khan was back now, hugging his hurt body.

"CHANGE IS THE ORIGINATER. IT IS THE DOOM OF ENTANS."

"It is Seranor's friend."

"IT MAKES HER WEAK, AS DO FRIENDS. YOU HAVE BEEN BLINDED BY YOUR WIND MASTERS AND FOOLED BY THEIR INSANITY. DO YOU KNOW WHAT SHE REALLY NEEDS, YOUNG SHEV'LA?"

"Nata."

"NO. SERANOR NEEDS STRUCTURE. IT IS WHY THE LAND YEARNS FOR ME. STRUCTURE ENABLES CONSTRUCTION.

ENABLES IMPROVEMENT. I DID NOT ARRIVE HERE BY
CHANCE. I WAS DRAWN HERE BY NEED. SERANOR NEEDS THE
STRENGTH OF THE ICE. THE PLANET NEEDS TO BE
RECONSTRUCTED. I WILL SAVE THEM FROM THEIR MISERY.
FROM THEIR EMPTINESS. FROM THEIR VOID.

"CONSIDER YOURSELF FORTUNATE TO BE ABLE TO JOIN
YOUR FATHER SO SOON. WHEN ENOUGH OF SERANOR IS
FROZEN UNDER THE ICE REALM, HER ENERGY WILL NOT BE
WASTED. I WILL RULE THE VERSOS WITH IT."

Khan sat up, fully recovered. "Deconstruction will
follow you until your realm of ice is but aqua that society
will use to drink and feed their plants. No matter I die or
live, Nata will not support you. She has been there since
the beginning and now I understand why. She is that
which you can never control."

"MANY THINGS YOU DO NOT UNDERSTAND. YOUR EXCESS
IDEAS LIMIT YOU. YOU ARE SELFISH, SHEV'LA, LIKE YOUR
FATHER, TULAI. IT IS BECAUSE OF YOU THAT YOUR FRIENDS
WILL DIE."

"Nata is what you can never contain. Change cannot
be contained. Cannot be structured."

"YOU WILL DO ONE MORE THING BEFORE YOU DIE."
Zorath curled the first finger on his left hand. Khan was
levitated up and pulled by strong force to the once blue
Nivian. "YOU WILL DIVULGE ALL INFORMATION THAT IRA
HAS GRANTED YOU. DO THIS AND I WILL EASE THE PAIN I
BRING UPON YOUR CERAMIN."

Khan felt his warmth get absorbed into the black
mass. He had passed the point of utter fear. Passed
insanity, reaching tranquility. The end had arrived.
Death stared at him. Sita smiled from behind. He would
die a non-conformist. "And if I resist?"

"THEN I WILL PRODUCE SUCH PAIN THAT THEY WILL PRAY
FOR THEIR QUICK DEATH." If there was one entan outside
of the inner circle then it was Khan, and Ira had shared

much information with him. Ira's reasons were not fully divulged but there was a strong desire to ensure that Khan knew. It came to him to now. Why did Ira trust him so, even from the beginning? There was something not said and perhaps it was too late for him to know in the path of death.

"For this reason you have kept me alive. For information."

"YOU ONLY SHORTEN THE TIME." Khan dropped to the ground. "I WILL HAVE IT NONETHELESS. IRA'S STRATEGY CANNOT BEST MINE."

"You cannot win, Zorath," started Khan. He had the chance to stand up for the hope that his non-violent father had. "Seranor is the creator of things. This my father knew and shared with you. He was the genius of this planet. But he did not know that he would release a murderer." Staring in the king's eyes without fear.

"YOU HAVE YOUR FATHER'S GENES – A TRUE GENIUS. THOSE THAT SUCCEED IN LIFE ARE NOT THE GENIUSES WHO ONLY KNOW CREATION. IT IS WHY THE KOZOTAL COULD NOT VANQUISH US. THEY ARE DISEASED WITH CREATIVITY. SUCCESS IS MADE IN ACTION. MADE BY EXTENSION. MINE ARMIES WILL BE THE ICE HAMMER THAT WILL SUBDUE THE PLANET. AND WHEN THE FROZEN EARTH CRACKS, THE SOUND WILL SIGNAL THE END FOR YOUR KIND AND THE BEGINNING FOR MINE."

"I will be recycled in the Versos like all else is."

"YOU ARE READY TO DIE. YOUR EYES SAY SUCH WORDS. THEY WERE ALWAYS YOUR WEAKEST POINT, SHEV'LA. YOURS AND YOUR FATHER'S. THE MISFORTUNE OF FAMILY KHAN— DENAR'KA." The Nivaton moved up close.

"Ira will stop you. He is aware of your tactics. Seranor will strike against you."

"I THANK IRA FOR SENDING YOU HERE AND FOLLOWING MY PLAN. THERE ARE MANY THINGS THAT IRA DID NOT TELL YOU."

"He has communicated what was necessary. I am alive, still, as are you though that may be a temporary situation."

Zorath: "Alive?"

Khan: "Seranor protects us. She always has."

Zorath: "What is life without milk in your veins? What is arvicity without the brightness? What is Shev'la without Seranor to feed you and to comfort you in the darkness? Do you know, Shev'la?"

Khan: "I am Shev'la Khan of Tulai and Lez-win Khan. And I am not your slave, dear Zorath. I cannot die until I have done what I need to do."

Zorath: "I will tell you and keep the suspense from your cerbind. Power is not taken. It is given. Yes. Seronians are weak because they defeat themselves. The ancient law of the Versos made it so. Power can never be taken by force. Oh, but there are ways to weaken and to fool those whose power you want.

"That is why Nivians are the supreme and guard the gate to stillness. We harvest power. That power, I tell you, will be drawn out of Her and she will succumb to my power. It was not a mistake that I came here for I knew that on this plane I could not die and could instead become a divine being, a God as you have put it. I was born a Nivian who wanted to become a king and changed his cerbind to become a God."

"I SHALL TELL YOU MORE TO SATISFY YOUR CURIOUS NATURE."

"There is nothing more." He was certain that Ira had been upfront and open. His party members were not so naïve.

"WHAT IS TRUE IS THAT SERANOR IS DEAD."

"Not possible. No. It is an impossibility."

"ALL THINGS ARE POSSIBLE HERE. FIVE DAYS AGO SHE PERFORMED HER LAST HALATION."

"Then Seragorn lives alone. How can this be?"

"SERAGORN LIVES BUT HE IS UNDER MY CONTROL. HIS MOTHER WILL NOT STRIKE IN HER DEATH AND THERE IS NOTHING TO REVIVE THE COSMIC SERAGON. SHE HAS OUTLIVED HER USEFULNESS AS HAVE YOU AND YOUR FRIENDS." He motioned the Nivaton. "TAKE HIM."

"By your command, my King," replied Denar'ka. Four armed zoldiers marched up by Khan. Seeing his time short and that his friends were still not safe as long as Khan held the tarc he pulled it out while Zorath moved away and Denar'ka managed the others. The tarc came out, his hands moving restlessly over it, disorganizing its frequencies and erasing the data. Once damaged enough he threw it hard toward the closest ice wall. Centimeters before hitting it stopped and flew backwards into the black hand of Zorath.

He threw the tarc to Denar'ka. "KEEP THIS—YOUR ACTIONS ARE FUTILE NOW."

On his wrists and ankles were placed rings of transparent ice. Held close together by an arvic force. A random morb was picked out and the same rings were placed on him.

"I've designed these myself," said Denar'ka. Once activated the rings kept a close distance to each other. The morb was forced to escape the device. As he fought and created resistance, the ring size decreased. Denar'ka pushed him more until the rings closed and both hands and feet were severed. The morb screamed in pain for only seconds before an ice fist quieted him. "So the wind can now be caught."

Zorath walked up to the three S4 zoldiers standing motionless along the far side. He looked once more at

Khan. The young Equist's white cloak billowing behind him. Defeat in his eyes. Shev'la Khan of inventor Tulai and mother Lez-win Khan, possessed by a deep-seated desire to satisfy his will as it pulled at him from every angle. Young master of the wind form on the path to insanity. Khan did not know defeat nor pain nor did he know of a secret that lay hidden in his very genetic fiber now. And if Zorath knew he would have slain him with his own spell to wipe every trace of his existence. A secret strength against the Nivian that his father so long ago masterminded. There would still be time if he and his friends could escape Vatu alive.

Khan was led to Level Three by Crispier and six zoldiers. He was placed in a prison cell made of hardened naqui, clarified to the point of absolute clarity. The floor was solid black and cool to the touch.

Chapter 26

THE THREE mercenaries who had escaped Khan's demise had not yet found a way out of Battlekeep Vatu. Guards were posted at every angle and portal. Patrols moved about ruthlessly searching for them. Using Boon's stealth methods, Griz and Alexan had managed to stay hidden and as long as their tarcs were not traced they would be safe but only for so much longer. This was the ice's domain. Ira's 12-hour deadline came closer. Decisions needed to be made.

"If he's not dead, he's caught; and if he's caught, he will soon be dead," Alexan said.

"He knew he wouldn't make it out," said Griz.

"But he knew that we would," replied Alexan.

"Farck it, I'm going after him!" cried Griz.

Alexan blocked his way but Griz threw him aside.

"Griz, don't go. We still have to get out. Khan wanted us to leave. If you charge in like this we will *all* die. Wait until we have a better position. I, too, want to go in but *not like this*."

The armored friend returned to the nearest gate, twisted it with his great strength then held it for several unspoken minutes before releasing his grip. "Morbfarcker!"

Boon had already extracted the ceramic spray can and readied himself. "Are you ready?"

"Wait," said Alexan.

"In case you haven't noticed Arvic Cerbi," said Boon, "time is running out. If we don't leave soon we're farcked both ways."

"Maybe Griz is right. We wouldn't be here without Khan. We wouldn't have this chance without him."

"I say death is a choice. And I choose not to die. Come on!"

Griz returned, resolute. "We do not leave without him or you leave without me."

"You see, he's chosen. It's you and me Alex. Four in, two out."

"Don't call me, Alex!"

"A thief can never be more than what it is—one who lives upon the lives of others. Go thief. And pray that none will live upon *your* life," said Griz.

s"If helmhead wants to jump to his death, I have no problem with that. Alexan, I'm sorry, so let's go!"

"Griz has made a valid point," said Alexan.

"About thieves?"

"No. About Khan. We must get him. What have I been thinking? I am Alexandrus Scaeval of House Scaeval and never in our entire ancestry have we abandoned a plan, idea or a friend. What have I become?"

"What is wrong with everybody today?"

"You are wrong, Boon. Khan has given much. But you are greedy beyond friendship. Selfish in every way."

"Wait just a minute! I've done the job I've been hired to do. We haven't encountered one trap—in case you haven't noticed—and we have two of three items in our hands. That's nearly 70% of our target. And we're still alive. That, to me, is all pretty good. Just because the so-called 'leader' wants to risk his ass doesn't mean that I have to die for him."

"What if that was you down there and Khan was up here. Then what, Thief?" said Griz.

"Stop calling me, Thief. The name is Boon."

"What is your real name anyway?" asked Alexan.

"It is my name."

"What is your real name?"

"Boon."

"Boon what?"

"Lafuratimus Boon, if you must know."

"Lafura—" said Griz laughing.

"Shut up, helmhead—Lafuratimus. Named after my father, Lafuratimus Illopotu."

"Interesting."

"What does all of this have to do with our decision to leave?"

"Everything, Boon. Fathers and mothers are those that we trust like our closest friends. Fathers...the ones we trust..." Griz firmly wrapped two hands around his helm and slowly pulled it off of his head. Boon could not stand to stare at it and looked away from its utter grotesque. "I owe my father for what he has done to me, for my disease.

"He abandoned me long ago just after he killed my mother. I lost everything then. All the love was gone. He left me after seeing the result of his work. I have grown to live with it but have never forgiven him. Never!" Griz was crying ruby red tears. They rolled onto his chest armor as he discarded his sweaty helm wet with milk. "I will not abandon my friend. I will put my life for his. It was Khan who showed me a new way to live. His love saved me. And you talk of his friendship as it is mud!

"You are the foulest mud and if we were anyplace different I would rip you limb from limb." Griz faced the thief. "Run thief but you can run your whole life and never arrive at your destination. I will stay."

Boon stood, head down and motionless for minutes before speaking.

Even the arvician stood silent. Griz hastily prepared himself for battle.

"When I was but a seed," Boon said, "we were poor and my second parents left me in their residence. I do not remember my early youth nor my first parents. It seems to have all begun those last few weeks. My father was troubled about something and his troubles grew every day...I was their trouble, the pain in their side...They left me there and did not ever return." He stared at Griz's dirty helm. The milk had dried over the face shield, rough dents and cracks had only half fixed themselves. "I have not spoken of this since that time and had wiped it from my memory."

"Then don't abandon your friend or you will become your parents," said Griz.

Boon crumpled into a pile of tears. He felt once again the empty pain inside his abdomen as he did the day he realized that his parents would never return. Emotions were hidden, disguises were well placed and life became an illusionary game where his objective was to survive. Thieving had become a way to tease attention, the attention he lacked his entire life. The attention of desire. Of love. The emptiness had never been filled.

"You did nothing wrong, Boon. As did I," said Griz, taking two steps closer. "If we leave it will be a mistake that we will carry for our lives. I already carry many of those mistakes. And look what has become of me. I am the nightmare in my father's dream. I produce the mistakes of my future seeds."

Three heads, friends of the windy warrior, kept their thoughts with stooped heads. Vatu was stirring and their tarcs sparked of attention. Denar'ka was honing in.

"Then let us not make another," said Boon. "Let us not produce any unnecessary mistakes."

"You will stay?" said Griz, asking for confirmation.

"Yes. Khan has sacrificed much for us. His life, in fact. I see that more clearly now. I owe him that much. We'll need some fresh ideas—Alexan?" The arvician had remained quiet knowing where his place was and wasn't.

"If what Khan said about Zorath is correct then he is needed. So there still may be enough time. I do not know how much. How long have we been in here?"

"Two hours," replied Boon. "An hour more to deadline."

"We make plans to retrieve our friend in economic time. Put away that can and let's get to work," said Alexan.

The three of them stood erect, stared at each others false eyes and raised their fists against the ice.

Chapter 27

ZORATH ENTERED the room where Khan sat meditating.

"Why do you come?"

"I SHALL LEAVE YOU IN DENAR'KA'S TRUST. MORE IMPORTANT MATTERS FIND ME."

"You will never find them."

"WHO? YOUR FRIENDS?"

"Not even your technology can trace them."

"DO NOT BE SO CERTAIN OF YOUR ABILITY. IN ANY CASE, YOU SHOULD NOT WASTE IT ON DEAD FRIENDS. YOU WILL NEED IT."

"I will not help you."

"YOUR EYES SPARKLE WITH TULAI'S STUBBORNNESS—"

"Dare to speak of my father in such way, you who have betrayed and stolen from the one who saved you!"

"NONSENSE! HE BETRAYED HIMSELF."

"No!"

"Do not drown yourself in his lies."

"He never lied. That is where his difference is with you."

"He did lie. The biggest lie of all."

"It was because of his honesty that made him creative. Truth breeds creativity."

"Look around you, seed of Tulai. Open your eyes one last time and see the beauty of my creation. Very soon this world will be swallowed into my very palm and all will be lost. And it was your hand that discovered my body and your father that released me. But he would have been one of many. It is the irony of Aquanomicus that all things – of opus and ora – may be free to become. This planet is a dream that I will control. Seronians lack desire for such things. They individualize themselves in the productization of society. Entans are the pity of the Versos and the reason for the struggle."

"This planet cannot die."

"You make the mistake of your father, you swim in an ocean of your own filthy lies. As he did until his death—"

"His murder!—He will be remembered."

"But you will not. Yours is the life of misery in which you hide, Shev'la Khan. You have abandoned one wife and a seed, leaving them to struggle alone. And you let another wife go. You left your friends to die in here. Who is left to love you?" Silence from Khan. "In the final minutes of your life, who will miss the great Khan? The luto designed for abandonment. The seed who abandoned his father at the time of his death. You hide in your stubbornness and all things you have touched have died or left." Khan, as much as he tried to calm his inner self, could not stop the wet tears from coming as each word from his enemy struck. The glistening King walked away. "AND FINALLY THE CURSE OF DEATH WILL ITSELF DIE. FITTING."

"Anativo!" shouted Khan in anger. Zorath stopped at the familiar sound of his first incarnation on Seranor. "If the Versos is nothing and I am but a dream then that makes you the greatest fool of all." Zorath ignored him. Khan laughed loudly, crying at the same time while he yelled out. "We fight for an illusion! We are illusions! I am the illusion! I am the illusion!"

He sunk into his cerbind floating across a span of aqua until he came to find himself resting upon an island, deserted of all but the soft clay floor. There he sat upon his island, wind at his face, ocean around, and himself rolling in the wet clay. Joyful. Soon his body was covered in the brown matter and it sucked at him, sucked his body down into it. Pulling the entire Versos with it, with Khan as the first. The only thing preventing its collapse was him. Khan's screams were drowned with clay as he vanished into the island and all went black.

FOR THE first time in his life Boon began to feel an attraction to this group of troubled lutos. Each character was composed of uniquely different ideologies and thinking about it rationally Boon found it absolutely odd that they could even remain together. He considered whether or not Khan played the essential part. It was not chance that brought them together. Other forces, still mysterious, were at play waiting to reveal themselves when all things were in place.

They exited onto the flooring. Level One was used primarily for storage. Sacks of frozen food, clay and ice, were stored on large ice shelves marked by strange symbols. Drinking aqua was encased in large kegs of purified ice, set on top of a flat disk five centimeters thick, with a long downward curved spout on one side, used for obtaining the melted aqua. The party stopped for a

minute and Boon decided to take a drink. It was very
fresh. Untainted.

"Where is he?" Griz said.

"Give me a minute," replied Boon, using his tarc to
trace Khan.

"Quick!" said Alexan.

"Wait," said Boon between sips. "You know, Alexan,
you have a serious character flaw. I don't know why
Khan puts up with it. But it's getting on all our nerves.
Drop the arrogance for a few minutes. You might actually
enjoy it."

"Coming from a thief, it doesn't mean much."

"You see, that's your flaw. You think that you are
better than us. I think that you are terrified that you are
just like everyone else, despite the fact that you're a
Kozoty."

"We are not alike. We can never be. I will forever be
different from you."

A shelf of ice came crashing down. "Shut up! The two
of you must shut up!" said Griz.

"Why did you do that?" said Alexan. By then it was
already too late, scores of pounding footsteps, armed and
armored, were heard not far from where they were.

"I've got it!—He's on Level Four. At least the tarc is."

Footsteps rounded the corner. Too close to exit without
a confrontation.

"We fight here. Take grounds," said Alexan looking
sternly at the clavus-luto.

First came ten morb lined-up perfectly in pairs. "Pil-
Nak-Dak-La!" Griz let loose the double-barreled rak
wiping out three instantly. Had his aim been better he
might have taken out twice that number.

The party was caught in milky hand-to-hand combat.
As the morb numbers dwindled to two, four cerbors came
marching in from behind. Spells against spells lit the

area destroying many food items. Frozen foods ended up cooked on the shelves. Ice turned to aqua. The wind shaft was melted shut at their backs and they were trapped.

Three cerbors formed in feromentan formation, collectively using their arvic ability to wipe out the infiltrators. Boon managed a poisoned strike crippling one while Alexan barely parried their first spell. Alexan cast out again finishing the remaining confused two morb that were about to pounce on him. Griz recovered from the previous morb attacks and hacked down the last cerbors only to replaced with ten zoldiers. Series 3.

Alexan called the ring's power. "Get ready to move!" he yelled. A spell of high intensity flared, a gamma ray, and cut through the floor whereby stood the zoldiers. The floor, from the added weight, groaned once and snapped like a ceramic plate on a rock face. All ten zoldiers crashed down to Level Two.

The three mercenaries ran to the stairs. Zoldiers from the basement came down. The three heroes leaped – Griz was assisted by a spell – to the third floor, then, only glancing at the broken zoldiers, leapt again down to the fourth and before they could manage to pinpoint Khan's exact location they saw a tall cerbor holding Khan's tarc. A score of zoldiers and three cerbors fell in from behind.

"Surprise, entans!" the cerbor yelled.

"Morbfarcker!" yelled Boon. "They're getting smarter by the day."

"Pil-Nak-Dak-La!" cried Griz. "Pil-Nak-Dak-La!" Noxy fire consumed the enemy's surprise.

Still surrounded by reinforcements, they took for cover in the low hum of factory machines.

Boon took pleasure in the argun but soon was back to his batier as the embedded spells ran out. Dead zoldiers were aqua behind him. Alexan did not hide nor play;

instead he stood against them in full pride casting arvicity left and right. "Sik-Nak-Dak-La! Birn-Nak-Dak-La!" Ice melted, zoldiers fell, and the factory was lit up.

The clavus returned to Griz's hands and sung through the cold air but he was over-matched by the zoldiers and too tired to continue for long at the rate of activity expenditure. He absorbed extra hits, milk flowed out his gray armor in larger amounts. A potion, his next to last, helped him to continue and just before he would need another he felled his nearest opponents. Reinforcements rushed into the fray.

Chapter 28

CONTINUALLY EMANATING cold from the floor brought the strong shivers that woke the young Equist. Sapped of his will on the ice nightmare of his dream. Footsteps came, he maintained his sleepy façade. Four morb and a cerbor. He could take them without shackles but was dead with them on. Better to wait.

The IRZ troops led him to an empty room except for a round table. Upon it was a gray full helm belonging to a familiar suit of plate armor, Griz's armor. Dried milk and dents covered it. The armor only regenerated itself while worn so he must have been hit first before it was knocked off.

Denar'ka appeared at the portal. "A memento your staff wanted you to have," he said coldly.

"My friend. He held it tight in one hand. "When is it that I will kill you?"

"In time you will die. You may feel comfort to know that your fate will be shared. We have cracked your loop and are welcoming your friends as we talk. They are so predictable." Khan whipped the helm at the Nivaton. He didn't feel the tightened rings hurting him this time. An ice blade fashioned from his enemy's own body cut a chunk of the face off before the helm tumbled into the wall. Griz's broken helm stared at him.

He was locked in the room for ten minutes. Had he been less infuriated at his opposition he might have sensed the strange arvic spells probing his cerbind. No matter. Equists were trained to dislodge organized thought and to attain the level of insanity. It was something that was well beyond the parameters of the equipment and left Zorath with no new information. It justified why Khan was hastily returned to his cell. Disparity grew in him and began rooting itself in his cerbind. His resistance flailed wearily.

"All timing is made perfect by its imperfect timing," he recalled what Nao had said during his training. This couldn't have been more correct. In his cell, sitting peacefully at the center was the smooth white flamma box. Its positive charge brought a fresh gleam of hope to Khan's half-closed eyes. He jumped at it.

"A gift," said the nameless cerbor.

Khan held it, crying tears of joy for the savior lost to thieves.

"You have returned to me. You have not forgotten me and never I abandoned you. Never. I'm sorry what I have brought to all around me," he said to Pyx. After holding her and staring at her in lost moments of pleasure, Khan decided that she held unfinished business.

He had unlocked the first two seals but the third
prevented him. It felt comfortable in his bound hands.
He felt its smoothness and its warmth and it flared in his
cerbind chasing out ideas of the dead. A wave of sweet joy
and cleansing passed through his whole body. He was
reminded of his youth with his father, the smiles in his
face; Mareenth came back holding his hand together with
Cal'la; even Sita smiled upon him and told him that his
newborn seedling was okay; and his friends, his next
family were not okay and were caught on Level Four,
surrounded by Zorath's troops. Their lives were near the
end. And as he dreamed, and regained the sense of who
he was, he saw the true power of Zorath and was
somehow connected with it.

Seranor's Box, sitting quiet on its own accord, then
opened and a bright flamma pierced him and all his
insides. Pierced every cosmic fiber of his porcelan flesh
and warmed his corius of all the cold that it kept.

As it opened so did the outside portal. Tens of armored
zoldiers burst into the cell room as if waiting for such an
action to happen and Khan took his advantage once the
cell door was unlocked. He lifted the lid on the box and
called her beauty out. Flamma, pure as from the first day
of creation flowed out like aqua in the air and blinded and
scalded all those of Zorath. Then Khan hopped, two-
legged, out the portal to the outside hallway. Denar'ka
approached from the west so Khan was forced to run east
to the center. As he hopped nearer he could hear the
battle of his friends one floor below.

Denar'ka ran after him followed by eight zoldiers.
More came down the stairs. Khan was trapped. And then
he saw Griz's fighting below. Fighting in fury. Griz
looked up to see his old friend. "Khan! We come! We
have not forgotten you!" Two morb engaged him. He

went berserk. Khan turned to the fast approaching Nivaton, smiling.

"Life goes on!" Khan cried out and lifted himself high into the middle of the complex nearly reaching the second level. His body twisted, not like before, but smoother and more succinctly. The wind form threw off the shackles and they landed below, defeated from their purpose.

He dropped to Level Four floating as the wind with the rage of a storm about to strike. Then the wind expanded and Khan released his fury of strikes upon his enemy. His hand became the blade, his movements became the battle cries. Morb limbs were cut off, zoldier heads rolled, the enemy was pushed back by the wind in the ice. Even Denar'ka felt its effects though he was the least affected.

His action bought his friends time to escape to the foyer between the fourth and fifth level as more troops replaced the dead. The hive vibrated. One by one, the three of them jumped down to the foyer. There they found a portal and entered.

Once they were safe, Khan dropped himself to the same foyer and moved toward the open portal. After the fifth step, Denar'ka landed to block his path. Too late. A cerbor from above sealed the portal connecting him to his friends. They could hear Griz's armored fists pounding holes in the ice. It was too thick even for his strength.

"You now owe me two things, Khan. The box and a match. But I only want one. The box I will retrieve when you are dead."

"Let my friends leave and I will fight you."

"Your friends cannot avoid their fate. My patience for you has been held far too long—Crispier!" The cerbor from before, shiny red beaked with a necklace, jumped down. "Send down, the naqui beast—Are you ready to die, Equist?"

"Are you?" Khan said.

Chapter 29

INSIDE THE lowest chamber there was an assortment of devices of both technological and arvic construct. On one end were six tall canisters with only two containing S4 zoldiers. At the halfway point was a wall with a central portal, ajar.

Boon used his IR to scan the area to little effect, though a signal that he had detected before showed up again and he downloaded a portion of it.

"There's no exit," said Boon after a quick but careful inspection. "They know it."

"We must get out now and hope that Khan can beat the Nivaton," said Alexan. "Spray the paint over here in the side wall. We must exit."

"Wait! The flashport is not responding," said Boon.

"What?"

"I kept a lock on the location and the signal...the signal is broken. It must have shifted or been moved."

"No one knew about it."

"Then it must have been something else. It wouldn't take much. Some shakes in the mountain could cause it. We can't get out without the connection and we can't go up."

"Then we are all dead."

"It is the hour of death," Griz said, repeating his favorite saying. His armor looked as if it had been badly painted in white.

"Find something else to say," said Alexan, thinking of a makeshift strategy. "There are only two ways out of here. Going up from where we came and through Ira's portal. With the naqui lake between us we don't have enough potions to do it. You have both seen what is behind this portal and it will be our death. We are not an army as Khan likes to believe. Our only and best way is to flash the farck out of here."

"Where is Khan?" said Griz.

"In case you forgot, the flashport is busted," said Boon.

"Then someone is going to fix it." He was looking at the two of them. "Someone with speed and stealth." His eyes passed over Griz's oversized, armored body and fixed on Boon.

"So now you need the thief again. But the thief refuses. I'm not going!" said Boon.

"I am *sorry* about my reactions before. Now go!"

"Don't push me around pridehead."

"Stop wasting time or we're all dead."

"First you abuse me and now you want my help."

"I don't want your help, you idiot! I just want to leave this foul place. Now go!"

"I'm not ready to go. Maybe there's a better idea waiting to be found in this chamber down here. We should look around—"

Griz, who had been leaning on a table trying to rest his injured and tired body, jumped up in full armor landing with a thud and grabbed Boon pulling him high above his head. Boon could not escape from his lutium grip.

"Fix the farcking port or I will end your miserable life right farcking now!" Griz was deadly serious. His temper had increased over the last tio so much that it even entered the party decisions. If Boon disagreed, he would have killed him then and there.

"Since you put it that way, okay." Griz, not able to restrain his fiery strength, threw Boon five meters into an open area. Boon landed on both feet. He was a little angry with Alexan but Griz was right.

"How do you plan to get me out, arvician?" A cynical question.

"Getting rid of you is the easy part. What's more difficult is finding the nearest air shaft. Get out your IR. We've got little time."

Boon's ingenious cylindrical device tracked a room just above the ceiling close to the west wall. It was much larger in size than the shaft, the IR indicated some kind of anti-naqui chamber. Perfect, thought Boon. After providing Alexan with some detailed information of its location, the Kozotian arvician prepared a spell then cast out a cone of flamma at the ceiling. The bracelet glowed yellow from the arvic discharge, nearing the last of its stored essence. When the cone stopped, Boon could see a small, finely sewn hole with an open area several meters in.

"That's the best I can do. Take this naqui potion—"

"I'll take it when I'm ready, thank you."

"Make haste like you've never made before. Our life is counting down in seconds. Three of us will come through. We'll monitor your tarc by the minute. Ira arrives in about half an hour so move." With that said, Boon was heaved up by Griz's hand and hooked into the hole with a singular climbing tool.

"Remember to bring back my equipment." Three seconds later he was gone.

"Two down, two to go," Griz said.

"If you keep guard, I will see if anything in this chamber can help us." Alexan didn't want to be around Griz. He was ready to kill something. Actually, he was readying himself for death.

Chapter 30

KHAN ASSUMED the wind stance as many times before but this time it was more unstable as Nao had tried to teach him. Focus replaced fatigue. The Nivaton's face grew intense and stood in solid form, a magnificent pillar in his domain.

Wind against ice.

In the background, Crispier rolled a black ball, no higher than half a meter in height, to the side wall. He placed a matching ring on his finger and shot out a ray of gray energy into the ball which became soft and jelly-like. Awakened from its imprisoned sleep, the black blob passed through the ice floor into Level Five to slay its unsuspecting victims.

Wind and ice – the free and the frozen – faced each other again. Khan's two-piece white suit rustled from the wind draft of the air shafts from far above. The air got trapped in the foyer and circled around, dancing for a way out like the Equist now faced.

Khan sank back into his own cerbind to pull out the tenseness and once done his body relaxed, loosened to be with the wind again. Exhaustion wanted to settle in him but he let it flow through him and did not resisted it. This was not the time of excuses. Here, now, was not only the match between wind and ice, it was that between opus and ora. It was the test long ago registered and unwritten. Nata and Niva watched. They would not interfere nor lose their focus on the larger aspects of Seranor's demise.

Denar'ka threw up his hand, clenched his one fist then slammed an open hand to the floor sucking the essence of ice into him. His body matched the color of ice. The Nivaton grew half a meter in height and his right arm became a double-bladed clavus. Cold, enough to burn naked skin, emanated from his body burning his clothes off in a bluish smoke as he rushed the young wind master.

Wind moves came easier to Khan lately as did confidence. He had grown comfortable with it. Those very abilities aided him now. Protected him from the first onslaught of attacks. Denar'ka was impressed. He did not stop. Would not stop until his enemy, the student of the master who rightfully denied him, was dead as dust.

Khan shaped the wind fashioning a batier from its shifty form and ripped the Nivaton deep. Chunks of flesh fell out only to be replaced by new flesh. He slashed again with similar results. Denar'ka struck, managing only to cut frosted clothes that snapped off. The two elemental masters danced around trying to destroy each other for many minutes. Finally, a surprise move caught Khan in a double-armed hug. Caught again. The Nivaton squeezed with the strength of a Serag. Khan's body began to collapse. The potion protecting his body against cold deteriorated as did the wind barrier.

A clunk on the floor by Khan's feet could not be heard over the pain. The white box fell out and slowly sank through the melting ice in the west chamber below.

He looked deep within to find his master's advice. Hollowness was the locked portal he tried to open. Denar'ka's body converted to naqui and, under searing pain to motivate him, Khan made his body hollow as Nao had instructed him.

"Wind in your eye! You will die!"

The cold essence filtered through him as aqua flows through a hollow pipe. The Nivaton squeezed again but only managed to squeeze a bag of wind without effect.

Finally, Khan expanded the bag and centimeter by centimeter Denar'ka lost his grip until he was completely off. He wasn't deterred and came again. Deadly strikes hit Khan burning his clothes from the naqui flesh and he watched the flailing arms bounce off. The clavus arm glanced off and Denar'ka fumbled with it.

Khan reformed his wind batier and ripped deep several times. Naqui flesh flew off burning the walls where it landed. The clavus changed into a spike and a thrust pierced Khan's abdomen. He stumbled before regaining his stance, the key to the forms.

He saw the burnt walls again and the naqui gave him an idea. Recomposing himself, he twisted his body when Denar'ka was close enough, overconfident that he would soon win, and wound himself into a tornado with Denar'ka inside. The Nivaton sprayed naqui sending spurts on every level as they ascended together.

Rising up high to the second level, Khan reversed course and then charged the naqui fighter toward the ground, Denar'ka's naqui body underneath him. Upon hitting the ground, a billow of steam, in all directions,

came out as naqui melted ice and two bodies burned
through to the level beneath.

Chapter 31

A BLACK jelly-blob had dropped into the chamber opposite the pillar. Griz, armed with his clavus, went to see what it was. The double-barreled rak sat quiet on the table he had just leaned on.

As he approached it, the blob grew into the shape of an entan, the clavus came up to greet the intruder. Pure black it was, shaped like a featureless entan, without fingers, toes, ears, eyes, or a nose. Just smooth kium skin.

The heavy clavus came down, strong enough to split any sized luto into two pieces, running diagonally from left shoulder to right hip. But not this time. As soon as the clavus blade entered the hard black skin, a spray of naqui came out covering Griz's right arm, scorching his armor. Griz, trying to avoid further injuries, pulled back while the blade was still lodged and snapped the tip of the clavus. The unhelmed warrior engaged the anomaly once more. "Die beast!"

Alexan heard the call of the wild from his friend even from within the second east chamber.

The naqui beast flailed two black limbs at Griz. The first hit squarely on the middle side, cracking ribs were heard from underneath the dented armor. The second attack glanced off his shoulder. The broken clavus came down heavily three times until the handle snapped and the head stuck into the floor.

Griz went mad, grabbed a small ice table as the naqui monster sprayed naqui from extended limbs. The table half dissolved and was dumped. The rak was nearby and Griz jumped for it but not before the naqui monster stretched out a limb to knock it away. Frustrated, the armored warrior picked up the heavy black thing, held it high. The right limb extended with a pointed end and pierced Griz's chest armor through to the back injecting naqui poison into his milk. It was not enough to stop the supernatural luto and he still managed to throw the monster into the far wall.

It recovered quickly and Griz had just enough time to retrieve the rak letting fly two noxy balls in succession. "Pil-Nak-Dak-La. Pil-Nak-Dak-La." He was badly injured and fought to get his balance. The first ball exploded behind the beast, melting ice and equipment. Alexan entered the west chamber, jumping to dodge the effects from the next ball. The second ball of noxy seared the beast and the shape became smaller returning to a large-sized spherical blob, regenerating rapidly.

"What is it?" Alexan asked, not sure what spell to cast.

"Farck if I know," Griz said, breathing heavy, milk pouring out.

Alexan considered a spell, his arvic stores were low and he couldn't cast the high level flamma that would certainly hurt the ice being. The black sphere vibrated and then started to grow again. "Tal-Nak-Dak-La!" Griz fired an ice slug at it forcing the beast to step back one step. Naqui sprayed out the crack in its armor before sealing itself up.

A white object fell from the ceiling just behind Alexan. The arvician went to inspect it.

"You're going to die!" yelled Griz. Just as the creature gained its full height again, he fired the last remaining noxy ball from the second cartridge. "Pil-Nak-Dak-La!" The naqui creature, aware of the weapon used against it, raised both arms and walked on. A ball of noxy fire burst causing extensive damage to walls, floors, shelving units, and the ice. Steam burst into the west chamber. All was a misty blue.

"That's a super-farck!" said Griz, confident of the damage he caused.

Alexan held the white box up.

KHAN DID not stop once through the solid ice floor. He kept his internal form hollow and focused a leg strike to Denar'ka's center then, once inside, he twisted, spraying his foe's naqui remains in all directions. The young Equist ended up spinning out of control into the central pillar in the chamber, semi-conscious, after hitting the floor. Another dream entered his mind. He was flying into the blue clouds in the sky, flying through them with his two seeds smiling that all was done and crying for Seranor's death. He was happy to be free at last. Free from the burden placed upon him.

If not for Griz's loud yell in the adjoining chamber, Khan may have never gained back his senses. The duel had left him dying but he couldn't stop now. Not if his friend was in trouble. A blue mist came out of the ajar portal.

He walked through.

Inside the misty, steamy chamber he caught the sight of the backs of Alexan and Griz. Hot aqua dripped from the ceiling. Many pieces of equipment had been melted and warped. Aqua puddles covered the floor. The plated warrior was down on both knees breathing heavily, coughing milk. Alexan was holding Pyx. Khan was happy to be back together with them.

"Griz, Alexan, it's me. What happened?"

Alexan pointed his head toward the center of the mist, holding the box in one hand.

From the steam came the sound of footsteps, heavy, hard and splashing through the aqua.

"It just won't die!" said Griz, getting up on his feet again.

Then the beast stopped, sensing something.

"The box," said Alexan.

"Pyx," said Khan.

"It is afraid," added the arvician. He stepped forward with the box and the beast retreated one step before lashing out an extended arm barely missing the arvician. The creature retracted then stretched out another limb striking Alexan in the head, sending him head over heels splashing to the ground.

Pyx flipped over and over in the air and Khan was there to grab her while dodging a similar attack on him. If it fears Pyx, then what lies inside may destroy it, thought Khan. He tried to somersault into a better position, but the flip ended short and he fell from a lack of strength. The beast jumped at him, knocking Griz in the chest.

Not so easily dropped, Khan rolled over and opened the box up.

"Now ice beast, be gone!" The brilliant flamma ray blew out encompassing the entire black skin. The beast groaned from intense pain, shrank and shrank until it was a small black ball then diminished into a large drop of aqua to join the large puddles on the floor.

Chapter 32

ALEXAN LAY motionless. It only took a light jarring on the shoulder from Khan to wake him. His right ear was still ringing from the lump on his head. Griz was propped up on a broken piece of lab equipment so that he could breathe.

"Where's Boon?" Khan asked, feeling all of a sudden dizzy, everything around him grew darker around the edges.

"He's fixing the return port," answered Alexan.

"We must go..." Khan on the verge of utter collapse. The internal bleeding from Denar'ka's pounding had taken its toll. The Nivaton did indeed fall under the fluidity and speed of Khan's hollow wind stance. The price paid was his dwindling life. "...did we win?..."

Alexan couldn't catch him before his body splashed in a puddle. "Griz, potion!"

Griz already had a potion out intending to drink it himself to prevent his own minute-by-minute death. His last one. A look at Khan was all that it took to change his cerbind. It was Khan who had saved him from the cult and it was his dying friend who now needed to be saved. He managed a sip before tossing a strong healing potion to Alexan. The sip refreshed him. The chilly feeling inside would not go away.

Khan woke up several minutes later, alive but far from healed. When he tried to stand he realized that his foot and ankle bone had shattered and gave out a shout.

Griz sat there thinking of Number 51. Maybe he wouldn't have a chance to see her again.

"Are you okay, Griz?" Khan asked.

"Just winded," replied the overgrown armored warrior, covered in frozen milk and ice, then went on. "Saranna. That's her name—Saranna."

"Who?"

"If something happened to me on one of these missions and I didn't get to taste another jug of fresh anaprimo, I would want you to tell her something for me. Tell her that she is the only luta that I will ever love. Tell her that for Griz. Tell her on the day I do not return."

"Do not consider death so early, old friend. We are nearly finished."

"Tell her so that she knows."

"When the day comes, she will know. Now look, it's not time for any of us to die so there's nowhere for you to go but to your favorite luta. It is Zorath who loses today."

"Enough of these ceramic moments. We must go."

"My thoughts exactly," replied Khan. He pulled out his tarc scanning for the connection. "Nothing. Boon, where are you?"

"I hate the cold."

"Next time we'll go south. I promise."

"Ira's potions are not as great as he thinks." Griz couldn't say the truth that he was in fact dying and didn't want to burden his friends with the bad news. Instead he sat, head up, shivering away the long minutes to his death. They still had to get out alive. He knew that he could hang on long enough to get out, maybe an hour, maybe less, but it was going to test him and it was the price of his killing. He had lived a life of neglect and pain starting from his father's experiments to his angry life as a plate-armored murderer for hire.

Thunderous footsteps loomed overhead. Battlekeep Vatu had come alive like a swarm of avian creatures who had been waiting too long for their meal. Alexan exhausted 95% of his remaining arvic stores sealing the existing three entrances to the fifth level. It was only a matter of effort and organization before another opening would be made. With Zorath gone and Denar'ka dead it would cause delays. Temporary delays.

"Alexan, we must use Septana to protect us," said Khan.

"We will leave soon," Alexan replied, in fear of touching the ancient relic again for the nightmares it would bring.

"Not until Boon is done. If they reach us like this we are all dead."

No response from the arvician.

Three worn lutos, mercenaries against King Zorath, locked deep inside an ice mountain five kilometers in, waited on the thief called Boon. A luto who had never in his entire life cared about anyone but himself. A team member upon whose success hung three lives and maybe his own and Seranor as well.

Ira's twelve hour deadline was coming to a close.

Time dissolved.

Less than half an hour to go.
The tarc still idle.
No connection.
No time.

Chapter 33

THE NAQUI antechamber that Boon entered after exiting
Alexan's makeshift tunnel led him to a double-sealed
portal. It was open after two locks moved aside from his
skilled hands. Thirty zoldiers in the small chamber
nearly stopped his corius until he saw that they weren't
moving. The synthetic ice soldiers were lined up along
the walls though were not alive, nor activated, yet. He
touched them, felt their cold skin. Punched one hard in
the head cracking its cheek. Disgusting. Dry inside.

He glared at the damage he had done. "The shell of an
entan and nothing more."

Boon studied their parts for apparent weaknesses.
Time was short and spared only the minute and a half he
had to wait for the naqui potion to take effect, then
stripped down to nothing. Reluctantly he left his

equipment with Griz and Alexan who were now left alone to tend to their own.

He tested the small pool of naqui under his feet. Just like cool aqua. Better not drink it, he remembered what Ira warned. An exit portal was not far off towards the furthest side of the corridor he entered. Once opened, it led into a smaller anti-naqui chamber then directly into the naqui lake. Pausing only a moment to wish his secret luta well he opened the portals and swam away. A white speck appeared in the large blue lake.

As he came out from the exit at Vatu, he could see thousands upon thousands of zoldiers inserted into cylindrical chutes with only their heads inside the naqui, breathing it and absorbing its essence. Maybe ten thousand zoldiers were neatly lined up around the base of Vatu. With another ten thousand on the other side, Vatu was a strong link in the frigid chain against Seranor. The central hive. Ira should have warned us, he thought, a swoosh of anger passed over him.

This wasn't so bad. Peace and tranquility under the naqui where nothing lived. He stopped to enjoy his naqui dream. As he closed his eyes to feel the total beauty of his submersion something grabbed his leg and, without delay, bit hard. He fought not to breathe in after expelling some air. A three meter serpent with fanged teeth ripped out a piece of his calf. Unarmed and defenseless Boon tried to swim away but the serpent was faster. He reached the surface inhaling as much as he could. A cool and slithery body wrapped itself around him dragging him under. His splashing and cursing caught the attention of the guards at the top and they alerted the rest of the keep at the top. Before he was completely intertwined inside the serpent's grasp he spun his own body and then delivered a direct strike to the nose of the creature stunning it.

He swam fast up to the smaller hole he remembered when they had slain the three snake beasts and climbed up the three meters of an icy face without problem. The serpent was gone.

Once out, he threw off all of the naqui thinking how smart Ira was and then began to move toward the large corridor. His body felt numb. Nine minutes gone.

Time was as naked and bare as he was.

In desperation, Boon didn't notice that his hair had turned green and his body tan in color. His body paint had been removed once more.

Boon ran, with a slight limp because of the gouge in his lower leg, at top speed to the flashport's location. Three minute sprints were followed by one minute jogging. This allowed him to stay on alert and to avoid surprise. Given a choice he would prefer the method of stealth. He spotted two guards ahead walking towards the cave opening. On his next sprint he planned his attack. Two surprise strikes, swift and direct, came from hand and elbow. Finally, a fight he could fight. Two morb guards dead before a sound was blurted. Thieves work the best by surprise. Lucky they weren't zoldiers. He grabbed one of their tarcs and a batier. The corridor was mostly empty but he heard the rising commotion from Vatu. The sound approached. They were coming after him. He ran faster.

Twenty-eight more minutes passed.

Heavy breathing.

Guard footsteps were heard from the distance.

Boon, who had never known what was a friend, hoped that his friends were still alive. Hoped that they would come out okay. To all be together again.

Arrival at the port. Red tears froze along his cheeks fearing time had run out.

Without equipment he would die where he stood.

Ira's cold-negating potion was still in effect. Hot breath the only sign he was alive.

His earlier notion was right, the flashport had become dislodged and putting it back together he found that it had been damaged by a fallen ice shard. Boon snapped a piece from the batier and tried to make it work. Three valuable minutes slipped by. He made a shoddy repair.

Were the others still alive? he thought.

The connection was fragile, but useable.

Chapter 34

KHAN, MONITORING the tarc each and every minute,
picked up the connection signal just as cerborian
arvicerers had regrouped and started blasting through the
seals.

"It is a day of death," said Griz. "Given the choice, I'd
prefer to die in battle." He glanced at one of the seals,
counting the time remaining before battle was upon him
once more. His own life was in decline and he wanted to
see it eye-to-eye with the sour-smelling, hybrid cerbors.
Then he remembered that he was not alone and grunted
in dissatisfaction. "This paint better farcking work."

Khan had picked up the spray can loaded with arvic
paint and covered an area the size of an entan on the far
west wall, adjoining the lake. Two minutes to wait. The

cerbors would have come through if Alexan hadn't whipped a spell into the cerborian mix. He conjured up an area effect (since he didn't know their exact positions) that dispelled all their castings as they created them. By the time the cerbors had figured out how Kozotian arvicity worked, the ice wall softened and morphed into a creamy yellow matter.

"Ira hasn't failed us, yet—Alexan, protect us," said Khan again, reminding Alexan of what must be done. Still no response. "Protect us and I can destroy this place."

"Is it your personal attack against Zorath or does our situation necessitate such oratic action?" In truth, Alexan dreaded Septana and the voices that would haunt him.

"It's necessary," Khan said. "We are in the midst of some kind of zoldierian factory. The very zoldiers that impose His will in our urbas." It's necessary and time is also short said Khan's tone and temperament. Alexan would not easily believe satisfying the wind maker with his pain and hoped that Boon was as efficient a thief as he had been in the past.

The arvic-laced paint dried, finally, just at the time the first seal blasted open sending ice chunks into the chamber. Masses of agitated troops roamed above them.

"Check that you've got your chute cards. Griz, go first," said Khan.

The plated warrior examined his chute card, laughing at its small size and probably more so because it couldn't give him what he really needed. He would not see 51 again, not as he had hoped in his miserable life of murder and milk; but if he was able to make it out there might yet still be that chance.

Griz, half-dead and terribly fragile, stepped through and tripped in the flashport hitting the circular rim of the port device on his way out where Boon waited anxiously.

Their exit was disconnected, again. The flat-faced brute then fell over and did not move.

KHAN'S AGILITY managed a one-footed hop with relative ease to a point where he could open Pyx. He listened to the enemy above. Cerbors would not blindly flash into this chamber for their chance of survival was low and without Denar'ka their leadership was broken and too disorganized for exact implementation. Killing the Nivaton bought them time but the enemy was regrouping and soon would snap the first seal, the only thing protecting the two of them right now.

The enemy had already blasted several balls of burning ice into the chamber, through some smaller openings, but luckily were not able to fix upon their position and ended up destroying more of the experimental equipment and the artificial cerbi. Limbs from the S4s were strewn about, one nearly hit Alexan in the face.

"You must use Septana," said Khan to the Kozotian. "I will release Pyx onto our enemy and rid this place from its oratic intention." Alexan just stared at the wind follower. Stared hard at what he was asking him to do.

"Do you know how to use it?" Alexan asked, referring to the white box in Khan's hands.

"I don't need to know."

"Be careful, Khan. These Kozotalian artifacts are far beyond what we can imagine. It is as if they were made 500 tios in the future. As such we cannot imagine their consequence nor their benefit."

"I just let Pyx do it. I am the medium of her destruction. She uses me to claim my needs."

"Be prudent," cautioned Alexan. "She will change you in ways you may not like. Enough wait. I will go before our enemy's aim gets better. We make haste."

If not for Boon's warning that followed next, using Griz's free tarc, Alexan would have entered the yellow portal without connection. The arvician was seconds away from almost losing his kol.

"Ignorant Thief!—Fix it!" yelled Alexan back through the tarc, shocked by his near-death experience.

"Hold on! Don't insult the one who saved your life," replied Boon. "Give me some time."

"This entire keep will come down! It will take us when it does; so move fast."

A BLAST snapped Alexan's body forward, caught off guard. Pieces of ice, a hardened ice interlaced with kium, splashed into the chamber.

"Get ready!—The seal is out," yelled Khan. He kneeled down, head up and held the orbis at an angle to the seal. "Let us serve each other, Pyx, so that we may both live."

Cosmic flamma warped the air around the two. The first wave of morb simply vanished from the white heat and, when the wide ray hit the stored energy crystalloids on the basement level, a loud explosion was heard. A set of three explosions followed, each larger than the other. Vatu shook. It rained morb, cerbors and zoldiers.

Alexan had no choice but to use Septana to protect himself and Khan. A hemisphere of ancient arvicity arose to shield them. The ceiling broke at the center and bodies came down bouncing off of the impregnable shield.

Another explosion erupted, louder than the previous. Chunks of ice walls and pieces of machinery crashed down. Battlekeep Vatu was disintegrating.

Their chamber walls split deep cracks where naqui poured in. The Level Five ceiling finally cracked and groaned one last time.

Vatu fell upon them.

"Boon! Fix the port or we're dead!" yelled Khan.

"It has been great working with you, Khan!" said Alexan, forcing the verse under the strain of Septana. He looked up at the mass that would soon fall upon them.

"We're not through yet!" cried Khan.

Vatu shook violently. The entire roof fell in and the arvician took the strain on his Kozotalian shield.

Khan: "Hang in there." Alexan sweated profusely as he fought to keep the shield up.

"Boon! Boon!" Khan yelled. "If it's not now, it's over!"

A moment of silence before the reconnection signal came back.

Khan pushed Alexan through and then fell in from behind just as Alexan lost his focus. Tens of thousands of kilos of ice mixed with zoldier and cerbor broke the floor, washed in a flood of pure naqui and unfinished zoldier carcasses.

KHAN HOPPED through to the other side, blocks of ice and debris followed them into the portal. Boon quickly broke the connection with his foot to stop the debris from continuing.

"What happened?" said Khan. He looked at the flashport then at Boon, nodding his head approvingly to his just action. "And why is your hair green and—"

"Griz is dying," said Boon with a tone of sadness he didn't think that he had. "That armor-plated shat is getting out easy."

Less than half a kilometer to go and the first wave of the enemy would fall upon them. Khan rolled Griz over on his back.

"Griz! Can you hear me? Griz! Griz."

"Go. I sleep in peace," said Griz, weak-voiced, unseen wounds under his whitish armor.

"It's not time to sleep, old friend," Khan said as he fought back the tears. Griz was dying. He looked at the other two – asking without words – for potions to heal his terminal wounds. Their heads shook slightly. Empty. *Damn!* They should have prepared better for this trip. "We have to go, Griz. We are not home yet. Just one more part and we'll be flying home. You must get up, now! Get up!"

Khan used a wind technique to help up the heavy fighter. The armor plates scraped together under the strain of the debilitated body. He looked more handsome without the helm. More real. Experience and readiness shown through. Griz blinked slowly as the noise from behind them increased.

"It is a day of death," said Griz. He smiled, not at his death, but at the trusted few who stood by him in the corridor of existence.

When Griz thought about the meaning and purpose of his life until then he could not summon an answer and it unsatisfied him; he imagined that it wasn't his life but that of another who had possessed him, since he had acted in ways suitable to ora and not the opus milk that circulated in his veins, and may have explained why the milk had ran forth to the outside. Even his very milk was repelled as if to remind him in dire action.

Life had a choice. Many choices, it seemed clearer to him now. For him all that remained was the choice of where to die and he decided that dying here was not what he wanted.

Most of all he wanted to be free from the burden of his murderous behavior. Free from the killing that he had taken upon himself. And he understood, with reluctant tears, that he would not see Saranna, his only love, after his freedom. When he came to this realization he felt numb and insignificant.

Chapter 35

BOON FINISHED dressing then grabbed the crystine pod he
had taken from when they first entered the lower levels.

Khan smiled: "We're going to need that. You have to
blow the corridor."

"I was thinking just that, but the whole thing will
collapse."

"That's the idea—Me and Alexan will take Griz. You
set up the explosives. Give us a three minute head start."

Boon tossed the pod up in his hands in anticipation.
"Two minutes at the very most. Go!"

"C'mon old friend, time to go home—Alexan!" The two
of them hauled up Griz and, shoulder to shoulder, started
running. Khan hopped on his one good foot. The wind
supported his other. A minute later Griz caught his own
feet and the three were off. Boon gave them the full two

minutes he promised, and by that point, he could see the white-eyed enemy approaching. Hundreds of them came at full speed.

When the pod exploded nothing happened but a loud bang. A pile of steam filled the corridor in both directions. The enemy stopped for several seconds and, thinking that they were safe, ran again. But the explosion had already set off a web of deep cracks in the mountain and as the enemy passed under the area where the crystine pod was set off, the corridor groaned once, then gave way.

THREE MEMBERS up front, one behind; the party against Zorath ran toward the cave exit to the outside, still untouched from the crumbling corridor. Inside the mountain's icy bowels the enemy was repulsed. Four beaten down adventurers, one trailing slightly, and their valuable cargo evacuated squeezing all the remaining strength that they could summon.

"Zorath is really gonna be shaken over this!" said Boon as he caught up to the others.

Griz: "Farcking ice head!"

As they exited the cave mouth, a snow avalanche closed the opening nearly sealing them in hadn't Khan not thrust them all forward with a strong, windy thrust.

A flat, 125 meter patio of icy rock lay beyond the door. The ice was a thin film that coated the rocky surface and would make it dangerous to walk over.

Alexan's stores, recharged enough for light spell work, allowed him to send up a pulse of flamma from which he could gain a better view of the surroundings. From where they were, the cliff extended out another half-kilometer to a point that then sloped down the mountain for another kilometer or more before hitting a sheer cliff. He noticed that a narrow ledge of ice sat at the bottom of the slope and was probably the only marker to separate the air and the mountain.

Khan made some estimations in his head as did Alexan and Boon to size up the effort required. Explosions were heard behind them as the enemy melted through.

"They're persistent," said Boon.

"We'll have to get down to the sheer ledge or our chutes will not carry us. Alexan, what do you suggest?" said Khan.

"I'm thinking. A flash could work but there are too many and my stores are far insufficient."

"We can slide down," said Boon. "We just need a flat board on which to do it with."

"And where—" said Khan.

"I could fashion them from the ice and snow," said Alexan.

"Do it and quickly!" Alexan went to work on the ice boards.

Shards of ice burst out from high above on the ice face above the wide opening that they exited. From behind the spray of ice and snow came a long and large ice creature. It floated through the air and headed with its large gaping mouth, towards Griz, who was the most stationary target. The others jumped to the side, Griz was too weak and slow so just turned to face the beast.

It caught him square on but he used his arms to prevent the jaw from swallowing him whole. Griz and beast rode the slope in a struggle. The beast's long and white tail thrashed down the mountain side.

"We've got to go now! Have you finished yet?" said Khan, desperate to save his dying friend.

"It's a little warped but it—" Khan had already grabbed it and jumped off. "It will only work if you ride it with the curve on the bottom. Too late. Khan already put the curve side up for stability and was chasing the creature's tail.

The other two boards, nicely designed, were finished. "Check your chute before you jump." Boon caught a glimmer on the rock. It was a chute card in the place Griz was taken from.

"He doesn't have his chute?!" yelled Boon. "Look!"

"Farck! Check yours."

"Got it. That's the last thing that I'd forget," said Boon.

"I'm not so sure about those two—"

A wave of arvicity passed over the arvician. A high level spell had been cast in the vicinity. He looked behind at the exit corridor. "Get out of here!" he screamed. Boon slid off followed closely by Alexan. Behind them was a hoard of zoldiers and cerborian arvicerers hot on their feet. Hot balls of noxy exploded behind them sending down an avalanche of snow.

GRIZ, ONCE again energized by battle, was just too weak to kill off the beast and each meter they slid he felt his life leaving him. The large jaw from the serpent tried to naw at him but could not overtake the super strength that faced it.

It was Khan who moved quickly onto the tail of the creature before his board snapped. He used his wind form to help him stay close to its cold body and worked his way to his brother. When he got to the head he leapt up and threw out a sharp foot strike, the unshattered one, to the base of what seemed to be the head. The wind sliced and severed the head from the tail which then went flailing wildly. But the head still clamped Griz. It needed focus. Khan looked up ahead. A few seconds to the cliff. He raised his right hand and snapped it down sectioning the head into two equal parts like a broken bowl.

Khan, Griz and two large pieces of an ice head slid off. Khan latched onto his friend and thrust his chute into Griz's hand, broke it and forced the feeble body to hang on. He held.

The pyramid chute and the large-sized entan caught cold air and slowed to a peaceful speed as Khan dropped without a chute or a ledge with which to keep him.

Two other desperate figures slid off the mountain into the icy darkness followed by masses of snow and rock and ice. Three pyramid-like chutes floated down, 4 meters on all sides, white as snow. Large, supernatural snowflakes drifting down from the dark sky.

One lone figure sped to his demise.

Just before losing consciousness for the last time, Griz mumbled four words: "I love you Ranna."

THE ICY winds at 7,500 meters up froze their wounds and their sweaty hair. All around them was darkness. Endless darkness as they floated into a new life. Above them they could still hear the rumbling of the mountain as it digested its contents for the last time.

Khan stabilized his fall and prevented himself from smashing into the mountainside. Once stable he quickly regained his stance and caught the wind beneath him and it carried him down. His fear of falling was preceding by the fear of dying.

He held onto the wild wind and could not help but think about one question: What path had they found? The team was sent in on a mission that would have killed any other. He was chosen for reasons Ira would not divulge and in convincing his friends to go they had joined him on his path. If Seranor was truly dead, as Zorath had said she was, it would only be a matter of time before Zorath once again gained his edge. The fifth level of the complex housed some new kind of zoldier, an improvement over the last which meant that even if the first wave was destroyed then a stronger, more capable army would replace it. Zorath would never stop until the planet was entirely his, until he could consume its power to eat his revenge. And Shev'la Khan, wind disciple to Equist Nao Li-Grum, was part of that process along with his compatriots.

By the time they had reached the 4,000 meter mark the winds became extremely volatile and Khan lost his balance. And he regained his fear of falling. He was tossed into the mountain's face several times, each time bashing him nearer into unconsciousness. Then he maneuvered to recover his stance but was twisted up by crosswinds and then began another freefall. Three large snowflakes followed from above.

Twenty-two minutes late for the rendezvous.

Ira wouldn't wait.

Khan's fall was so fast that he could not see, only to feel the blinding wind's cold burning his extremities. He concentrated hard without result. The 500 meter mark came and this time, seeing his possibilities slim, he relaxed and made himself hollow as when with Denar'ka. As Nao taught him. His balance returned and he regained control of his fall. In fact, he was no longer falling but flying in the wind's caress. In his joy of such control he decided to dance with Nata and to enjoy her beauty. She sung into his ears and he felt her love.

The ground, a flat white, came into view. Soon enough his friends glided passed him. They too were pleased and called out in excitement though none could here it quite clearly. It was there that Khan saw Griz's limpness and his out of control chute. He raced to his aid in the cover of darkness.

Chapter 36

HAPPY TO be on solid ground Boon kissed the white snow, temporarily mistaking it for his luta. Alexan landed second with quiet displeasure.

The mountain rumbled.

Two minutes later, Khan landed safely, standing on one leg and using the wind for support to land in the soft snow. Griz semi-crashed into the snowy ground 10 meters from Boon's flank. He was dead before he hit but thanks to Khan was not splattered on the rocks below.

"What are you doing, Helmhead?" cried out Boon.

"Griz!—" said Khan.

"I'll see if Ira is around," said Alexan and pulled out his tarc walking into the darkness, still bright to his white-cupped eyes.

Khan skimmed the surface wind over to the hunk of armor face-down in the snow hill. A pillow of snow covered his scorched and dented armor. He had been through war. Khan, with one good foot, slipped on a stone and landed squarely on Griz. Not a movement. No sound. The armor stopped regenerating. One eye cup had been ripped off in the fall. The black girdle around his waist was hot to the touch. Khan carefully pulled off the other eye cup. The eye, like the first, was also closed underneath.

Fear hit Khan like being drowned in aqua and not able to breathe.

"Griz? Griz?" No pulse. Body cold. A naqui pus coming out from under his armor. The mark of the naqui beast. "Poison!" *Dead.* Khan yelled out. The others felt the pain in his voice. His most trusted friend, gone.

Boon ran over.

"Griz, you cannot die," cried Khan. "Not now. We've made it. We're out. We'll go south where it's warm. I heard of some buried treasure guarded by beautiful lutas..." Khan sat holding him. Boon stood around them, head bowed for his fallen friend.

From the moment Khan accepted the death of his brother and looked upon his travels at an angle that he called his path to enlightenment that possessed him in his early youth, he was terrified by the straight-faced fact that he was responsible for another death. Destiny – but a word to mean only one thing for those associated with the young Equist, the seed of Tulai Khan: death. For all those who accompanied this luto were sure to die.

Khan suddenly felt he was a luto who had surrendered all that he believed and loved for all that could and might not be. Had he given so much to his disillusionment? He had forsaken himself as a Seronian who once followed the ways of opus, of balance and of respect for life, and in so doing he gave in the respect of his own being and created a hole in which those around him would also face what he faced, and in this cosmic certainty that he now blamed himself with he knew that it was Anativo who had opened the door to the impossible, had broken the gate between all things real and unreal. The more he cried inside the more he swallowed the facts facing his kol for the very first time since his family was murdered: Zorath must be vanquished and it must become his mission in life to remove the poison that infests Seranor. And maybe, he thought, if I am cursed with death then to put myself around the Nivian shall in turn cause his death and so we shall all be freed from the suffocation of ice.

FIFTEEN MINUTES later, Alexan walked over with Ira. He had waited. He never waited for any others. Two plainly armored henchtans followed by the Levin's side. Two steps behind was a heavily armored fighter with a superior batier strapped on his belt and a heavy shield in his left hand with the Seronian Torq. Beside him walked a two meter tall female Kozoty, perfect as a snowflake and even more captivating.

Khan wore frozen tears.

"We have to go, Khan." Ira's words were softer than usual. He called the two armored henchtans to take Griz and handed Khan a potion. "That'll fix your leg. There's nothing I can do about Griz now, sorry. We move. Zorath's armies have been driven back and now he has no more to replenish his dwindling forces. He is stopped. You and your team have succeeded as I knew you would."

The white box came out of Khan's pack and was handed to Ira. Alexan carried the two Arvinstrum relics.

"These are our friends. This is Teramon and this is Falantia." He pointed to the armored warrior first then to the Kozoty.

Khan nodded in greeting. "I am Shev'la Khan and these are—"

"We know who you all are," Falantia said, stopping the introductions short.

"Without all seven" (Ira pointed to Alexan with his two relics) "he is doomed to fail. And now that the Orbis is once again under protection, our planet is safe," Ira said.

"But Seranor is dead," said Khan.

"Who has spoken such words?"

"Zorath."

"He lied. She is in pain and dying, but not dead."

"Like the pain in my chest?" said Khan. Knowing that Seranor was alive did not remove the fact that Griz wasn't.

Ira touched him on the back of his shoulder. "Death is life to some. We are still in danger here. We should go."

"Ira," said Boon, "I found a low frequency flamma signal when the zoldiers were around. It might be a communication or control signal."

"Show me!" Boon pulled out his IR and transferred the data to Ira's tarc which then displayed it. The small flamma screen lit up. "You're right, but it's encrypted by photonic bursts. Look here. The signal becomes larger at these points."

"Data transfers," said Khan without even looking at the image and before Boon could speak. "I noticed when we entered Vatu."

"You could have said something," said Boon.

"Their system uses an alien photon key to pass instructions between the flammascopes and zoldiers. It's very sensitive."

Ira wanted to know: "Can you break it, Khan? Can you disrupt it enough to hurt the Armies of Zorath?"

"It's not easy."

"But can you do it? We mustn't drift at times like these." He could see the wind maker having a hard time with the loss of his friend. On top of that, they had just survived the infiltration and escape of one of the Kium King's most heavily gaurded outposts 8,000 meters in the middle of an ice mountain – but need preceded want. "Can you bypass the photon key?"

"It's not easy."

"You just said that!"

"It is the first time that I have ever seen such a system. I understand the theory of it but the photon spectrum of flamma is very nasty. Photons are sensitive and if you upset them enough they will disintegrate and never surrender the message you seek. Their communications grid uses a central photon messaging system with its own key in addition to minute photon bursts for each zoldier. The system is designed to collapse, if I am right in my early estimations, like a lake of thin ice that carries a Serag. One or two steps may be okay but the chance of the ice breaking increasing in probability in magnitudes with each step."

"We will use this against his Army of Naquior. Keep it close by." Ira wasn't going to waste any more time with Khan's current disposition. "It is really late. I detected Zorath's presence some time ago then lost it after the quake. I have arranged flashport several hours from here—We move! Pick him up," he said, pointing to Griz's body.

The leader of the Terium knew that Zorath could trace them. Even his own defensive spells, thrown in the vicinty, could not displace all their presences as they had been designed to do. It was likely that Ira could displace himself but that would be futile with so many others around, defenseless against the forces that would be used against them.

The Nivian would be able to extract inconsistencies in the spell fabric and, by deduction alone, could find the ragged warriors. That would put Ira in a very uncompromising position and the Kozoty didn't like to be in such situations as they tended to produce unstable outcomes and could turn the balance one way or the other.

Chapter 37

FALLING SNOW rained down on the heads of eight standing figures at the base of the mountain as it growled from the residual shocks inside its core. Hot breath billowed in short puffs from their tired faces. Khan's breath was more erratic than the others. He eyed his friend, his brother, and could not accept the results as they were. After all they had been alive to witness and to fight against, one of them had been removed from the equation; the very reason that he had initially refused to go. Instead, it was not the ill-fated Khan who was to die rather the one whom he loved. Another of his family taken from him. Abandoned once more.

Griz's body, wrapped in cracked plate armor, painted with dried and frozen milk – missing his full helm, a trademark – was hoisted up by the two henchtans and readied to be carried off to a waiting talin. Snow flakes began to pile themselves upon his still body, layer upon layer as would a blanket from a mother in a time of caring.

Suddenly, a thunderous wave of white flamma ripped through the air bearing down on the exposed targets. Phosphorescent zamma, the same that first cut the planet at the time of Seragorn's birth 1,300 tios back in history, reached to an area only meters above their heads and without warning was absorbed by the instantaneous arvic shield that came up to protect them.

Alexan, without thought or active reaction, had sunk his fists into Septana as if by natural instinct and saved all of their lives. The defense sucked his own essence and he dropped to his knees into the wet snow and skid back some 4 meters from the violent force. Seca's heat melted the snow and ice and rock around them all. The land became gouged by molten white fire.

All of them spun around in every direction to find who was attacking them. Ira already knew who it was and focused on finding the Kium King.

"You must prevent another attack like that," said Alexan, head still down and in a breathless voice.

"Anativo has returned to extinguish us," said Khan, remembering the annihilation of his family and friends in Ulaq. "He has returned!"

"Zorath!" cried Ira, withdrawing his arvic batier to the unwelcome guest. "Prepare to fight!—Boon, give the IR to Khan. Khan, you must break the encryption. I sense zoldiers coming—crack their code and they will crack. Find it or they will find you." Ira turned left and right to bark his commands. "Teramon, Falantia, come."

The others heard the sounds of zoldiers 9 seconds after Ira.

Khan, worried about whether they would make it through the next few minutes, took the IR. His foot and ankle had completely reset from the potion.

A loud voice echoed at the wide pass, carried by the wind, and spoke with total conviction: "YOU WILL ALL DIE FOR YOUR INSOLENCE! YOU WILL RETURN TO CERAMICO AND WILL GIVE YOUR KOLS TO ME!"

The two henchtans holding Griz's body laid it down carefully then readied themselves.

"Whatever happens, do not give him the relics," said Ira to all of them. He was running alternative strategies simultaneously in his head, drawing the best possible conclusions. He did not like the fact that he was best capable of fending against the blackened Nivian. It unnerved him to conclude that and also gave him pleasure to know that he could speak for his dead father. *Finally*. "Alexan, can you maintain this shield?"

"I think so, but not another attack like that. My stores are too low to—"

"Take this potion," said Ira, tossing a small vial to one of his henchtan who then fed it to Alexan. "It will replenish some of your lost arvic stores. The rest be ready. We must win this day for Seranor. Think not of yourselves. Think beyond yourself this day and we may yet conquer the conqueror. Waist no breath and move in certainty."

TWO HUNDRED plus zoldiers from all sides marched up to surround the remaining eight. Leading the ranks of zoldiers was Avar-Sint. His rader was in hand and his armor began to glow radiant green.

Hovering high above their ranks was the Kium King. A black void in the air. In his right hand he held Seca.

She beamed metallic silver. The air surrounding her blurred in her presence unable to contain her cosmic beauty all in one mouthful.

Ira walked out first, followed by Teramon and Falantia. The Kozoty straightened to his full height striding in long and measured steps.

"I am Ira of House Levin, seed of Amid and Tamil Levin. It was my father Amid who let you live. And it will be his seed who will see you die." Ira showed his black batier, so heavily embedded with ancient arvicity that when he released her from her binding she became a translucent white. "Quel is slayer to the ice!"

"THE LEVINS – AS ALL BEINGS OF THIS FUTILE PLANET ARE – ARE *WEAK* AND POWERLESS TO STOP ME. I HOLD SECA, THE CARVER OF PLANETS. STAND BEFORE ME JUNIOR LEVIN AND YOU WILL BE FIRST TO BE VANQUISHED."

Zorath flew forward until he was over snowy ground. Ira flashed out and back in directly in front of the Nivian. A white batier swung with fatal accuracy and precision upon him.

Chapter 38

ALEXAN COUGHED milk, voices filled his head, this time voices of love, and told him that he was the protector of opus. He was the arvicity. And he held on not knowing anything else.

Inside Alexan's shield, Khan used the IR and Ira's tarc to break into the reams of photonic code. He worked fast to adjust for the flammic emissions and then once the colorized communications grid was exposed, he moved into the encrypted areas.

Encryptions were generally the same to him and only made difficult by the number of twists and folds in the flammic architecture. Once flamma was folded it could not be unfolded or the signal would collapse and remain permanently untouchable. Photon transmission keys, a highly developed form of secure transmission, were not of Seranor and, luckily for him, had incorporated similar technology to what his father once used when he was a much younger seedling, much improved in technological function though technology was like the talin; it was a carrier and no matter how advanced that carrier was it operated on the same basic principles.

Using Ira's tarc, an advanced model that was lighter and more robust than his own, Khan managed to expose the key signaling areas, the ones that maintained the instructions that served the zoldiers. The message of instructions, from his rapid scanning, were telling the zoldiers not only how to behave and for communications purposes but also the instructions, probably sent from one or two flammascopes nearby and inserted within the existing wave so that it could not even be identified, were telling the zoldiers how to regulate other functions like naqui circulation and bodily regeneration. If this was true and hidden inside the signal was a layer of light that controlled zoldierian life, then Khan was to find this mechanism and to sabotage it as fast as fast could be.

His mastery of cryptography unfolded the complex encryption – Boon's nimble fingers maintained its opening using the tarc's crystal – and layer by layer he broke through the signal and into the pool of photon codes. Once fully made bare and realizing that it was impossible to deactivate each and every zoldier, he inserted a black light – known as a *void* to code breakers – that entered the zoldier's communication network and proliferated into each of the distributed units. The void would space the set of instructions controlling their metabolic functions and would interrupt their protocols so that all things would be divided and made erratic. It was like inserting an advanced nervous disorder into a being who had no nervous infrastructure with which to support it or to get rid of it. This also avoided the highly sensitive nature of photons since it did not measure nor change the photonic keys; instead, it just inserted an undetectable, insignificant blank space that the key would not sense.

In essence, the wind maker launched a Serag onto the frail ice lake and this Serag was given sharp footwear devices with which to cut the surface of the ice without falling through until all the ice was cut and the entire lake would collapse together with the beast—but only after the beast had sabotaged the majority of the network.

The zoldiers, once lined in perfect columns, began to shift and move as they experienced a bad case of emotional outpouring. They were forced into anger, sadness, and remorse without the ability with which to release such emotions.

FOLLOWING IRA'S signal, Teramon and Falantia engaged Avar-Sint. The Sint walked calm and usual when facing his two opponents. Falantia was an arvician of great ability and her partner Teramon was master batierstan of Seranor. It was Teramon who had first challenged a Sint, though failed in his execution because he was unprepared. This time, with help from the Terium, Teramon was well prepared and would not succumb to failure a second time.

Ceramic weapons, enchanted with arvic intentions as well as pure arvic spells clashed between the mighty three.

Teramon had bore deeply into the Sint even before he had a chance to regenerate his wounds while Falantia parried his spells and struck with her own devastating lists.

By the top of the third round the Sint fell back hard in his regenerative death. Avar-Sint was lifeless and cold but he was healing rapidly.

Teramon had been hit twice by the rader, pieces of his porcelan had fallen as had pieces of his armor.

Falantia, knowing what must be done, quickly cut the girdle with a glistening blade and removed the ring as Teramon grabbed the rader and hauled up the body onto his massive shoulders.

QUEL SANG as she attacked, a haze of white and blue filled the area around Ira and Zorath as opus and ora clashed. Tens of seconds passed, Ira grew weary against Zorath and if not for his arvic items he would have died.

A subsequent blast from Seca directed at Ira missed and hit Alexan's cosmic shield. The two henchtans were caught outside of the protective barrier, they were running to help with the fallen Sint, and were obliterated into air molecules.

By the top of the fourth minute, a sweaty Ira had disarmed Seca from Zorath's hand and Quel had severed one of his three kium fingers. Ira had already sustained several arvic wounds but by committing to such a move, he was vulnerable to attack. A spell hit him, absorbing his life-force into Zorath's ring.

"YOUR RESILIENCE IS AT END, LEVIN!"

The Kozoty spun and with Quel's help managed a two-handed thrust into Zorath's black chest, hoping to disrupt the spell caster, before losing grasp of his weapon. The enemy reeled back in obvious pain from the slayer of ice though pressed on with his concentration. Quel was pulled out, dropping to the ground. *Farck.* The wound was slowly healing.

"GODS CANNOT BE SLAIN. I AM A GOD! AND THOSE WHO DO NOT SERVE THEIR GOD SHALL SURRENDER TO THEM AND THEIR MIGHT."

Ira resisted with his remaining strength against losing his kol and was slowly dying by its potent attraction. The area upon which Quel rested had melted the snow until Seranor's skin was naked once more.

Chapter 39

ALEXAN RELEASED the shield and sank down into the snow. The cosmic essence had consumed his own and once fully extracted he could no longer continue to channel the Kozotalian power. By this time, it was fortunate that Khan's cryptic maneuvers could be harvested and the zoldiers, now within killing distance of the last few survivors, began to shake violently and reacted to each other swinging wildly into their own ranks.

Khan left the IR with Boon as Ira drifted into the nexa. His blinding wind blew Zorath's clothes but did not cut his focus. "I am the wind!" yelled the Equist. The wind force rose in strength and upturned several large stones that came hurtling towards the former Anativo. At last, the spell broke and Zorath stumbled backwards as he disintegrated the boulder that had knocked him.

Ira submitted to the comfort of the snow beneath his feet.

"Wind in your eye! You will die!" The wind Equist rolled his arms in aerodynamic execution, rotating the cuffs of wind into a blade and propelled that windy weapon at the unbalanced foe. The wind force cut into the custom made kium, into Zorath's mid-section and ripped through the unbreakable ice material until a mortal wound almost tore the being into two halves—but Zorath was mortal no longer and his body was only a tool of destruction. You may break that which is mortal but not the immortal. It did manage to stun the Kium King.

Khan wasted not one ounce of time, not one measure of space, as he twisted himself into the wind, into Nata, with a volatile force yet unseen. He remembered his father, his brothers and his mother. He remembered the pain that was brought upon him and so inflicted it to the Nivian who had caused it. Nata was his revenge.

Zorath was twisted around and upside down before he had a chance to retaliate with his own attacks. Nata was not so easily deterred. She swallowed the Nivian demi-god into her mouth and lifted him high up the mountain side.

In a large crevasse between two mountains, Khan dropped the unwelcome alien deep into the ice then cast his cyclone hair at the mountainside and released an entire glacier upon the semi-conscious, and once all powerful, Zorath. The mountain roared and trembled as snow and ice fell to bury once again the Nivian who came by his own invitation.

WHEN ALL was done, the mountain slept after its fury; and the zoldiers, once a coordinated military force, washed the ground as aqua when the void separated their artificial genetic functions that caused their own destruction.

"The storm has come," said Ira, as he slushed through the zoldierian aqua, semi-recovered from his deadly battle.

"It is Nata's will," replied Khan.

"Yes. And it is your will to be Nata."

"I could not accept your death before my own."

"It is because of you that I breathe. It is also why we have netted ourselves a third piece to the Arvinstrum." Ira re-sheathed Quel then picked up Seca from the ground and held it out. "An exchange for the life taken."

"I would happily trade back 100 Seca's for the life of my brother," said Khan, solemnly.

"It is unfortunate that we can only choose one and not the other."

Avar-Sint's body was strapped to a talin. Teramon, whose wounds from the Sint had now been regenerated, carried Avar's rader. Falantia took his ring and girdle in a pack. Griz was laid down on a talin also.

Boon noticed the chain formation, under Griz's body, of a girdle melted in the snow attributing it to the sheer weight of the armored luto than anything else.

Chapter 40

NINE TALINS in all, with rider silhouettes, save three, glided off toward the warm south, toward the public reaction that awaited them in the urbas. Four heroes had been born, four shards in the back of the downed Nivian King, four pieces in Seranor's puzzle.

Change was Nata's gift to the planet. All things were made of change. It was in transformation that life continued. Snow continued to rain down on the riders as the landscape changed from its paint. Khan listened to the snowflakes as they passed the air while they rode and looked as the familiar wind wound its way between their perfect crystalline structures. Sometimes snowflake would hit upon snowflake and the perfection would be lost only to be replaced by more of the same.

What is it that puzzles me? Khan said to himself, estimating that there had been no resolution this day, no resolution and only change to which would once again present new circumstances that would challenge him.

He looked back and saw the icy temperatures freezing the zoldier aqua pool into a sheet of ice covering thousands of square meters at the foot of the mountain they had just left. The falling snow covered the memories and after two hours all was an omniscient white. Again. The snow blanket put the mountain to sleep.

"Oh, Khan. Rest your concerns in our ride home," said Ira from up front. "We should be happy this day and for what has come of it."

"You are right, Ira. You are right," said Khan, adjusting his posture in his talin.

His Kozotian friend did seem to be able to read Khan even though he demonstrated no apparent caring in his features. He understands more than he shows, he thought. Perhaps we are like snowflakes and in all our perfection there is one truth that pervades us all and that is our temporalities for we, like the snowflake, are falling through the skies and though beautiful are made so in a temporary fashion – even beauty cannot last forever. And the more beautiful that we are made the shorter our existence seems to be as if we become more fragile and our perfection cannot be contained for lengths of time that we wish.

This new concept, at least new to my own cerbind, does not give me the comfort, as I had hoped it might, any more than the removal of my enemy did. Whether we fall a straight line or are shifted by the wind's caress does not matter to me anymore. There is certainty in suffering and the greater the exposure to its effects the less its effects are felt.

If there is no real end in the change of all things, then it is okay for me to acknowledge the very changes presented to me and in their acceptance to make my own will a part of that change. The threat of ice shall remain as long as Nivians exist and there will always be the light from the Kozotal to shine upon the planet we call Seranor, and it shall be that She cannot be destroyed by anything but Herself.

Is it me and my friends who have been summoned – by her – to assist? I must consider this possibility and, rather than to fight against this flight path, I should not create struggle, but; instead, to know that if Seranor has chosen me in some obscure way then I am honored by this choice, and my life becomes meaningful to know that my snowflake – filled with imperfection and vulnerability – is made all the more perfect in its decision to act and it becomes strengthened by this very act; I am made stronger by my decision to become convicted of my strengths and committed by my weaknesses. These are the things that prove that Seranor cannot ever die nor can her seedling, Seragorn.

We are the dream of this planet. We are the life that, in turn, keeps *it* alive. If that is what we are, dear Seranor, then I will share in your dream – no, I will create a new dream, one filled with all possibilities, and we will dream together.